THE SILENCE

THE SILENCE

Sarah Rayne

This first world edition published 2013
in Great Britain and in the USA by
SEVERN HOUSE PUBLISHERS LTD of
19 Cedar Road, Sutton, Surrey, England, SM2 5DA.

British Library Cataloguing in Publication Data

Rayne, Sarah.
  The silence.
  1. Haunted houses–England–Peak District–Fiction.
  2. Horror tales.
  I. Title
  823.9'2-dc23

ISBN-13: 978-0-7278-8248-6 (cased)
ISBN-13: 978-1-84751-474-5 (trade paper)

All Severn House titles are printed on acid-free paper.

Severn House Publishers support the Forest Stewardship Council [FSC], the
leading international forest certification organisation. All our titles that are printed
on Greenpeace-approved FSC-certified paper carry the FSC logo.

Typeset by Palimpsest Book Production Ltd.,
Falkirk, Stirlingshire, Scotland.
Printed and bound in Great Britain by
MPG Books Ltd., Bodmin, Cornwall.

ONE

Edinburgh,
8th March 20—
Dear Emily,

It seems that after all these months Stilter House can finally be sold. At last! I know probate can take a long time to obtain, but I had begun to think those solicitors were deliberately dragging matters out.

However, I think that before we put the old place on the market it would be as well to get the furniture removed. Aunt Charlotte had several very nice things, and I wondered whether we could ask Brad West's wife – widow, I should say – to take a look at them. You remember her? She recently moved to Oxford and has a small antiques shop there, so she would be a good person to consult. Also, family is family, and I dare say Nell has found things difficult since Brad's death. It would be nice if we could put a little business her way.

Fondest love,
Margery

Edinburgh,
12th March 20
Dear Emily,

I'm glad you agree about arranging for Nell West to provide valuations for the contents of Stilter House. I'll write to her at once.

I don't think we need worry over what Charlotte used to say about the house. She was always a touch eccentric and given to imagining she saw things. I always thought she simply needed stronger reading glasses.

And even if there was ever anything in Charlotte's stories (and nothing will ever convince me there was), Nell would only be there for a day or two.

I hope your leg is better – although that new treatment sounds very odd. I wish you would trust conventional medicine more. Do remember how much money you spent with that peculiar man last year, who claimed to have healing hands, and left you with ingrowing toenails and the poorer by £500, to say nothing of his being so very *familiar* with you during the massage part of the procedure.

Margery

Edinburgh,
13th March 20—
Dear Nell,

I wonder if you would be free to undertake a small commission in the near future?

You may remember Brad's Great-Aunt Charlotte, who lived in Derbyshire? Brad used to spend some of his school holidays with her at Stilter House. Sadly, she died last month, although she was 95 so it wasn't entirely unexpected, and vigorous and utterly *compos mentis* to the last.

I'm executor of the estate, together with Brad's other aunt, Emily, and one of those house-clearance firms will be clearing everything out. However, the solicitors suggest a professional appraisal of the contents first. Is this something you could do? The estate will cover your fees and travelling costs, of course, and if there's anything you think you could sell in your Oxford shop we could arrange that.

I enjoyed the photos you sent of Beth. She has a strong look of Brad, and I shed a tear on his behalf seeing the likeness. Those wretched motorways, so dangerous, and he was always such a good driver, it still angers me to think what happened to him.

If ever you and Beth can visit me, you would be given a very warm welcome, but of course it's a long way up here and my house is on the north side of Edinburgh.

Much love to you both,
    'Aunt' Margery West.

Nell read Margery West's letter twice. Was it a genuine offer or was it Brad's aunt trying to help her a little? She remembered Margery, and although she had never met Charlotte, Brad had often talked about staying at her house in Derbyshire for school holidays. He had been taken to see ancient caves in Dovedale and the Blue John Mines, which he had loved. But best of all, he used to say, was the discovery of a piano at the house and Charlotte arranging music lessons for him. It had been a revelation to learn how to make music for himself, he had said. After that first time he had always thought of the house as magical.

Nell stared thoughtfully out of the window of her shop, which looked onto Quire Court. At this time of the morning fresh spring sunlight lay in chequered patterns over the quiet old stones. It was not a time when ghosts might be expected to be around, although any ghosts that walked through the court would be civilized and polite ones. If Nell had believed in ghosts she would never be worried by the ones that might haunt Quire Court. But there were other kinds of ghosts . . .

She read Margery's letter again, and the memories of Brad flooded back, painful and intrusive. *I'll never forget you*, said Nell to Brad's memory, *and I won't let Beth forget you, either. But I don't want you walking in and out of my mind, just when I'm starting to put my life back together – just when Beth's getting used to having no father – just when I'm starting to be so very happy with Michael.*

She would accept Margery West's request. Beth deserved even this small contact with her father's family. She had only been seven when Brad died, and photographs and handed-down memories were no substitute for the real thing. It left such a blank if a child did not know one half of its heritage – you had only to read about adopted children seeking their birth parents in later life. And Brad had talked about Great-Aunt Charlotte with so much affection and gratitude that Nell would like Beth to see the house.

'I've written to accept Margery's offer,' she said to Michael that evening. 'It'll only mean two or three days, and Beth's school breaks up for Easter next week so she'll come with me.'

'How about the shop?'

'If I drive up to Derbyshire early on Sunday morning, Henry Jessel at the silversmith's next door would look after the shop for Monday and Tuesday,' said Nell. She hesitated, then said, 'How tied up are you with College things? Would you like to come with us? The house is in the Peak District – it's a gorgeous part of the country.'

'I don't think I can manage it,' said Michael. 'There's a lot of end of term stuff to deal with.' He did not say it, but Nell felt him thinking that to accompany her would be an intrusion into Brad's world, and that he had no place there.

So she said, 'You've got the new Wilberforce book to finish, as well.'

'I have, and I suspect,' said Michael, 'that I'm running out of things to write about Wilberforce. There are only so many things a badly behaved cat can get up to in the space of thirty-five thousand words for eight-year-olds.'

'Did C.S. Lewis run out of Narnia tales?'

He smiled at her. 'No. But I'll stay here with Wilberforce – the fictional one and the real one. Where exactly are you going?'

'It's a small Derbyshire village called Caudle Moor. The house is called Stilter House, and it was built for a Ralph West. 1900 or thereabouts. Margery West sent me a copy of the deeds of the house and some of the early paperwork – builders' estimates and architects' reports and stuff like that.'

'Stilter's an odd name for a house,' said Michael, glancing at the large envelope on Nell's desk.

'I think stilt can be an architectural term. Something to do with pillars or piers.'

'It's still curious,' said Michael. 'I like Caudle, though.'

'It's an old name for a medieval posset,' said Nell, who had looked it up, guessing Michael would light on the name. 'A kind of egg-nog.'

'Did you hear that, Beth? You're going to Egg-nog Village for Easter.'

Beth, who had no idea what a posset or an egg-nog was, but who loved new words, beamed.

'I think,' said Michael thoughtfully, 'I might send Wilberforce on a visit to a tabby-cat aunt who lives in Egg-nog Village.'

'Aunt Tabitha,' said Beth, at once.

'*Yes.* Where's my notebook. Let's work that out now.'

After Michael had left and Beth had gone to bed, Nell explored the contents of Margery West's envelope. There was a slightly dog-eared photocopy of the title deeds, and Margery had included copies of the initial building orders and architects' reports. 'Which might be useful in dating some of the contents,' she had written.

Nell unfolded the first of the letters, which was from someone called Samuel Burlap.

Dear Mr West,

I have made time to look at the land you have purchased, which is known locally as Acton Field. I have paced it out myself, east boundary to west, and north to south, and it is some three-quarters of an acre, which I believe will do very well as a site for your house. The ground slopes steeply in places and there are, of course, still parts of the old Acton House that stood there. But we can demolish what's left of that, and if we site the house on the crest of the land you will get a view over Pickering's Meadows that will be something beautiful, such meadows being a sight to behold of a summer morning.

Mr Archibald Filbert of Derbyshire is preparing plans for a house and they will be ready in one month. He is a good architect, although a bit modern for some folks. What I recommend for your house, sir, is good Derbyshire stone and clay bricks, together with sound, properly weathered, English timber.

You will recall that the extension I built at your work-place in Derby two years ago was mostly in stone, and how very pleasing it was when finished.

Respectfully yours,
    Samuel Burlap,
    Builder.

Directly beneath this was a letter from the modernist architect, Archibald Filbert. Unlike Mr Burlap, who had written in careful and deliberate blue-black ink, Mr Filbert's missive was written on one of the new typewriting machines.

> Dear Mr West,
>
> I have to hand the plans for your new house on Acton Field in Caudle Moor, and believe you will be very happy with them. It is a traditional design, since you say you will be employing Mr Samuel Burlap for the building, and he may find it a perplexity to follow plans for a modern dwelling, being what you might term set in his ways, although a very good builder.
>
> I shall be pleased to discuss the house plans with you at a time and place convenient to you.
>
> A note of my charges is included with this letter.
>
> Assuring you of my best intentions at all times,
>
> Archibald Filbert (R.I.B.A.)

The small warfare between these two gentlemen amused Nell, and she turned to the next blue-black ink missive, to see what else the traditional Mr Burlap had to say.

> Dear Mr West,
>
> I have to hand your letter of 12th ultimo, and if I may make so bold, I suggest you take *absolutely no notice whatsoever* of the letter sent you by Prebendary Gilfillan. Most country districts have a few old legends, but the Acton land is no more haunted than my vegetable patch and there will be no ghosts to trouble you. If I may make so bold, sir, Prebendary Gilfillan is a gossiping nuisance with an unhealthy preoccupation with the past.
>
> Trusting you will also forgive my referring to a clergyman in such terms, but if Edgar Gilfillan has been nearer to a cathedral than a day-trip round All Saints in Derby, I should be very surprised indeed. Not wishing to be uncharitable, but I know the Gilfillan family well. They have lived in this area for many years and were always ones to present themselves as saintly.

Begging pardon again for plain speaking.
Very truly yours,
    S Burlap

Nell considered investigating the rest of the envelope's contents, in case there was anything from the saintly Prebendary who had apparently issued ghost warnings to Ralph West, but it was already half-past eleven which was late enough if she and Beth were to set off at seven tomorrow. She slid the letters carefully back in the envelope and put the envelope in her suitcase for tomorrow's journey to Caudle Moor.

But, drifting off to sleep, Samuel Burlap's words slid in and out of her mind.

The Acton land is no more haunted than my vegetable patch, he had written. *There will be no ghosts to trouble you . . .*

What ghosts? What ghosts did people think had troubled the land in the past?

TWO

T he drive to Caudle Moor was enjoyable. Nell and Beth played I Spy-type games as they went along, and stopped for an extra breakfast at a motorway pull-in, which Beth loved because she liked speculating where all the other people were going. Nell phoned Michael to say they were over halfway there. His phone went to voicemail, but she left a message and said she would ring again when they arrived.

As they left the industrial areas of the Midlands and crossed into Derbyshire, the landscape gave way to gently undulating countryside with rolling farmlands. There was a faint, early morning mist, and tiny B-roads branched off, with signposts marked with names that could not possibly have existed anywhere other than England: Wincle and Danebridge and Ramshorn. Beth read these out with delight, and she and Nell made up rhymes about them. It was something Brad and

Nell used to do on long car journeys, but it no longer felt
lonely to be doing it without him. Beth's idea of rhymes was
simplistic, but Nell heard, with a pang, that she had her father's
way of catching a resonance.

Beth said it was pretty cool to be going off like this on the
very first day of the Easter holidays, and double-cool to be
going to a house where Dad had stayed.

'I found a photo of him taken at Stilter House,' she said,
not looking at Nell.

'I didn't know we had any.'

'It was in that old suitcase. It's a really old photo and it
says "Stilter House" on the back. He looks about my age so
it must have been taken *years* ago, and— Why are you
laughing?'

'I'm not. Tell me about the photo.'

'He's sitting at a piano, and I know it's Dad on account of
that photo we've got in the frame when he was ten. He looks
exactly the same.'

'I don't remember ever seeing any photos of Stilter House.
Did you bring it with you?'

'No.' Beth retreated into silence, and Nell did not press her.
They still had private areas where Brad was concerned –
memories which were not automatically available for discussing.
This appeared to be one of those areas for Beth; she sent her
mother one of her enigmatic smiles, and reached for the MP3.
She's tuning me out, thought Nell. Fair enough.

It had begun to rain as they pulled off the motorway and
the signpost to Caudle Moor was half hidden behind dripping
trees, but Nell saw it in time and turned in.

'Almost there,' she said to Beth.

Almost there . . . Had Brad thought that when he came here
for holidays all those years ago? Had he travelled along this road
– perhaps on a bus or in an adult's car – a delighted eight or
nine year old, looking forward to going to the house with the
magical piano? The rain was still pattering down and the car's
windscreen wipers clicked back and forth in time to the words.
Almost there, almost there . . .

Caudle Moor was a speck of a place. There was a little
main street, a straggle of shops including a minuscule

supermarket, a pub, and a tiny police house overlooking a green.

Nell said, half to herself, 'And they say English villages like this don't exist any longer.'

'Maybe this one doesn't exist all the time,' said Beth hopefully. 'Maybe it's magic and it's only there for people who know where to look.'

'We have to turn right into Gorsty Lane,' said Nell, smiling. 'I can't see it – oh, there it is.'

Gorsty Lane was narrow and fringed by hedges and tall trees that interlinked their branches overhead, creating a green tunnel. With sunlight dappling the road it would be lovely here, and in a short time there would be a froth of white elderflower on the hedges and a haze of bluebells in the distant woodland. *Oh Brad*, thought Nell, *why did you never bring me here? Didn't you want to remember this place?*

I remember, I remember, the house where I was born . . . The words of the old poem slid into her mind. Brad had not been born in Stilter House, but it had formed a large part of his childhood. Nell was starting to feel as if he was very close to her – not the Brad she had married and loved, but the child he had been.

They glimpsed a scattering of cottages, looking like dolls' houses set down in fields, but Stilter House, when they reached it, was neither a cottage nor a dolls' house. There was a weathered gate with the name tacked on – Beth scampered gleefully out to unlatch it and Nell drove through. As she waited for Beth to close the gate, she leaned forward, trying to see the house, but it was veiled by the rain and the trees. But on the left she could make out a high garden wall, the bricks mellow and crusted with moss and ivy. There was a latched door set into the wall halfway along and Nell stared at this and thought, *What would I do, if that door swung open now, and a boy with tip-tilted eyes like Beth's and a flop of soft brown hair walked out . . .?*

I remember, I remember . . .

Beth got back into the car, smelling of fresh rain and clean hair, and Nell suddenly wanted to hug her because she was all that was left of Brad. But Beth hated what she called slop, so Nell drove forward trying to avoid the worst of the ruts. And there, through the rain, was Stilter House.

On a sunlit day, Brad's childhood house would be friendly and welcoming, the grey stones and mullioned windows glowing with light and warmth. Seen through an April rainstorm it was dour and remote. The trees surrounding it were bowed over with rain and thin branches reached out goblin fingers to the windows. The rooms behind those windows would be dark, and the tapping of tree branches would sound like someone asking to be let in.

It was larger than Nell had expected – what was once termed a gentleman's residence – and it stood in substantial grounds. *Three-quarters of an acre, and if we site the house on the crest you will get a view over Pickering's Meadows . . . And there will be no ghosts to trouble you . . .*

Nell said cheerfully to Beth that this was much grander than she had expected – she had never known Dad had stayed in such a terrific place.

'We'll unload everything and set out the sleeping bags, then we'll explore, shall we?'

They were going to stay in the house. Nell had thought this would make it easier and quicker to work through the contents, and Margery West had written that even though it had been empty for over a year it should be perfectly habitable. But seeing the house, Nell was not so sure if it was a good idea.

Margery had sent a set of keys and had arranged for the electricity to be switched on. Nell unlocked the front door and the mustiness of a long-empty house greeted her. She stood for a moment, feeling the house's atmosphere engulf her. It was a quiet house, an elderly lady's house. *Great-Aunt Charlotte*, thought Nell, *I think you lived a gentle, slightly old-fashioned life here. You visited friends and they visited you, you dabbled in local gossip, you read books, and enjoyed music . . .*

Music . . . A faint sound stirred deep within the house, not exactly music, but something that might once have been music. Nell glanced down at Beth, but Beth was looking about her with bright-eyed interest, and did not seem to have heard anything. Probably it had been the rain trickling through gutters.

The fresh rain scents were already filling up the hall, and the slight mustiness was dispersing. Rooms opened off the main hall on each side, and at the far end was a stairway with a carved banister, worn smooth by age. Had Brad slid gleefully down that, and been indulgently told not to in case he fell off?

Nell shook off the images, and said, 'The kitchen will be at the back, I should think. Let's take the box of food in and make ourselves a drink.'

The kitchen was a large, rather old-fashioned room, high ceilinged and stone floored. There was an oak table at the centre and a huge dresser against one wall. The dresser might fetch a very good price, thought Nell, eyeing it, and so might the gorgeous blue and white china set on it. It looked like Minton.

Thankfully there was a fairly modern gas cooker, together with a microwave and an electric kettle. Nell turned on the tap and the water ran rustily into the deep old stone sink, but then cleared. She let it run a while longer, then filled the kettle and switched it on. There was a fridge which she also switched on; it would take a while to get properly cold, but when she explored the rest of the kitchen, there was a narrow stone-floored larder with a marble slab where they could put the butter and milk for the time being.

She was setting out the provisions when she heard the music again, and this time it was certainly not rainwater. This was someone playing a piano – a piece of Mozart, Nell thought. Beth was nowhere to be seen; most likely she had been exploring the house and had found the piano. Nell listened for a moment, thinking Beth must have been practising diligently. Leaving the kettle to boil she went out into the hall, calling Beth's name.

The music had stopped, but Beth called out from one of the rooms and Nell made her way down the shadowy hall, trying to see a light switch, but not finding one.

Beth was in a big room on the left of the hall. Rain rippled down the windows, bathing the room in a faintly greenish light as if it lay at the bottom of a deep lake. But even like this, it was a lovely room, high ceilinged and with deep bay windows. At the far end French windows overlooked a small terrace with mossy steps, and a jutting chimney breast was flanked by shelves stacked with books and what looked like music scores. Near the French windows was a low, dark, gleaming shape. Charlotte West's piano – a baby grand – the piano that had been such a part of Brad's summers.

Beth was perched on a music stool, beaming and Nell started to say, 'So you found the piano—' Then stopped, realizing that the piano's lid was shut.

In the same moment, Beth said, 'I was going to play something to surprise you, but it's locked and I can't find the key.'

There would be a perfectly logical explanation. Nell knew this. She had certainly heard piano music only minutes earlier, but it could have come from anywhere. A car could have been parked nearby – she had not yet worked out exactly where Stilter House was in relation to the bewilderment of lanes, but it was possible that one side of the house was closer to a road than she had realized. Or there could be a property nearby with a radio on and a window open. In this rain, though?

Still, it was important not to alarm Beth, who was already looking puzzled, so Nell said, 'We'll hunt for the key later and you can surprise me then.'

It was only when they were back in the kitchen that she discovered the kettle, switched on a good ten minutes earlier, was stone cold. Nell swore at it, then apologized to it – which made Beth giggle – and flicked several switches. Lights, cooker, even an iron. Nothing. Obviously Margery's instructions had become lost or misunderstood.

'OK,' she said to Beth, 'there are two things we can do. We can try to find a local pub or a b&b with a room—'

'That'd be boring. I *like* it here, it's Dad's house.'

'Or we can stay here and light candles.'

'Could we? I'd like that'

'Well, let's find out if it's practical,' said Nell, opening cupboard doors. 'Because if there aren't candles or matches—'

'We could drive back to the village and buy some.'

'Yes, but . . . No, it's all right, there're candles and matches in this cupboard. So far so good.' It was April, the middle of an English spring, the evenings were light and even with the teeming rain it was not cold. What about cooking though? There appeared to be a gas supply, but was it connected?

'We could send out for pizzas,' said Beth hopefully, as Nell wrestled with the gas cooker. Beth loved sending out for pizzas which she considered a grown-up thing.

'There's no phone and the mobile signal isn't working – I tried a few minutes ago.'

'We could *drive* out for pizzas,' said Beth, not to be daunted.

But the gas cooker worked. 'It's looking good,' said Nell. 'Let's see if the gas fires work. It might be cold later.'

Two of the rooms had gas fires; one in a small sitting room overlooking the gardens, the other in the music room. They looked to be the same vintage as the cooker, but they both leapt reassuringly into life. Nell sat back on her knees in front of the piano, the gas fire leaping warmly, and smiled. 'Two days of candlelight, then.'

'Good.'

'Let's sort out the bedrooms now.'

The bedrooms were large and Beth wrinkled her nose at the furniture.

'It's pretty grim, isn't it?'

'People pay money for grimness these days. And some of it's beautiful,' said Nell, running her hands over a small bow-fronted bureau.

In a small room overlooking the back of the house were bookcases filled with children's books. Beth instantly sat down to examine these, and Nell saw that the titles and authors were from the 1930s and 1940s. Enid Blyton's school stories and some of the Greyfriars books. There were also some Elinor Brent-Dyer and Angela Brazil titles; Nell thought Brent-Dyer went back to the 1920s, and Angela Brazil was as far back as 1910. She would look more closely later, to see if there were any first editions. She paused, looking about her. Had this been Brad's room when he stayed here? Had he gone to sleep reading one of those books about long-ago childhoods, and had he woken to that view over the lanes?

Leaving Beth among the jolly hockey sticks of Blyton's and Brazil's girl boarders, she investigated the other bedrooms. A large one at the side of the house had twin beds, and Nell thought she and Beth could sleep here. And by the time they had spread the sleeping bags on the beds, eaten a picnic lunch and explored Stilter House more fully, it began to feel friendlier. Nell made a start on the inventory, working through the rooms systematically.

It was annoying to find it was impossible to make a phone call, though. The mobile signal appeared to be out of range, and the landline was disconnected, of course. But there would be a phone box in the village or at the local pub, and Nell could phone Michael from there tomorrow. She was glad that at least she had left him a message earlier on, so he would know they had got here.

Edinburgh,
April 20—
Dear Emily,

A nice note this morning from Nell West to say they're setting off for Stilter House on Monday. She will provide a list of anything she thinks is worth selling through the conventional antiques circuit, together with photographs and an estimate of the figures we can hope to achieve. She's going to stay at Stilter for a couple of nights while she makes an inventory; it sounds as if she likes the idea of Beth seeing the house where Brad used to stay as a child.

She seems interested in the house's history – she says all houses have a story to tell and she likes trying to find those stories – and she's going to read the copies I sent her of those old letters and accounts Ralph West kept. She says if there are any receipts it might help date some of the contents and provide a provenance. I haven't said anything about the blue and white Minton, because we both know the story of how *that* was supposed to have been acquired. Personally, I never believed it of Charlotte's mother – she was far too ladylike to smuggle out an entire Minton dinner service during a Townswomen's Guild tour of the china factory. There are thirty-two pieces, for goodness' sake!

In answer to your question, no, I have not told Nell about Esmond. As you know, I was always firmly of the opinion that Charlotte imagined all of that.

I certainly do *not* think you should try cosmic surgery for your leg, whatever cosmic surgery may be. It sounds extremely suspicious. Have you thought of acupuncture? I believe the Chinese are very wise in these matters.

Fondest love,

Margery

Edinburgh,
April 20—
Dear Emily,

I like your suggestion that we make a small bequest to Beth. I'll ask Nell to look for something in the house that can be kept until she's older. And we might set up a small savings account for her with a portion of the house sale proceeds.

But I think you're overreacting in saying Nell shouldn't stay at the house after dark, and that Beth shouldn't go to the house at all. But you were always given to dramatic behaviour – that's not a criticism, dear, just a statement of fact. Nell and Beth will be perfectly all right.

Margery

THREE

Michael Flint had had a mixed weekend. It was the last few days of Hilary Term, with all the end of term activities enlivening Oriel College. Students wandered in and out to say goodbye, or include him in various farewell activities.

Owen Bracegirdle from the history faculty held a Sunday lunch buffet in his rooms, which had been intended to go on until a decorous mid-afternoon, but ended up lasting until six o'clock. Michael returned to his rooms to learn that Wilberforce had spent his own afternoon in pitched battle with the ginger tomcat belonging to Oriel's chaplain, with whom he was currently conducting a territorial war. It was unfortunate that this latest battle had taken place in Oriel's chapel, which, as the porter said, could not have been much more public, and it a Sunday, to boot.

'And the yowls Wilberforce let out when we hauled him out, Dr Flint – well, you'd have thought he was being gutted for violin strings.'

'I will gut him for violin strings if he does it again,' said Michael wrathfully, and bundled the unrepentant Wilberforce into his rooms before seeking out the chaplain to apologize, during which he found himself agreeing to pay the vet's bill for the ginger tom's bitten ear.

On the crest of this incident, he wrote a new chapter of the current Wilberforce book, in which the fictional Wilberforce signed up for a Japanese martial arts class, the better to deal with the ever-inventive mice who plagued his life, but found himself in the wrong schoolroom learning Oriental flower-arranging by mistake. Michael emailed this to his editor, intending her to deal with it on Monday, and was slightly disconcerted to get an almost immediate reply saying she was currently in America, but would read the new chapter that evening in her hotel because Wilberforce would make a welcome diversion after schmoozing book buyers and reviewers.

After this he checked his voicemail and was pleased to hear Nell's voice with a message timed just before ten that morning, telling him they were on the outskirts of Bakewell and they had had an uneventful journey, but the phone signal was getting a bit erratic, so she was sorry if she sounded crackly. She would try to phone again later.

Michael was just relenting so far towards Wilberforce as to give him a bowl of his favourite tuna chunks, when the phone rang. He hoped it would be Nell, but it turned out to be Henry Jessel from the silversmith's shop adjoining Nell's.

'Michael, I'm glad to catch you in,' said Henry. 'I looked into Nell's shop earlier – she left me a key and asked me to check answerphone messages fairly often, because she's hoping to hear from those Japanese customers who might buy that Regency desk. They haven't phoned, but there's a message on the machine that I'm worried about, and I don't know what to do. I tried to phone Nell, but her mobile's inaccessible.'

'She left a message earlier saying the signal was erratic,' said Michael.

'I dare say there's acres upon acres up there that are out of reach of a signal. I emailed her as well, but I don't know if she's taken her laptop – or if she'd check emails anyway.'

'I think she was taking it, but she might not check emails until this evening, or even tomorrow,' said Michael. 'What's the worrying phone message?'

'I think you need to hear it,' said Henry. 'Is there any chance you could whizz over?'

'Now?'

'Well . . .'

Michael glanced at his watch. It was half past eight. 'All right, but I'll have to get a taxi,' he said. 'I've been sloshing vino at somebody's lunch since midday. I'll be there as quickly as I can.'

On the way to Quire Court he tried Nell's mobile again, but it was still inaccessible. A nearby church clock was chiming nine as he crossed the court; Michael had never identified which church this was, but he always liked hearing it. He liked Quire Court as well, which was a small quadrangle near Brasenose College. He had the feeling that it was one of the corners where fragments of Oxford's long and vivid history had collected, and that one day those fragments might overflow, in a glorious confused cascade of Norman invasions and Saxon settlements, and civil wars and dreaming poets and quarrelsome academics.

There was a notice on Nell's shop saying that from Monday to Wednesday all customers should please go to Henry Jessel, at Silver Edges, next door. Michael, who had a key, let himself in, enjoying the familiar scents of old wood and beeswax, and the bowls of dried lavender which Nell always placed on the choicer tables or desks she was selling. At the moment there was a round cherrywood table and a set of chairs in the main window, as well as the Regency desk, earmarked for the Japanese customer.

As he went through to the office at the back of the shop Henry came bustling in, his elderly cherub face worried.

'I saw you arrive and I'm so glad you've come, Michael, because I haven't known *what* to do.' He indicated the answerphone. 'It's a most peculiar message. The caller phoned twice, I think. The first time she didn't speak – as if she hadn't expected to get a recording and it disconcerted her. The second one is about fifteen minutes later.'

'As if she had to prepare what she was going to say?'

'That's what I thought. Here goes.'

As Henry had said, the first call was silent, apart from a faint crackle from the machine. It cut out, then went on to the second one. It was unmistakably an elderly lady's voice – but it was not the quavery voice of weak old age; it was a vigorous, decisive voice. Michael had the impression that she might be reading from some notes.

'Nell,' said the voice. 'This is Emily West – Brad's Aunt Emily. I hope you remember me – we met a couple of times, and Margery has arranged for you to list and value the contents of Aunt Charlotte's house. I'm very glad about that, although I should think it will be quite a task because Charlotte lived at Stilter House since she was born, so there will be a lot of stuff.

'I have written to you, but as I haven't heard back I'm concerned my letter might have distressed you. Or perhaps I've simply got your address wrong and you haven't received it yet, which is why I'm phoning. Nell, my dear, I strongly advise you not to stay at Stilter House itself. There's a very nice pub in Caudle village and they let out perfectly comfortable rooms. It would reassure me very much if I could know you and Beth will stay there.

'Lots of love to you both. Here's my phone number in case you haven't got it. I'll be away for a few days at a health farm. Only a small place, but I'm told they do some marvellous things. I'll be back on Thursday.'

The message paused, but Emily West did not hang up. Michael glanced quizzically at Henry, who held up a finger, indicating, Wait.

Emily's voice came again, a little breathless this time.

'Please don't stay at Stilter House, Nell. Because whatever Margery may say, Esmond never left Stilter House. He is still there. Charlotte knew it and I know it. And Beth is so very like Brad was at that age.'

The dial tone returned as Emily hung up, and Michael looked at Henry in bewilderment.

Henry said, 'You see what I mean? It's so peculiar, I don't know whether we ought to tell Nell about it. Always supposing we can reach her.'

'Nor do I,' said Michael, frowning. 'But she was going to stay at the house – Stilter House – I do know that.'

'Is the call genuine? I mean – is Emily West genuine?'

'I think so. She's the elder sister or cousin of the aunt who set this up. That was Margery West.'

'Emily sounds perfectly lucid and intelligent, doesn't she?'

'Well, yes. That last part though – she sounded as if she said all that on an impulse. As if she'd written out what to say, then gave in to some impulse.'

'That's what I thought.'

'Is there a time on the call?'

'Yes, wait a minute – eleven o'clock this morning,' said Henry, having peered at the machine's display screen. 'Are you going to ring her back?'

'I think I'd better try. She said she was going away, but I'll phone her. What time is it – quarter past nine? That's not too late, is it?'

'Try anyway.'

But when Michael rang the number Emily West had given, there was no reply.

'Then she's gone to her health farm,' said Henry.

'I'll try again in the morning,' said Michael. 'And I'll try Nell again later, but I don't want to alarm her. I'm sure it's nothing.'

'The letter Emily mentioned might turn up tomorrow, as well,' said Henry. 'Nell did tell me to open anything addressed to the shop – particularly anything that looked urgent or important. I'll phone you if it does arrive.'

'It might give a bit more information,' said Michael.

'Do let me know if it's anything dramatic, won't you,' said

Henry hopefully. 'I love a bit of drama, and you don't get much drama flogging silver and engraving charm bracelets and watches. Well, it depends on what people want engraving. You wouldn't believe what some of them ask for and half the time they can't spell it anyway.'

Michael stayed long enough to hear some of the more scurrilous tales about Henry's customers, then went back to Oriel where he tried Nell's mobile again but still with no success.

He ate a belated meal in his rooms, and tried to work on Wilberforce again, but Emily West's phone call kept intruding, and he was aware of an uneasy prickling at the back of his mind.

It was, of course, some fantasy imagining of an elderly lady; Michael thought he would not pay too much attention to it. Or would he? Emily West's words ran through his mind yet again. *Esmond never left Stilter House,* she had said. The prickle of unease increased, and Michael thought if he had not made contact with Nell by this time tomorrow, he might try to track down Margery West.

It was all nonsense, of course, and he was overreacting. Nell would phone tomorrow, and in any case she would be home on Wednesday evening, and they would have supper together. Michael would cook for them as he always did when Nell had been away on a buying expedition, and she would relate all her exploits as they ate, which was also a small tradition. This time he would try not to have a culinary disaster, although it was remarkable how easily things got burned in his cooker, or did not cook at all.

But the words on the answerphone kept replaying. *Esmond never left Stilter House . . .* And, *Beth is so very like Brad was at that age . . .*

Esmond . . . The unease at the back of his mind stirred again.

Nell and Beth had scrambled eggs for their supper, after which Beth seemed happy to go up to bed. She had picked out one of the children's books, and Nell had found a box of old-fashioned night lights in a cupboard which would be quite safe for Beth to read by. She tucked her in, left her absorbed in the long-ago world of plucky schoolgirls to whom rap and boy bands and text-speak would be a foreign language, and thought she would take a look at the rest of the children's books while she was up here. It was already almost dark, but if she lit a couple more candles she would be able to read titles and authors.

The small bedroom, lit by the candles, had a comfortable atmosphere. Nell sat cross-legged on the floor in front of the shelves, enjoying sorting through the books. There were complete sets of Enid Blyton's Malory Towers school stories, as well as the Brent-Dyer and Angela Brazil books. The Angela Brazil ones were cloth covered, and appeared to be first editions. Nell listed all the titles carefully, recording the ISBNs and dates of publication, and thought she would photograph the covers and the end papers tomorrow, in order to discuss them with the bookseller in Quire Court when she got back.

She was just reaching for a copy of *The Water Babies*, which was surely considerably older than the other books, when a sheet of ruled paper, covered with a child's writing, slid out of it. Nell, supposing it was a home-made bookmark, but interested in the child who might have placed it there, unfolded it.

It was not a bookmark. It was a letter, and it was dated twenty-five years earlier.

Dear Esmond,

I know you'll find this, because The Water Babies is your favourite book and you'll read it again really soon.

I'm very sorry I won't be at Stilter House to know about the secret you promised to share with me, but I have to go home early tomorrow morning, because my father has just heard he's being posted to Germany. My mother phoned earlier to say so – it must have been while we were playing the duet. Aunt Charlotte says I'll be going to Germany for my next school holidays instead of coming here.

I wanted to say goodbye, because I know you hate it when people go away without saying goodbye. But I will come back one day, and we'll play some more duets and I'll practise extra hard so I can keep up with you.

I wish you had told me what the secret is!

From Brad West.

It was a long time before Nell laid the little note down, and when she finally did so tears were streaming down her face. *So you do haunt this house after all*, she said to Brad's memory. *And you had a friend here called Esmond, and you used to play the piano with him. And when you were nine, Brad – the age your daughter is now – you left Esmond this note inside his favourite book.*

She dashed the tears away impatiently, and reread the note, touching it with her fingertips as if a trace of Brad might linger on it. It was so easy to imagine two boys playing in the gardens at Stilter, exploring the lanes – perhaps for blackberries in autumn or birds' nests in spring – and picking out a duet on the piano. Having their childhood secrets from the adults . . . Esmond, whoever he was, must have come here often and been made very welcome to have been in the habit of borrowing books from this room. Nell held *The Water Babies* for a moment longer, then replaced it on the shelf.

The room was dark now, and rain had started to lash against the windows. She snuffed the extra candles, and went along to the large bedroom. Beth was asleep, the Malory Towers book upside down. Nell stood by the bed for a moment, looking down at the small figure. Beth's hair was ruffled on the pillow and she was not quite smiling, but she looked as if her dreams were pleasant ones. Nell felt the ache of Brad's loss all over again. She wanted him to be standing next to her, to share this moment with him, to look down at their sleeping daughter and then to exchange smiles of mutual congratulation. For a moment she thought something sighed in the room's shadowy corners and she turned sharply, but there was nothing. Brad was not here, despite that fragment of memory he had left in his note. He would never smile at Beth again and it was stupid to wish for what could not be. She touched Beth's face lightly, then went downstairs.

The little sitting room was snug, the gas fire popping gently and casting a warm glow of light. Nell thought she would have a final cup of coffee and see if the candlelight was enough for her to type her notes onto the laptop, hoping that would help drive back the clustering memories. But it did not, and after ten minutes she gave up and switched off the laptop.

The best way to deal with a ghost was probably to confront it. Very well, she would confront Stilter House's past, which was also Brad's past and see if the memories could be diluted that way. The wodge of papers Margery West had sent were inside the laptop case, and Nell drew out the sheaf of letters sent to Ralph West during the building of this house.

April 1900
Dear Mr West,

We have finally levelled the site, apart from the old outbuildings and I shall use casual labour to demolish those. Even as I write, the apprentice, Adolphus, is taking messages to the labouring gang, who live in and around Caudle Moor, offering them the work.

Yesterday I paced out the footings again. I like to be sure everything is in order and make it a rule to double-check everything – a fact which doubtless you will recall I employed during our first meeting in Derby.

I'm afraid we have had Prebendary Gilfillan on the site again. Might you have a polite word with him? I am sure he is welcome to walk on your land, but it distracts the men when he begins praying and intoning rituals, saying the ground must be purified of its evil, and the unquiet spirits banished. Last week Mr Filbert and I were discussing the best place to site the mains drains, and the Prebendary walked along a trench my men had dug out, reciting the Lord's Prayer as he went, with several excursions into the Twenty Third Psalm. I am a reasonable man and accustomed to working in all kinds of conditions, but psalms in sewer trenches are not what I care for.

Respectfully yours,
    S Burlap,
    Builder.

April 1900
Dear Mr West,

I am sorry to report a problem with the demolishing of the outbuildings. The boy, Adolphus, delivered the messages

to the local labouring men as per our arrangement, but none
of them seem to be available for hiring.

Two plead illness, viz., to wit:

1. A stiff neck running down both arms, making it
   impossible to swing a sledgehammer and the pain cruel
   as charity.
2. Wife sick something chronic, and cannot be left.
   (The wife in question is, I am afraid, a little too fond
   of frequenting the local hostelries, although it is
   ungenerous of Prebendary Gilfillan to say she will be
   flat on her back from an excess of gin. Although sadly
   probably true).

In addition, two more men have apparently accepted
other casual work, in one case emptying the cess pit on
Sir Beecham Bondley's estate, in the other lime-washing
Sir Beecham's buttery which seemingly stinks to high
heaven on account of four cock pheasants and six
partridges having been left there by the gamekeeper last
autumn to ripen, but overlooked, resulting in the carcasses
ripening to putrefaction level.

If we are to finish the house by the end of the summer,
I cannot take my men from their work to demolish the
outbuildings. I recommend, therefore, that we leave them
be. They are some distance from the house, and perfectly
safe, particularly if I secure the loose sections of roof
slates and nail up flapping windows.

I await your instructions, and am, as always, your
obedient servant,

  S Burlap,
  Builder.

April 1900
Dear Mr West,

I have to hand your letter of yesterday's date and am
glad you agree we should leave the outbuildings in place.
They could easily be demolished at some future date.
Also, if you plant a climbing ivy or a nice Virginia creeper
on the south wall you will hardly see where the roof has
fallen in over the coal shed.

I remain, dear sir, yours respectfully,
   S Burlap,
   Builder.

FOUR

Nell laid the letters down. They had served their purpose a little; Brad's ghost had stepped back into the shadows, and the ghosts of Samuel Burlap and Ralph West were more prominent.

The renewed hints in the letters that the land was haunted were intriguing; it might be interesting to delve deeper into that. But probably the trail would be too vague, and most old and remote country houses had a legend attached to them.

Nell wondered what relation Ralph had been to Brad. Great-grandfather? Great-great uncle? She must ask Margery. Perhaps she and Beth would find some photographs of Ralph or his family while they were here. Part of the reason for coming here was to give Beth a few memories of her father's family.

She reached for the next letter, which this time was headed: *Doctor Brodworthy, The Surgery, Caudle Moor. Consulting Rooms open 10.00 to 12.30 each weekday. Members of Mutual, Benefit 'or Friendly Organizations, and Oddfellows Societies, seen on Wednesday afternoons by appointment.*

May 1900
My dear Mr West,

   I write at the urgent request of a patient, Mr Samuel Burlap, (Builder), to inform you that work on your new house on Acton Fields has been temporarily delayed due to Mr Burlap's indisposition.

   I am hopeful that this will only be a short delay; however, there has been an incident of the most unfortunate kind, and Mr Burlap is presently incapable of overseeing the work. Being a prudent man, and a moderately prosperous one, he has paid into the Good Fellows Mutual & Benefit Society, so is assured of proper care.

You will appreciate that I have a duty of confidentiality to my patient, and trust you will accept my assurance that the illness is in the nature of a temporary disturbance of mental facilities, and that after a judicious period of rest and calm, Mr Burlap will resume his duties.

I am, sir, very sincerely yours,
E Brodworthy. M.D.

Clipped to this letter, with a pin that had rusted into the paper, was what appeared to be a report on Mr Burlap's condition, sent to the Good Fellows Mutual & Benefit Society, again on Dr Brodworthy's headed notepaper.

May 1900
Sirs,

I beg to enclose a note of my charges for treatment for two weeks to one Samuel Burlap of Caudle Moor in the County of Derbyshire, Mr Burlap having, as I understand it, been a member of your esteemed Organization for several years, and you being therefore bound in honour to attend to my fees.

As per your Rules and Terms, I enclose my report on Mr Burlap's condition, and as your Rules also request in a case of mental disturbance, his own statement.

Your early settlement of my fee will oblige.

Yours very truly,
E Brodworthy. M.D.

The fee that the good doctor had apparently deemed appropriate on this occasion was one guinea, and although Dr Brodworthy's report did not appear to have survived, Samuel Burlap's own statement was there and clearly had been written down verbatim. Nell, scanning the first few sentences, received a brief image of an earnest clerk seated at the corner of a desk, scribbling for dear life everything that Burlap said.

> Report in re: Mr Samuel Burlap.
> Statement made by Mr Burlap to Dr Brodworthy, on 23rd April 1900
>
> I'd like to make it clear, that I'm as sane as ever I was and as sane as any man. I'd like that written down in this statement, clear and bold, so it's properly understood.
>
> I dare say the Mutual & Benefit people are used to mad people protesting their sanity, and I dare say they'll read what I have to say and remember that the asylums are filled to the eaves with poor souls who believe themselves sane.
>
> Or they might think I was drunk, so I'd like it set down that I enjoy a glass of ale of an evening, but never in excess. It'd be bad for my business if folk thought I had taken to drink. It'd be even worse for my business if they thought I had taken to seeing things as weren't there – things I know can't be there, never mind all the nightmares and fears a man pushes down into the depths of his soul.

Nell paused for a moment, listening to the storm that was still lashing rain against the windows of Stilter House. It was the kind of night when you were glad to be safely indoors. She got up to make sure the window was firmly closed, then reached for the papers again, wondering whether to postpone reading the rest of Burlap's statement until tomorrow – or even to take it back to Oxford. But she was curious to know what had happened to Mr Burlap and it was only a quarter to ten, too early to go up to bed.

> I dare say it might also be wondered if I'm what they call malingering. But I'm not a malingerer and never will be, having been brought up strict Presbyterian by my mother. Mr Ralph West is paying a fair price for his house, and a house he shall have, never mind if half the ghosts in Christendom rear up to gibber at me.

The next line was crossed through, as if the clerk or secretary had written something down, and Samuel Burlap had wanted to withdraw it. Nell held the paper closer to the candle and thought she could make out the words, 'Even if they're ghosts I might recognize . . .' But the scoring-out had been done firmly, and she could not be sure she had deciphered it correctly.

This is what happened to me on Tuesday evening.

By six o'clock I had finished my day's work on Mr West's house, and I was pleased with what I had done.

Building a house is a remarkable thing. It's like seeing a living creation emerge and know you've been the one who created it. Maybe artists painting wonderful pictures feel like that, or people who write books or poetry. I wouldn't know about that, though, for my mother didn't hold with such stuff, and I was brought up in the belief that proper work for a man is building and carpentering and smithing. Farming, too, of course. I'm none the worse and likely the better for having such an upbringing, and I should have brought up my own children in the same way, had Mrs Burlap and I been blessed with any, which we have not, although I should not like it thought I was ever neglectful of my marital duties, or Mrs Burlap unwilling. You'll excuse my mentioning that.

But when it comes to my houses – well, I always feel a pride, and I like to know people will live in those houses and weave their own histories. History isn't always what's written in books or taught in schools. The history of ordinary men and women is embedded in walls and floors and timbers of buildings.

I set off to walk home that Tuesday night, thinking of nothing more than the rabbit pie Mrs Burlap would have ready for supper. It was twilight – that part of the day when fanciful folk tell how the shadow beings gather, waiting for the night to fall so they can walk abroad. A lot of rubbish, but it's an hour when a man might, if he was so minded, imagine he saw things that were not there.

What I saw first, though, was the house – Mr West's

house, *my* house, as I still think of it. I should explain here that it's nearing finish. We've got what you might call the shell erected, but we still have to put in floors and inner walls and ceilings.

But seen from Gorsty Lane in the spring twilight the house had taken on a different look. For the first time, it looked to me as if it were distorted. As if something had wrenched at the carefully placed joists and joints, and pulled them all a fraction out of true. So strong was this impression I wondered if I had made a mistake in my measurements, or if Mr Filbert's plans had been wrong. But I knew I had made the most careful calculations, and Archibald Filbert is diligent and methodical.

But the impression of something wrong persisted. The central portion juts out from the main frontage, and on the first floor are two tall windows on each side of this section. Standing in the half-light, those windows took on the appearance of huge, grotesque eyes, as if the house was staring down at me.

There were no lights anywhere, and no sounds, but I knew someone was nearby. I knew it in the same way that you enter a darkened room and need no light to tell you someone's there.

However, I'm a practical man, so my first thought was a practical one. If there's anyone here, I thought, it'll be gypsies or tramps. They'll be scouring the place for items to make use of or sell – workmen's tools, or even a sack of mortar or a tub of paint. I was angry more than anything else, and I went toward the house at once, for I was not having my careful work disturbed and my tools stolen. Nor was I giving much attention to the creeping unease that was stealing over me, at least not then.

But the uneasiness increased with every step. I was not frightened of louts – I've sent many a one about his business. This was a different unease, a cold prickling nervousness, a feeling that something was warning me of danger close by. They tell you that our long-ago ancestors, living in caves, had an extra sense which we've almost lost today – a sense that warned them of danger. I don't know about that, all I know is that as I walked across that piece of land it felt as if something was crouching in the shadows watching me. But nothing moved until I came level with the house. Then something darted across the shadows, its shape so blurred I was not sure I had seen anything at all. A trick of the light, or a breath of wind stirring the silvered trees, creating an illusion, that's what I tried to tell myself, but I did not really believe that. As I stood there, the movement came again, and this time I knew it was not a trick of the light. It whisked across the darkness and into the straggle of outbuildings on the far side of the house.

I went after it. I don't pretend to be especially courageous, but I hope I'm not a coward, and most of my mind was still angry at this intruder who was daring to scavenge among my careful work.

I want this next piece written down firm and exact, as I'm telling you.

As I went towards the old outbuildings, I heard music. Someone playing a piano. That was impossible. Ahead of me was the shell of Ralph West's house and behind and all around me were the dark, deserted lanes. It was impossible that someone could be playing a piano so close to me. And yet there it was. Light, delicate music. But cold. No, I can't explain how music can be cold, but so it was. Like the snapping of icicles in the depths of winter.

Fear swept over my entire body, because I knew I was hearing music where no music could exist.

FIVE

*M*usic where no music could exist . . .

Nell read these last sentences again, a pulse of unease beating in her mind. That's what I heard earlier tonight, she thought. Music inside this house. Music where no music could exist, because the piano is locked up and we haven't got the key, and there's no electricity on for radios or stereos.

There would be a logical explanation for both incidents, though. The music Nell heard would have been a car radio in one of the lanes, and Samuel Burlap, despite his protestations had most likely had a few drinks. She laid the papers down, leaning her head back, staring into the gas fire. She was starting to feel sleepy – it had been an early start to the day and a long drive and there had been a mixture of emotions waiting in the house. In a moment she would put Mr Burlap away and go up to bed. In a moment.

The flames of any fire – even a gas fire – conjured up pictures, evocative, comforting. Brad would have known this room. Had the fireplace been open then? Had Charlotte West lit a fire in the evenings, and had the seven- or eight-year-old Brad stared into its depths and seen the pictures children did see in firelight? Goblins' caves and fiery mountains and sala-manders . . . You did not see caves or mountains in a gas fire, but there was still a sense that there might be something on the other side of the flames.

The room was warm and although rain still beat against the windows, it was a soothing sound, mingling with the soft hissing of the gas. Nell's eyelids felt as if weights were pressing down, and although she was not quite asleep, she was no longer fully awake. She was in those borderlands where reality and dreams blur and blend, and where the impossible knits itself into the possible. Where soft music weaves itself into the dream patterns and the dreamer's awareness.

Music. It tapped against her mind. She liked music. She and Brad often used to go to concerts, and one of her favourite memories of him was of a night when he had sat down at a friend's piano and played Scott Joplin, amidst a lot of wrong notes and laughter, and how he had gone on to sketch out a few notes of Dvorak's *Humoresque* before closing the piano with a flourish and saying he was years out of practice. It was one of the memories that had led her to suggest piano lessons to Beth.

It was not Scott Joplin or Dvorak she was hearing now though, and when she opened her eyes, it had gone. *I was half asleep and I dreamed it*, thought Nell. *I probably translated the sound of rain into music because of Burlap's statement, and because Brad wrote that letter to his friend Esmond about playing duets.*

She was about to dismiss the whole thing and get up from the chair when the sound came again and now there was no doubt about it. It was light and fragile, but it was unmistakably someone playing a piano. The music was delicate but intricate, Chopin, perhaps, or Debussy. Nell might almost have suspected Beth of creeping downstairs and finding the piano's key, but Beth's playing was certainly not of this standard. Was this the music Samuel Burlap had heard over a century earlier?

Panic threatened, then Nell remembered she did not believe in ghosts or ghost-music. Summoning up all her resolve, she reached for one of the candles, and went out to the hall. The candle flame sent shadows leaping across the darkness and the music wove itself in and out of the shadows, as elusive as quicksilver. *And colder than ice*, thought Nell, repressing a shiver. *Burlap said it was cold, and now I know what he meant. But this can't be Burlap's music. Maybe I'm still asleep and dreaming.* As she went towards the music room, this last possibility seemed very likely, because the whole setting was so much the traditional walk through the haunted house it was almost too good to be true.

Could it be Beth after all, perhaps suffering from some form of sleepwalking? She had had a series of nightmares a couple of years ago – could they be returning in the form of sleepwalking?

The front door rattled as a strong gust of wind blew against it, and for a moment it was as if someone was standing out there, trying to force the door open. The candle flame flickered, and in its erratic light Nell saw something crouching at the far end of the hall. A small figure – hunched by the wall, its face turned towards her. Oh God, someone had broken in – someone was huddled in the dark corner, watching her . . .

She began to retreat, her heart racing with fear, praying the candle would not snuff out and leave her in pitch darkness.

And then the flurry of wind died down and the flame burned up again, and she realized all she had seen was the squat shape of the old umbrella stand. Optical illusion, Nell. Get a grip. But surely to goodness you were entitled to imagine you saw nightmare things in this setting?

The door of the music room was ajar, and she took a deep breath and went towards it. The shadows were deeper here, but she could see the piano from the doorway, the silken wood gleaming, but the darkness twisting so thickly around it that it was impossible to make out details. Was it open? Was someone seated on the stool, reaching out to the keys? She took a step further into the room, and as she did so, the curtains stirred in another draught of cold air. The candle flame went out and darkness closed down. The music stopped as abruptly as if a door had been slammed.

Nell gasped, but forced herself to stand still until her eyes adjusted to the dimness and she could make out shapes in the dark room. There was no one here – she was sure of that. She groped her way towards the pale outline of the French windows, so she could open the curtains and get enough light to see her way back to the hall.

The left-hand curtain came back with a scraping rattle, and although the rain was still sheeting down outside, the room lightened at once. Nell reached for the other one and drew that back.

Standing pressed against the glass was the figure of a woman, her hands lifted as if to bang against the glass, her eyes wide and staring, her face thin and ravaged, clotted strings of darkness clinging to her like ancient dregs.

Nell cried out and stumbled back, knocking against the piano. It gave a faint thrum of sound, and then, incredibly and impossibly, the figure vanished. It did not walk or run away; it simply disappeared between one heartbeat and the next, leaving only the rain streaming down the glass panes and the dark, drenched gardens beyond.

Nell's legs were trembling so violently she was about to fall over. With her free hand she grabbed the edge of the piano and half fell onto the stool. She was icily cold and she wrapped her arms around her body in the classic gesture of trying to

force warmth back. After a moment she got up, forced herself
back to the French windows, and peered into darkness. But
there was only the pattering of the rain and the sound of the
trees moving in the wind, and all she could see was her own
reflection, slightly ghostlike in the blackness.

Probably she was the one who had been sleepwalking, rather
than Beth. She had slipped into a dream and the music had
been part of the dream. But she had no sense of waking from
sleep, not like the hero in Keats' poem who after meeting his
dream-phantoms, wrote, 'I awoke and found me here on the
cold hill's side—'

And *now* she was thinking like Michael, who would find a
romantic quotation in any situation, and would probably recite
lyric poetry on his way to the gallows. But the thought of
Michael was instantly comforting, and Nell felt better. There's
no one out there, she thought. It was the rain making a peculiar
pattern – it *melted*, for pity's sake!

She groped her way along the dark hall, lit a fresh candle
in the little sitting room, and made her way up to the bedroom
she and Beth were sharing. It was stupid to wonder if that soft
piano music had woken Beth, because it had not existed. And
of course Beth was all right; she was still soundly and contentedly asleep, exactly as Nell had left her.

She went back downstairs. She would finish reading Samuel
Burlap's statement before going to bed herself. Because either
Burlap or Dr Brodworthy would surely end in giving an explanation for the music, and once Nell had read that she would
be able to sleep soundly.

> After I listened to that frozen music for a little while
> I summoned the resolve to go down to the outbuildings.
> They're only three or four low small structures joined
> together by their walls, each with its own little latched
> door. They more or less mark the boundary on the
> western side of the land and they're partly hidden by
> overgrown hedges. There's an old wash-house, a
> dilapidated earth closet, and a couple of stores for coal
> or logs. The largest is a game larder where the birds
> would be hung after a shoot, or where poultry would

be plucked before going up to the house for table. It was this I investigated first.

I knew about game larders. There's one up at Sir Beecham Bondley's house and my mother used to help in the kitchens when they had house parties and shooting parties. When I was old enough she sometimes took me with her.

'You can run errands, Samuel,' she'd say, and I rather liked scurrying around the fine estate and delivering messages to kitchen staff where I might be given a handful of raisins if cook was baking a cake, or to the beaters who would sometimes give me a sliver of cheese or the corner of a pasty from the bag-dinners they took out with them. I never told Mother; she would have been annoyed; she would have seen it as charity. I sometimes told Father though, and he always grinned and said, 'Sounds good. You have to take what you can get in life, boy.'

The game larder on the Acton land was much smaller than the one at Bondley House, of course, and the door was almost hidden by a thick mat of sour-smelling ivy. It hadn't been disturbed for years, that ivy – no one could have got in there without leaving tracks. But there are times when the body acts independently of the mind, and before I realized it, I was clawing at those crumbling leaves. They came away in huge, dry swathes falling from the door and the surrounding wall, the stalks splintering like small sapless bones. And there was the door, a thick old oak door, scarred by time and weather. There was an old ring-latch; when I grasped it, it scratched against my hand, but when I pushed hard it swung open, and thick, stale air came at me.

It took several minutes to pluck up courage to go inside. I had to keep saying to myself that there would be nothing in there – there could not possibly be anything.

Thin moonlight lay in bars across the stone floor, and dirt and grime crusted the walls, and it was a terrible, evil-smelling place, as I had known it would be. Black iron hooks protruded from the ceiling, and there were deep shelves, topped with slabs of old, cracked marble.

Ahead was an inner door with a small grille about two-thirds of the way up – that was where the meat and game was kept. The grille was to allow air in. There were four or five thin bars across the opening to keep out birds and vermin.

I could no longer hear the music, but a faint movement came from beyond that grille – barely visible, hardly more than a rippling of the shadows. There's nothing in there though, I thought again. You know that, Samuel Burlap. But the impossible music was brushing against the silence, the notes trickling through the darkness like frozen cobwebs or the tapping of dead fingernails against glass. Or like wasted hands scrabbling on a prison door, trying to get out.

As the thought formed, the movement came again, more distinctly this time. A woman's face looked out at me from behind the grille.

She was standing up against the door, her hands curled round the bars of the grille – she was gripping them with such fierce strength I could see her knuckles standing out white and taut. I could *see* them, I'm telling you and I could see her, just as clearly as I can see you now and that desk you're sitting at, and those pages your assistant's using to write all this down.

I think I called out, although I couldn't tell you what I said. I do know that I seized the door handle and wrenched at it with all my might – like the outer door it was stiff and half-rusted into place. Years, I thought wildly. It's been like this for years. Dear God, does that mean she's been there all these years? *Alive in there . . .?*

The door was held in place by two thick black bolts, one at the top, one at the bottom. You'll think the outside of a door a strange place for bolts, and so it was. It wouldn't take anyone half a second to know they were intended not to keep something out, but to keep something in.

My hands were shaking, but I drew both bolts back and the door came open with a shriek of old hinges, and showers of rust and dirt. Spiders and black beetles scuttled away, and I went in.

The room beyond that old, bolted door, was empty. *Empty.* And yet, as I stood there, I knew something was in there with me, and I felt a cold black despair – as if all the light and life and colour was draining from the world.

I know that sounds pretentious, but it's what I felt. I felt a hopeless, hard misery chipping slivers from my soul. I knew I should never be able to get those lost fragments back.

I suppose you want me to describe that woman? Well then, she was thin and not very old. Her skin was pale as if something had leeched all the life from her, and her eyes were huge and dark like black lamps, and if ever there were nightmare eyes – eyes that would stare at you in your sleep and haunt you in your waking hours . . .

And even though she vanished when I opened the door – vanished as completely as if she had been made of cobwebs that shrivel in the light – I know that once she had really been there. Once, she had been imprisoned behind that door. I *know* it, just as I know my name is Samuel Burlap and my father was Jack Burlap.

And there was the music – the music I thought never to hear again.

Note by Dr Brodworthy: The patient here broke down into complete incoherency. A bromide was administered, and an arrangement made with the note-taker to return in two days' time to complete the statement.

Nell thought the trouble with seeking reassurance was that you never got it, in fact you usually ended worse off.

It was probable that Burlap had simply seen a real intruder on the building site, and did not want to admit the intruder had eluded him. And again, it was possible he had been drinking.

But what about the music? Burlap had heard the music, and Nell had heard it, too. Music that could not have existed on that long-ago night. Music that could not exist tonight.

At this point she reminded herself that she had been half-asleep, and that she had undoubtedly imagined the whole thing.

Stilter House's eerie half-light did not help, either. If the house had been properly lit, none of this would have happened. This made her feel so much better she reached for the candle again, resolving to prove to herself that the music room was entirely normal and free of all unearthly presences, with no ravaged-faced females peering through the windows. She would do that, then she would go to bed.

But the minute she opened the music room door she was aware of something different. What was it? Had something been moved? Nell moved the candle around to see more of the room, and suddenly knew what had changed.

The piano lid, unquestionably locked earlier and the key nowhere to be found, was open. Nell walked nearer and it was then that she saw music propped on the stand. Had it been there earlier? But she was sure it had not.

The music looked old; the edges were curling and the pages faintly foxed. It was a Chopin Nocturne, composed in 1833, the opus number and key printed at the top.

Across one corner, in neat, careful writing, the ink faded to brown, was written, 'Esmond.'

SIX

Michael spent an uneasy night. Emily West's words replayed in his mind over and over again. *Please don't stay at Stilter House,* she had said. *Esmond never left Stilter House . . .*

It was absurd to read anything sinister into this, but he could not forget that the last time he had felt this particular unease, it had heralded a deeply unpleasant – nearly fatal – encounter with an ancient force that dwelled within a deserted old house.

Monday morning brought an email from his editor who had read the new instalment of Wilberforce's adventures, but said that while the idea of Wilberforce performing clumpy ju-jitsu and karate among the chrysanthemums would certainly make for terrific illustrations, did Michael think suggesting martial arts to seven year olds was the right way to go? Perhaps he could rethink that one, could he?

Michael cursed, and got up from his desk to try Nell's mobile again, but it was still inaccessible. Next, he tried Emily West's number, but there was still no reply.

He returned to the computer and had just opened the file containing Beth's idea for Egg-nog Village and Wilberforce's Great-Aunt Tabitha, when Henry Jessel phoned.

'I think that letter from Emily West has turned up,' he said. 'It's a Scottish postmark and the address is handwritten. I haven't opened it – it's a large envelope and it feels as if there's an enclosure. If it's going to be opened at all I'd rather you were here.'

'I can come round now,' said Michael, glancing at his watch.

'Can you? I'm about to open my shop, so I'll leave the letter in Nell's office for you. Call if you want me.'

When Michael reached Quire Court, Henry waved to him through his window, but there were two customers with him, so Michael went straight into Nell's shop. The letter with the Scottish postmark was there, as promised. Reading the contents would feel like an appalling intrusion, but in view of Emily West's phone call, and since he could not reach Nell herself, he could not see any alternative. And supposing Nell or Beth were in some kind of danger?

Before he could change his mind Michael slit the envelope and drew out the two sheets of paper, clipped to several sheets that looked as if they had been taken from an old exercise book.

He set these aside and focused on the letter itself.

'My dear Nell,' wrote Emily West in a clear, firm script. 'First, I must tell you how very pleased I am that you stay in touch with me, even though we haven't met since Brad's funeral. I so enjoyed the photos you sent of Beth last Christmas.

'I expect you know I'm an executor of Aunt Charlotte's will – Brad's great-aunt she was, of course. I'm not a very active executor, I'm afraid – Margery is doing most of the work. She has such energy for business matters.

'I'm so pleased you've agreed to value the contents of Stilter

House, but you'll have quite a task on your hands, because
the place is full from cellar to attic with all kinds of things.
(If you find a Minton dinner service do be careful about selling
it, though, because there's always been a suspicion in the
family that it wasn't come by entirely honestly.)

'My main purpose in writing is to advise you *very strongly*
not to stay in Stilter House overnight. Charlotte and I often
talked on the phone, and I used to stay with her two or three
times a year. Most of what she used to say can probably be
put down to what Margery called her fey attitude – she was
always a little vague, dear Charlotte, but it was part of her
charm. But she was always very clear and very definite about
one thing, and that was Esmond.'

Esmond, thought Michael, aware of the jab of unease again.
He read on.

'At first I thought it was a neighbour's child Charlotte was
talking about. "Esmond is a strange, silent child," she used to
say. "He comes here to play the music to me." Charlotte was
very fond of children, and they always responded to her so
well. A crying shame she never married and had several of
her own. I asked where Esmond lived, and Charlotte looked
surprised. "He lives here," she said, as if she thought I should
have known. "It was his house when it was built all those
years ago. 1900, that was."

'A peculiar statement, but it didn't worry me overmuch,
because Charlotte used to have exceptionally vivid dreams,
and several times she was convinced she had "seen" people
who could not possibly have been there, generally because
they were all dead. "I've been seeing great-grandfather," I
remember her saying after her afternoon nap. Or, "D'you know,
I believe my cousin Mary sat in that chair earlier today, you
remember her, she died in a boating accident."

'I reasoned – so did Margery – that Esmond was another
of these daydreams. We hoped she would forget about it, and
for a time it seemed she had.

'But when I stayed at Stilter House last year, Charlotte
asked me to find an old address book from one of the bedroom
cupboards. She suffered a bit with arthritis, you know, so stairs
were a struggle for her at times. I wanted her to try a herbal

rub which a charming young man had recommended that very month – shockingly expensive, but it contained distilled orchid essence, which accounted for the cost, of course, and the young man was able to get several bottles at a discount price. But Charlotte held by wintergreen and some unpronounceable pills which her GP prescribed.

'I went up to find her address book; she said it would be in the bedroom at the side of the house – the room Brad always had. "His" room, he liked to think it, and so it was, with books and games and so on for him during his holidays. He generally had holiday homework, too – compositions or nature study projects – and there was a small desk by the window for that.

'That's where I found the composition he wrote just before his ninth birthday. It was in an exercise book at the very back of the cupboard, behind the address book I was looking for. I saw his name on it, and – I'm not ashamed to admit this – I took it to read, because I was always so fond of him and it felt like a small memory from his childhood.

'Nell, my dear, I've hesitated for a very long time before sending this to you, because I fear it will revive all the sadness. But I think you need to know what Brad wrote about Stilter House before you go there. So here it is – the pages from the exercise book. The composition Brad wrote all those years ago. I don't know what to believe or what to think, but one thing seems clear: Esmond wasn't just a figment of Charlotte's imagination. Brad saw him as well.'

Michael laid the letter down, and looked at the sheets of lined paper, covered with a child's careful writing. I can't read that, he thought. It's too private. But I can't just shovel it in the post to Stilter House for Nell to read without any prior warning.

He looked back at Emily's letter. 'Esmond' could have been written off as the too-vivid imaginings of an elderly lady, prone to daydreaming, perhaps caught up more with the past than with the present or the future. Except for one thing. Brad West, it seemed, had seen Esmond as well.

With the feeling of stepping into a dark and uncomfortable place, Michael reached for the pages and began to read.

Brad West, age 8¾. Composition for English. My Summer Holiday.

Most summers I go to stay with my Great-Aunt Charlotte, who lives in Caudle Moor. We go to see caves and mines, which are really old and spooky, and you could have a lavishly good horror film in them.

Aunt Charlotte lives in a house called Stilter House, and I have my own room there with a desk and books which she keeps for me. The books are old, all fusty-smelling and splodgy, but that's good, on account of you know you're reading about the old days. People in those books went to different kinds of schools and ate different things, and they didn't have TV or anything, and they said things like, Gosh and Golly.

There are two very good things about Stilter House. One is that I have a piano at the house and Aunt Charlotte has let me learn how to play it. I played something by Mozart this summer. The man who comes in to teach me every Thursday afternoon said Mozart wrote it when he was nine, so it's extra good that I'm playing it now I'm nine too (in September).

The other good thing is that I see my friend Esmond when I come to Stilter House.

Esmond isn't like anyone else, not people at school, or anywhere I've ever been. He doesn't speak, but we have a private sign language. He comes to Stilter House when no one's about, because he doesn't like being around when the grown-ups are there.

He always waits for me in the piano room. He knows a whole lot about music and he plays much better than me. He's really good at playing Chopin. But I know tunes he doesn't, so I'm going to learn some to play for him next holidays.

Soon Esmond is going to tell me a really big secret that he says only he knows. I hope I can stay here long enough to find out what it is.

The composition ended with that, but there was a final page of Emily West's letter, which Michael now read: 'As you'll perhaps know, Brad had to leave Stilter House very suddenly when his father was posted to Germany. He spent most of his holidays over there. I think he used to visit Charlotte in later years, but only ever for a day – never staying overnight.

'But you see Brad, too, met "Esmond" – he played music with him. As to Esmond's secret, I have no idea.

'It doesn't seem as if anyone ever read that essay, but if anyone had, I think it would have caused considerable unease. Even all these years later I'm uneasy – for you, but especially for Beth. I don't know what Esmond's intentions towards Brad were. And if he is still there, thwarted of Brad he may turn his attention to Brad's daughter. Nell, dear, I do know how peculiar all this sounds, but please believe that I'm very concerned for you.

'I hope we can talk about this before you go to Stilter House. I'll be away for most of next week – at a new health farm. They get you to inhale the smoke of burning pine, and also make you to walk round a spiral in the grounds for 20 minutes to exercise your ear muscles.

Fondest love to you and Beth.

Emily.'

Michael laid down the pages. There must have been two boys called Esmond, he thought. That's the only explanation. There was one who lived there in 1900, and another in Brad's time. Perhaps it's a local name or something.

He locked up Nell's shop, thanked Henry Jessel and promised to recount the whole story very soon, then took the letter and its enclosure back to College, which was already moving into its holiday mode, where it felt and sounded and even smelled different.

Wilberforce had gone to sleep on Michael's desk, on top of a memo from Oriel's Director of Music, marked 'For Immediate Attention.' It was only when Michael shooed Wilberforce off to get to the memo, that he saw the phone was registering a new message. He put the memo aside, pressed Play, and was relieved to hear Nell's voice.

'Michael – sorry I couldn't phone until now – the signal here is so poor it's almost non-existent, and I've had to drive to the village pub to call you. I got your message from yesterday though. Henry Jessel left one, too. Everything's fine – although there's no electricity on so we're eating by candlelight. Pity you aren't here to share that, because you're one of the last surviving romantics, aren't you? But we're going to have lunch here later and they'll let me use their Internet connection. I want to send photos to one or two colleagues – there are a few things that are a bit outside my province. I won't ring your mobile because you either won't have it switched on, or you won't be able to find it, but if you get this message in time you could email me. Beth's emailing you anyway – she won't tell me what it's about, she says it's a big secret. She's written it all out to copy-type so you'll probably get quite a missive – you know Beth! I'm guessing you're planning a surprise for my birthday next week, so I'm not going to pry and spoil it. Hope to be back on Wednesday evening.'

It was annoying to have missed Nell's call which she had made while Michael was in Henry's shop, but it was very good to know she was all right – that she and Beth had spent an apparently untroubled night. Michael was inclined to believe Emily West suffered from a too-vivid imagination, or even that the orchid essence had been laced with cannabis.

He felt he was now free to give his mind to College matters, and he reached purposefully for the Music Director's memo, which bore one of Wilberforce's paw marks where Wilberforce had absent-mindedly walked across some spilled marmalade in the kitchen. The memo, which fortunately was still readable, turned out to be a tentative request for Michael's collaboration on a publication the Director was writing on the influence of the Romantic Poets on late-nineteenth-century music. Was there any chance that Michael might be free this afternoon for a preliminary discussion?

The request was rather flatteringly couched, and the Director was a person of considerable repute in music and academic circles, so Michael thought he would probably accept, although he could not, for the moment, think how he would balance it with Wilberforce and Caudle Village, to say nothing of his normal term's work. Wilberforce sold to a surprisingly large number of gleeful seven year olds, and the

Director's book would sell to a small number of earnest but influential academics, so there would be two lots of kudos to be gleaned next year. Michael spent ten minutes feeling pleased with himself, then remembered that Tennyson had said that pride was often the cap and bells for a fool, after which he banished the delusions of grandeur and turned his attention to emailing Nell.

He spent ten fruitless minutes trying to explain about Emily's letter and Brad's essay, before realizing that to abruptly confront her with the words of her dead husband via the Internet was unthinkable. In the end, he sent a brief message, saying he was looking forward to seeing her and hearing about Stilter House, and to stay in touch when and if she could.

This dealt with, he ate a sandwich lunch, thought what a good idea it would be to tidy his desk for the end of term, and made a half-hearted start which he abandoned after ten minutes when he came upon some draft notes he had made for a lecture on Beowulf, which contained several interesting references he had forgotten jotting down. This naturally led to a search of his bookshelves in order to track down the original sources, and almost made him late for the meeting with the Director of Music.

The two of them spent an absorbing afternoon, enlivened by several large glasses of sherry, which the Director thought an appropriate tipple for half past three, although his idea of measures was generous in the extreme so that Michael returned to his rooms slightly light headed from half a pint of sherry on an empty stomach. But his head was pleasantly full of Byron and Berlioz, Faust and Gounod, and he sat down to record the gist of the discussion while it was still fresh in his mind. It was getting on for five o'clock, so he thought he would make a few notes for the current Wilberforce chapter, then dine in Hall. First, though, he would check his emails to see if the promised note from Beth was there, and if Nell had replied to his own earlier message.

There was nothing from Nell, but Beth's email was in the in-box. She had sent it from The Pheasant, clearly delighted at having had a grown-up lunch in a pub.

Hi Michael

This is from a pub called The Pheasant. I had chestnut soup for lunch, then chicken in mushroom sauce, then Bakewell tart and I'm stuffed to the eyebrows with food.

Stilter House is a really good place and this morning after breakfast I met a boy who lives somewhere here. I don't know where his house is, because he just walked into the music room while Mum was in the attics, sorting out stuff. There's a brilliant piano here, and he played it, then we played a kind of duet, only he's a lot *lot* better than me, which is double-gross because I think he's only the same age as me. So I'm going to practice extra double hard this afternoon because he's coming back tomorrow. He didn't speak, but what's weird is I understand what he means without having to speak.

I don't think he wants anyone to know he was here, so you mustn't tell, and specially not Mum, because I'm not supposed to talk to people I don't know. Anyhow, he showed me some music and it's got his name written on it, so I know what he's called.

He's called Esmond.

Lots of love from Beth.

The thing that initially slammed into Michael's mind was the way in which Beth's words echoed those of her dead father, twenty-odd years earlier. He reached for Brad's essay. 'He always waits for me in the piano room, and we play stuff together,' Brad had written. Beth, twenty-five years later, had said, 'He just walked into the music room . . . We played a kind of duet . . .'

Alarm notes began to sound in Michael's mind. Emily West had said in her letter that she was afraid that Esmond would come back for Beth. And Beth's email said Esmond was coming back tomorrow.

Emily was fantasizing, thought Michael determinedly. So was Charlotte when she talked about Esmond. Beth has simply met someone with the same name. It's just a local name, that's all it is.

Then he thought, But supposing it's more than that?

SEVEN

Nell had managed to forget about the eerily insubstantial music, and she had managed to convince herself that there was nothing sinister about finding the piano open last night. Probably it had never been locked in the first place and the lid had been jammed. And there was nothing sinister about the music with Esmond's name on it, either. It was twenty-five years since Brad had known Esmond, so if the music had belonged to Esmond, of course it would be old and a bit faded.

She and Beth had slept well in the deep old beds, and the kitchen was warm and friendly. As she made toast and poured cereal into bowls, Nell thought how impossible it was to believe in disembodied piano music, or figures made of rain or cobwebs who peered through windows.

How about that other ghost, though? How about Brad? If he was here at all, he was very faint and faraway. I'm not exactly over you, said Nell to Brad in her mind, and I probably won't ever be, not completely. But I can think of you without that wrenching despair and loss.

After breakfast she and Beth drove to Caudle Village where she was able to phone Michael, and leave a message on his voicemail. After this she and Beth bought more candles and matches from the tiny supermarket, along with two electric torches.

Back at the house, she worked her way through the downstairs rooms, listing furniture and silver and china, photographing several more pieces, and making notes. The house was warm and filled with morning sunlight and it was remarkable how little the lack of electricity mattered, although sorting through some beautiful damask table linen stored in an old sideboard, Nell thought it might soon become irritating. But for a couple of days it was quite fun to camp out.

Beth spent almost an entire hour typing an email to Michael

on the notebook computer which was her most prized possession. When Nell reminded her the notebook was on battery
and could not be recharged until they got home, Beth said,
solemnly, that an email to Michael had to be properly written
on account of Michael knowing about English and stuff. You
had to spell words right and things for him.

'You have to do that for everyone, not just for Michael,'
said Nell, smiling. 'But I know what you mean.'

At half past twelve they returned to the village, where the
landlord of The Pheasant was happy to let them use the Internet
connection. Beth sent her email and Nell sent various
photographs to colleagues, mostly of items that were a bit
outside her area of expertise. There were some paintings, and
a pair of what she thought were patch boxes – tiny enamelled
containers that would have contained beauty patches for elegant
eighteenth-century ladies. There was also the piano, of course;
that was a very specialized area. She wondered if she would
want it herself and thought she would not. If Beth's interest
in music progressed she would buy a brand new one, with no
vagrant memories embedded in its depths.

There were a couple of emails in her own inbox, one from
Henry Jessel and one from Michael, but Henry only said there
was no word yet from the Japanese customers about the
Regency desk, and Michael's message merely said he looked
forward to hearing from her soon.

The Pheasant was bright and welcoming and the landlord,
whose name was Joe Poulson, was interested to hear they were
staying at Stilter House. A grand old place, that was, and
everyone had known and liked Miss West.

'Lived at Stilter all her life,' he said, proffering the menu,
which modestly announced itself as providing fresh,
home-cooked food. 'A very nice lady. I dare say the house
will have to be sold, will it? Pity to see it go out of the
family – it was as much a part of Caudle Moor as my own
family – my wife's family too, for they've lived here just
as long. Folk don't bother about that kind of thing much
nowadays, do they, but I like the feeling of – well, conti-
nuity I suppose you'd call it. You'd like a table overlooking
the market square for your lunch, maybe? And I'd

recommend the Bakewell tart. You can't come to this part of the world and not try Bakewell tart.'

They ate their lunch in the tiny dining room, the Bakewell tart was pronounced delicious, and Mr Poulson's wife came beamingly out of the kitchens, to accept their appreciation. They were please to come again, and try the Ashbourne ginger-bread next time.

It felt nicely familiar to drive back along Gorsty Lane; to recognize a home-made sign to a public footpath, to point out to one another the cottage Beth had said was like a dolls' house. The door at Stilter House gave its distinctive little creak of old hinges when they unlocked it, and the house's individual scents greeted them.

Beth went off to the music room to look through the music. There was a hugely big stack of it inside the piano stool and on the shelves, she explained. She would be very careful with it, but there might be stuff Dad had played and she could play too. It was great that Mum had found the piano key, wasn't it? Nell was aware of a stir of unease at this innocent remark, but she ruffled Beth's hair, which was about the only caress Beth would tolerate, and went up to check the bedrooms. Tallboys and ward-robes sometimes contained odd, overlooked things of value, but there did not seem to be any in Stilter House's bedrooms. There were no pieces of Limoges glass or Hilliard miniatures; no lions or witches waiting to pounce, only a couple of forgotten fur coats smelling of mothballs, and several dried-out lavender muslin bags of the kind once used to scent wardrobes.

Late afternoon sunshine trickled through the latticed windows and lay in diamond patterns on the floor, and as Nell made notes, she thought about Samuel Burlap's statement. She had glanced rather cursorily through the rest of the papers to see if there were any more of Dr Brodworthy's distinctive typed pages, but there had not seemed to be. And I don't really want to know anything else, thought Nell. If Burlap succumbed to some form of insanity, I'd rather not know. He built a beautiful house, and I think that's what he'd like to be remem-bered for, not for some weird hallucination of a ravaged-face prisoner in the old game larder. And the music, said a voice in her mind. Don't forget he heard the music, just as you did.

As if the thought had given substance to the memory, the music was suddenly with her again, distant but unmistakable, and Nell laid down the notebook and pen and sat very still, her skin tingling. Was it happening a second time? Burlap's chill faery music that he believed had brought the ravaged-face woman back into being? The music that existed where no music could exist . . .

Except that this music she was hearing could exist, of course. Beth was investigating the music in the piano room, and clearly she had found something to try for herself. Nell relaxed and sat on the window seat to listen, smiling to hear Beth's small hands stumbling over a section, then replaying it more accurately. She did not recognize it, but it was light and clear, the kind of simple or simplified piece Beth's teacher used to lighten the tedium of scales. Nell thought she would go part-way down the stairs and listen quietly, so that later she could tell Beth how much she was improving.

She sat in the window seat on the half-landing to listen. Beth was certainly improving. Her teacher had tentatively suggested she be entered for one of the children's music festivals, but Nell was torn between wanting Beth to shine, and concern about pushing her into a limelight she might not want. She leaned against the window recess, enjoying the music and the faint scents of old polish and oak brought out by the afternoon sunshine.

The music seemed to be reaching its end, and Nell went down to the hall and pushed open the music-room door. Sunlight poured through these windows, as well, momentarily dazzling her vision, but through it, it was possible to see the small figure at the piano, silhouetted against the oblong of the French windows – a figure so small it had had to pile up several cushions on the stool to reach the keyboard.

Nell blinked and put up a hand to shield her eyes from the strong sunshine. It was Beth, of course, and yet . . .

And yet it somehow seemed wrong for Beth. There was the silky brown hair and there was the familiar tilt of the head which meant Beth was concentrating on something important. She was concentrating fiercely on the music now – so much that she had not heard Nell come in.

Behind her the door swung in on its worn hinges, and at

the sound, the music stopped abruptly. There was a blur of movement within the sunlight. The small figure jumped down and ran towards the open French windows, then paused and looked back, straight at Nell.

It was not Beth. It was a young boy, about Beth's age, with the same colour hair as Beth's. He paused in the doorway, looked back at her, then darted into the gardens.

Without realizing she had been going to speak, Nell said, 'Brad . . .' The name came out like a ghost-whisper, like the cobwebs of old memories, not quite frayed to insignificance yet still capable of hurting. It lay sadly on the old room, then Nell was running through the French windows and across the small terrace outside, half falling down the moss steps. She stopped at the foot, trying to see into the overgrown tangle of garden, but there was nothing. The boy had vanished, as completely and as suddenly as the rain-figure last night. Nell came back into the room, trying to calm her tumbling thoughts.

She closed the French windows, turning the key in the lock.

'Beth, were you playing the piano earlier this afternoon?'

It was half past six and Beth was helping to make sandwiches which they would have for supper, with tinned soup.

Beth was buttering the bread, not looking at Nell. 'I found some old music so I tried a bit of it. It was quite hard, though, so I didn't play much. And it was a bit cold in there so I took my book into your room with the gas fire. Why?'

As far as Nell knew, Beth was completely truthful, so she accepted this at face value. And since mention of an unknown child being in the house might frighten Beth, she said, 'I thought I heard you playing. You're improving by leaps and bounds.'

'Am I really?' Beth looked pleased. After they had eaten, she went back to the little sitting room to finish the Enid Blyton book. It was pretty good, she said, when Nell asked what she thought of it. 'Only they're so gross, some of those girls. They talk about having maids at home. I don't know *anyone* who has maids, do you? Well, except at Oxford, and that's not the same, is it?'

'Oxford's a law unto itself.'

'I'll finish it though, on account of wanting to know what happens.'

'While you do I'll go up to make some notes about the rest of the books,' said Nell.

'Are they worth a lot of money?'

'Some of them might be. So don't spill anything on that one. Call if you want me. I won't stay up there long, though. It's already starting to get dark.'

As Nell sorted through the books, the image of the boy at the piano was strongly with her. Michael had recently been absorbed in Longfellow's poems, and there had been a line he had liked and had quoted: 'All houses wherein men have lived and died/Are haunted houses . . .' And then something about, 'The stranger at my fireside I cannot see . . . There are more guests at table than the hosts invited . . .'

It was an unnerving idea however you looked at it. And what about the stranger at the piano? Was it conceivable that the boy in that dazzle of sunlight could be a lingering fragment of Brad? A shard of memory still lodged in the house?

I think there are a few strangers at the firesides of this house, thought Nell. But I don't think I'd mind if they were a link with Brad.

It was then she heard Beth scrambling up the stairs, shouting to her. She tumbled into the room, white-faced and clearly frightened, clutching at Nell's hands.

'Sweetheart what's wrong?'

'There's someone outside.' Beth's voice was shaking, and fear jabbed at Nell.

As calmly as possible, she said, 'Are you sure? What did you see?' She knelt down, holding Beth's hands tightly. 'Darling, you're perfectly safe. Just tell me what you saw.'

'I went back into the music room so I could sit in the window and read. Then I thought I'd have another go at that old piece of music. I thought Dad might have played it so I wanted to play it as well. And I got a bit more of it this time, which was pretty good, but then there was a kind of movement from the garden—'

'Through the French windows?'

'Yes. At first I thought it was just a bush or something blowing across the glass. Only,' said Beth, on a sob, 'when I looked, it wasn't. It was a woman – Mum, she was standing right up against the window, pressing against the glass, and she had this thin, *thin* face, and hands that sort of scrabbled at the glass as if she was trying to get in . . .'

'She can't get in,' said Nell, as Beth faltered. 'Whoever she was, she couldn't possibly get in. Everywhere's locked up. We're absolutely safe – we couldn't be safer.' But we're not, she thought. I can feel that we're not.

Beth said, 'I 'spect we could just tell her to go away, could we? Only she might come back. Like – when we're in bed and it's dark, and if she got into the house . . .' She broke off, her small face crumpling.

'That won't happen,' said Nell at once. She was listening for sounds from downstairs as she spoke, but there was nothing. 'I'll go downstairs now to sort it out,' she said. 'You stay here.' She saw Beth's scared expression, and she said, 'Bethy, listen. This was the room Dad used to sleep in. So you sit at the desk – I'll bet he often sat there – and I'll be straight back and everything will be fine. It'll be someone who's lost and come up to the house to ask for directions or something like that.'

But despite her words, Nell's heart was thudding as she ran downstairs, and she was strongly aware of Stilter's isolation and the non-existent phone signal. Probably there was no one out there. Yes, but you saw someone last night, said her mind. And Beth saw something just now, and she isn't given to wild flights of imagination.

It was growing dark and Stilter seemed to be sliding down into its semi-haunted twilight state. Nell cast a swift glance towards the music room door, then darted into the kitchen to collect one of the new torches. Back in the hall she thought something moved beyond one of the narrow panes of glass at the side of the front door – a faint shape that might be a human hand or might be a tree branch. There was the sound of rain pattering against the windows. Or was it rain? Mightn't it be fingernails, tapping to see if anyone was at home . . .?

Nell took a deep breath, reminded herself that the torch was heavy enough to use as a weapon if necessary, and went determinedly towards the music room. She stood warily in the doorway, shining the torch all round, every nerve tensed. But nothing moved and nothing seemed out of place. Bay window, chairs, tables, bookshelves, piano which was open with Esmond's music still propped up on the stand. Gripping the torch more tightly, she turned its light onto the French windows. It sliced a triangle of sharp brilliance through the violet and indigo shadows, but nothing seemed to be out there. Had the woman Beth saw gone away, as she had last night? Nell had a sudden wild vision of some poor half-mad soul in the grip of a freakish compulsion to walk through Stilter House's gardens every evening at the same hour.

She turned back to the room, trying to decide how safe she and Beth were and wondering if she dared go all round the house to look into each room. She was just checking the catch on the French windows when there was a movement behind her. Nell whipped round and something stepped out from the shadows and walked towards the piano. The torchlight fell on wild unkempt hair and mad, staring eyes, and on dreadful thin hands that reached out greedily. Nell gasped and raised the torch in instinctive defence, backing away, praying to reach the door before the woman pounced, somehow managing it. She slammed the door hard, then ran across the hall and up the stairs as if all the demons of hell were at her heels, calling to Beth, not caring if her voice gave away her exact whereabouts.

Beth answered at once. 'I'm here. What's happening?' Her voice was scared, but she was clearly all right, and Nell fell thankfully into the room.

'It's all right, we're quite safe. But we're going to drive to the village.'

'Is it the woman I saw?' Beth hopped down from the window seat, her eyes huge with fear. 'Did you see her?'

'Yes. She won't hurt us, though. Most likely she'll have run off now,' said Nell, hoping Beth would accept this. 'But she seemed confused, so it'll be better if we get to the car and fetch help for her. We'll go quietly downstairs, and all you've got to do is keep tight hold of my hand and do exactly what I tell you.'

'You promise it's safe?' said Beth, her eyes huge.

'I promise it is. Double treble promise.'

As Nell led Beth to the dark landing, her mind was racing ahead. She always put the car keys in the side pocket of her handbag, but had she left the bag in the sitting room where she had been working, or looped over the banister at the foot of the stairs when they came in earlier? Let it be on the banister, she thought.

'Beth, I'll snatch up my bag from the stairs and we'll go out through the front door. If the bag's not there it'll be in the little sitting room, and that'll mean a quick sprint down the hall and out through the garden door. All right?'

Halfway down the stairs Nell saw that the music room door was partly open, and her heart leapt with fear. I left it shut, she thought. She's come out of that room. She's somewhere in the house.

The foot of the stairs was in shadow, and for a moment she thought her bag with the keys was on the banister after all, but as they neared the stairs she saw it was only a scarf. She tightened her hold on Beth's hand, and pointed to the hall. Beth nodded, understanding, and they went towards the back of the house. Please don't let her be here, Nell was thinking. Please let us get out of the house and to the car.

It was like one of the old children's games, where you had to cross a piece of land without being caught or seen. The hall seemed to stretch out and out, like the distortion in a nightmare, and there was the strong feeling that she and Beth were not alone. It's the stranger at the fireside, thought Nell. The guest who wasn't invited, but who's here anyway . . .

Here was the sitting room at last, and there was her bag on the fireside shelf. She picked it up, and turned to indicate to Beth that they would go out through the scullery.

There was a whisper of sound from the dark hall and a blurred movement, then the woman was in the doorway, her face in shadow, black rain clinging to her. For several dreadful seconds Nell froze, then Beth gave a sob of panic and her mind snapped back into place. She thrust Beth behind her, then bounded forward and slammed the door hard. There was no lock, but she was already seizing the edge of a small settle, and dragging it across the door to form a barricade. Blessedly Beth seemed to understand, and threw her own small weight behind the task.

'That cupboard as well,' gasped Nell. 'Push it hard against the door. Good girl. We're safe now.' She took a deep breath, then, as calmly as she could, said, 'And get my phone from my bag, will you? There might just be a signal.'

'There isn't,' said Beth, having found the phone and tried it. 'It says "Out of reach of signal". Mum, what are we going to do? Will she go away—' She broke off and in a terrified whisper, said, 'The door handle's moving. She's trying to get at us.'

But Nell, who was still leaning hard against the makeshift barricade, had already felt the slight shift of the cupboard, and she turned to stare in horror at the door. The handle was twisting back and forth and a thin line of black was appearing around the frame. Nell grabbed her bag from Beth and slung it over her shoulder. In a low voice she said, 'We're going to get out through that window, and run to the car, and drive to the village. You can climb through the window, can't you?'

'Yes.'

'Good girl. Quick as we can.'

The window was quite a small one, criss-crossed with leaded lights, but Nell thought that pushed open to its full extent they could both get through.

'It's stuck,' said Beth in panic, as Nell wrestled with the catch.

'No, it's just a bit warped.' As Nell renewed her attempt to force the latch, the settle was pushed even further away from the door, and the gap around the frame widened again. Fear lent Nell strength; she thumped the window catch with her fist, and it gave way. Cool night air, with rain inside it, came in.

'You first,' she said, lifting Beth onto the narrow sill. Beth swung her legs over, and jumped onto the grass four feet below. 'Easy,' she said. 'Come *on*, mum.'

Nell followed, landing on the soft grass. Rain blew into their faces, but it was a good feeling. We're out of her reach, she thought. We'll get away.

The window was on the side furthest from the drive, but they only had to go along the path and through a wrought-iron gate and they would be at the front of the house and within sprinting distance of the drive.

'Move slowly and quietly,' said Nell in a whisper. 'Then she won't hear where we are.'

It was not quite dark, but the rainstorm had brought a dull uncertain twilight that hung over Stilter House, turning the trees into grotesque figures waiting to reach down to scoop up unwary humans. Beth cast a scared glance at these and clung tightly to her mother's hand and Nell hated Stilter House with fierce intensity.

The rain had stopped, but moisture dripped from the trees in an eerie rhythm. Nell opened the side gate slowly so the hinges would not squeak, and closed it behind them. Once clear of the house the dripping leaves seemed to take on a different pattern – the pattern of soft footsteps following them. She shot a quick look back, but nothing moved, and every step took them nearer to the car and its safety. Here was the shrubbery – in the smeary half-light it was a dark mass of lumpen shapes. Could the woman have crept around the other side of the house and be hiding there?

She said, very softly, 'Beth, we're almost there. There's the car, just beyond the bushes. I've got the keys ready – we'll simply dive straight in and drive away. Everything's going to be fine.'

As if to mock these words, a thin high sound sliced through the night. It might have been the sonic screech of a bat, or the squeal of some small vulnerable creature resisting a predator, but Nell knew it was not. It was the sound of the iron gate being opened. The woman was in the dark, dripping garden with them. As Nell half-turned, the figure was there, silhouetted against the night, lifting up her hands – hands that held something black and ancient, something that was made of twisted iron, and brutal spikes. She began to walk through the trees, holding the dreadful thing out before her, as if she was displaying it for Nell, as if she was saying, 'Look at it, *look at it,* because this is what's waiting for you . . .'

Nell felt, rather than heard, Beth's gasp of fear, then they

were both running towards the car, no longer caring about being
heard. Once Beth skidded on the wet grass, but Nell pulled her
upright. She risked a glance over her shoulder, and for a
split-second there was nothing to be seen, then between one
heartbeat and the next she was coming towards them through
the trees. The rain clung to her outline, gleaming coldly, and
Nell pulled Beth over the last few yards to the car. Her hand
was shaking, but she pressed the key tab, and the car's lights
blinked as the auto-locks released the doors. They tumbled
inside and Nell fired the engine and revved it, cursing that the
car was parked facing the house. Was there room to turn without
reversing? No, the drive was too narrow, and she might hit the
rockery or one of the trees and puncture a tyre or do something
to put the car out of action.

The woman was advancing and there was no time to execute
a precise three-point turn. Nell threw the car into reverse and
backed down the narrow drive towards the lane as fast as
possible. The exhaust made clouds of smoky vapour on the
damp air, and the reversing lights glowed. Into this smoky,
red-tinted glow, came the wild-haired figure, indistinct through
the rain-spattered rear window, but black and forbidding, still
holding out the lump of spiked iron.

There was a moment when Nell thought the woman was
not going to move and that she would either have to stop or
reverse into her. She touched the brakes warningly, and as the
brake lights glowed, quite suddenly the woman was no longer
there. Nell's heart jumped. Had she hit her after all? No, she
could not possible have done; she would have felt even the
smallest impact, and the woman had been several feet away.

'She's run away,' Nell said, forcing her voice to sound calm.
'It's all right, Beth – we're absolutely safe.'

In a frightened whisper, Beth said, 'She had something in
her hands. She was sort of lifting it towards you. What is it?'

'I don't know.' Nell manoeuvred the car the rest of the way
to the lane, then drove away from Stilter House at top speed,
swerving around the sharp bends, praying not to meet another
vehicle, constantly looking in the driving mirror to see if they
were being followed. This last was the height of madness, of
course, because unless the woman had a car of her own, which

surely they would have seen, she could not be following them.
But Nell kept looking.

'Where are we going?' said Beth. Her voice sounded tight,
as if she was determined not to cry.

The main thought in Nell's mind had been to get away from
Stilter House, and for a moment her mind was blank. Then
from nowhere came the obvious answer. 'We'll go to The
Pheasant,' she said, and with the words came the image of the
low-fronted old pub and its feeling of warm security. She felt
instantly better. They would be safe at The Pheasant.

Beth seemed to pick this up, because in an almost normal
voice, she said, 'That'd be brilliant. Because even if that woman
did try to get in there, she'd never get past that man who
served our lunch.'

EIGHT

Joe Poulson at The Pheasant would certainly not allow any
menacing or burglarious people through his doors, and was
shocked to his toes to think of Mrs West and her small
daughter enduring such an ordeal.

'Out there on your own, and there's nothing worse than a
deserted old house for attracting odd people.' He reached for
a pot of freshly percolated coffee and poured out two cups,
adding a generous measure of brandy to Nell's. 'For the shock,'
he said, firmly. 'I'll phone Sergeant Howe at the police station
at once. He'll go out there and take a look round, but it's my
bet it'll have been nothing worse than some nasty tramp.'

Nell, drinking the coffee gratefully, thought, *Could* it have
been something so relatively innocent as that?

'Whoever she was, she'd have thought the house was empty,'
said Poulson. 'And she'd think to herself, Aha, this will do
me nicely for a night's kip.'

Nell said, 'I'm hesitant to go back – tonight, at any rate.
Your sign outside says you do bed and breakfast. Is it possible
we could have a room?'

'Indeed you can,' said Poulson, beaming. 'There's one double and one very small single, so maybe you'd prefer to share the double. There's twin beds in it, and my wife can have clean sheets on in ten minutes.'

Nell, thankful she had been able to snatch up her bag containing her wallet with cash and bank cards, said that would do very well indeed.

The room turned out to be whitewashed and chintz-furnished, with oak ceiling beams and a huge fireplace with a copper jug filled with dried flowers. Poulson's wife, who seemed to be a lady of few words but serenely plump disposition, unlocked the room, indicated the bathroom next door, and murmured that there could be a bite of supper in half an hour if that would suit.

'We don't have to go back to the house, do we?' said Beth, after Poulson's wife had gone. 'That'd be double-bad.'

'We're definitely not going back,' said Nell.

'Good. Will the police catch that – um – woman?'

'Oh yes,' said Nell, at once. 'They'll know the area – they might very well know who she is. You don't have to worry about any of it. There are some peculiar people in the world, and we happened to meet one.'

'I don't mind so long as we don't have to go back,' said Beth, bouncing on one of the beds. 'I like it here. What will we do for pyjamas and toothbrushes and things?'

'It won't hurt you to sleep in your vest for one night, and we'll ask if we can have an apple each after supper instead of brushing our teeth. Tomorrow I can go back to the house myself and collect our things. It'll be all right, though,' she said, seeing Beth's expression. 'I shan't go on my own.'

'You're phoning Michael,' said Beth, as Nell reached for her bag and felt inside for the phone.

'Yes.' Nell was slightly annoyed to find herself behaving like the classic wimpish heroine seeking masculine comfort, but she suddenly wanted very much to hear Michael's voice.

But Michael's direct line at Oriel College was switched to voicemail, and when Nell dialled his mobile number that, too, went to voicemail. She left a brief message on both numbers to say they had removed to The Pheasant in Caudle Village for tonight, and added the number.

It had been unreasonable to expect Michael to be on hand at the exact minute she wanted him. She was perfectly able to cope with this situation, in any case; she did not need a knight in shining armour dashing up to her rescue, and there was also the point that Michael would most likely get lost on the road between Oxford and Caudle, because he had the worst sense of direction Nell had ever come across.

Michael knew his judgement might have been affected by sloshing down the Music Director's sherry during the afternoon. But he reread Beth's email, and then he reread Emily West's letter and Brad's essay, and although individually the contents of the letters were not particularly sinister, put together they seemed to him to take on very menacing shapes.

He considered Brad's essay. Brad had written that Esmond always waited for him in the music room. 'He doesn't speak,' Brad had written. 'We have a private sign language.' This was not particularly strange or unusual. Children did make holiday friendships and have private languages, although nowadays those languages tended to be spattered across social websites.

So far so good as far as Brad West was concerned. But then more than twenty-five years later, Brad's daughter had sent an email in which she talked about Esmond in exactly the same way. 'He walked into the music room,' Beth had said. 'He didn't speak but I understand what he means without having to speak.'

It could still be coincidence. Just about. Beth was a modern child, but she had a rather endearing liking for the worlds of long-ago children; she loved *Alice's Adventures Through the Looking Glass*, and she adored C.S. Lewis's Narnia books, and Pamela Brown's *Blue Door Theatre* series. But Michael did not think Beth would have dreamed up a ghost-companion, at least not in the space of twelve hours, and even if she had, she would not have given it the same name as her father's long-ago friend.

What about Great Aunt Charlotte? She had seemed to know about Esmond, and Emily West, repository of Charlotte's slightly fey stories, had sounded genuinely fearful that Esmond might come back for Beth. And according to Beth, Esmond, that elusive silent child, seen by three different people at three different time spans, was indeed coming back to Stilter House.

It's too many coincidences, thought Michael. I can't ignore them. He wondered if he could track down a local police station and ask if they would check on the temporary residents of Stilter House. But when he tried out a possible dialogue for this, it sounded so nonsensical, he abandoned the idea, and instead dialled Emily West's number again. There was still no reply, so he searched for a number for the other aunt – Margery, in Edinburgh. But he had no address and there were so many Wests listed for the area, it would take hours to work through them, by which time it might be too late to do anything else.

I'm building this up into something absurd, he thought. It's gothic fiction – the ghost-child who appears at intervals. But this is Nell, said his mind. And Beth. And if there's even a tiny possibility that they're in some kind of danger . . .

To go mad-rabbiting up to Derbyshire because of an elderly lady's imagination and a long-ago schoolboy's essay was the height of madness. But by half-past six Michael knew that unless he could reach Nell by phone, he would have to do just that.

This fact finally faced, he hunted out road maps to see exactly where, and how far, Caudle was. He found it with difficulty – a tiny place on the southern edge of the Peak District. Nell had said the journey was just over a couple of hours and when Michael checked with an online route planner, this was confirmed. But route planners never seemed to allow for mundane things such as diversions or traffic hold-ups, so he would add an extra half an hour for that, and he had better add a further half hour for taking a wrong road, because it was remarkable how often roads and road signs could be misleading. He zoomed into the directions as far as possible and was gratified to see that Stilter House was shown, and that it was in Gorsty Lane.

What about all the sherry he had drunk with the Music Director? How far over the limit was he for driving? He tried to calculate times and quantities, and thought he might be borderline. Would a train journey be more sensible? More to the point, would it be possible? He wrestled with rail helplines and websites for fifteen minutes, before concluding that Caudle was simply too far off the beaten tracks and that it was completely off any National Rail tracks as well.

Was there anyone he could ask to drive him? Most of the dons were either immersed in end-of-term tidying-up or interviews or had already left College, and Michael was not keen on involving any of them in this peculiar business anyway. The majority would probably smile rather pityingly and later tell one another that Dr Flint was off on another of his peculiar exploits again, and before Michael knew it, he would be summoned to the Dean's study to be told College was a hotbed of gossip about his ghost-hunting activities and had he considered the effect on his students.

Surely if he ate a substantial meal in Hall and set off just after half past seven the sherry should have dissipated, and with reasonable luck he would reach Caudle by eleven. He might be able to raise Nell by phone before then anyway and not need to make the whole journey.

He emailed his editor to say he would send the chapter on Wilberforce's visit to Great Aunt Tabitha by the end of the week, and, to indicate he was working diligently away, added that he was, in fact, visiting the real Egg-nog Village for a day or so.

Oriel turned out to be serving a very substantial chicken casserole with accompanying vegetables that evening, so Michael had a large helping, followed it with some fruit salad, hoped this was blotting up most of the sherry, and went off to ask the porter to put out Wilberforce's food for the next twenty-four hours.

'I'll certainly do so, Dr Flint, although it wouldn't matter if I didn't, for that animal would eat human flesh if it was offered him and there was nothing else available,' said the porter.

Michael agreed, handed over several tins of Wilberforce's favourite cat food with a bottle of milk, and added a ten-pound note for the porter's trouble.

After this, he threw a few overnight things into a bag and checked his phone for messages and his computer for emails. He had hoped to hear from Nell, but there were no phone messages at all, and his inbox contained only one email, which was from his editor who liked to keep her authors on their toes by firing off emails at hours when most other people regarded work as being over for the day. She was, she wrote, intrigued to hear he was visiting the real Egg-nog Village and eagerly awaiting the new instalment of Wilberforce and Great Aunt Tabitha. She had already alerted their illustrators to Aunt Tabitha's recent creation, and would soon be sending over some images of Tabitha herself, suitably adorned with mob cap and pince-nez. As a PS she added that Michael should not forget he could claim the cost of his journey against income tax as 'Allowable Research'. Michael could not decide if this was a polite way of telling him his publishers were not going to foot the bill for the trip to Derbyshire. He locked up his rooms, and set off.

Sergeant Howe from Caudle Moor police station was large and reassuring. He arrived at The Pheasant after Nell and Beth had eaten their meal, and said he had taken a good look round Stilter House and its grounds and had found no signs of intruders. Likely there had been a gypsy wandering around or a tramp, that would be what Mrs West had seen, and very alarming for her too, he did not doubt. But whoever had been there earlier was definitely not there now.

It seemed to Nell that Sergeant Howe's bovine eyes flickered towards the hovering Poulson and that something passed between them. But Poulson only said, warmly, that this was very comforting, and they were much obliged.

'Shall you be going along to the house again tomorrow?' asked Howe, buttoning his notebook into his tunic.

'Yes, I'll have to. I've still got some sorting out left.' Nell did not say that the prospect of returning to Stilter House was a daunting one.

'Then I'd suggest I come along with you, or that my constable does,' said the sergeant. 'Just to be sure, you know.' He prepared to take his leave, having refused – with palpable reluctance – Poulson's offer of a pint of home-brewed. 'Stilter's an odd old place. Joe knows that better than most of us, don't you, Joe?'

Poulson nodded solemnly, and the sergeant said, 'Old Caudle family, Joe and his wife. Always been a Poulson here at The Pheasant. And Joe's wife had a grandmother—'

'Great-grandmother, if you don't mind, Fred, and maybe one or two more greats, in fact.' Poulson winked at Nell and Beth. 'No call to make my wife older than she is.'

'A great-great-grandmother who lived and worked at Acton House – that's the place that was on that land before they built Stilter.'

'In service to the Acton family, my wife's great-great grandmother,' nodded Poulson, who was polishing glasses. 'A Stump she was, and that's a good old name hereabouts, for all the teasing it gets. She was housekeeper to the Actons. Eliza Stump, that was her name. As for the Actons themselves, they were a well-respected Derbyshire family.'

'Apart from one of them,' put in Sergeant Howe, and Poulson said – a bit hastily, Nell thought – that every family had one rotten apple in the barrel.

'Very rotten indeed, that particular apple,' said the sergeant caustically. 'And we've got the records of the trial in police archives as proof. Didn't you have an ancestor who was on that jury, Joe? Yes, thought I saw the name Poulson when we transferred all the records onto computer last year.'

Nell was about to ask what the trial had been, when she saw that Beth was listening, huge-eyed. So she said, 'You've both been very kind, and I'm sure there won't be any more trouble at Stilter House. We'll be leaving tomorrow afternoon anyway. But I'll take up your offer to come out to the house with me tomorrow, if that's all right, Sergeant?'

'Nine o'clock suit you?' said Sergeant Howe.

'Yes, certainly.'

Nell glanced at Beth, but before she could say anything, Poulson said, in his comfortable voice, 'I dare say Beth might like to keep my wife company in the kitchen for an hour or two tomorrow?' He smiled at Beth. 'There's talk of a new batch of Bakewell tarts to be baked. My wife would welcome a bit of help with that.'

'That'd be extra double-cool,' said Beth at once. 'Um – could I do that, Mum?'

'Yes, but you're not to get in anyone's way.'

'I won't, I really won't. Thank you very much,' said Beth to Poulson, who beamed and said what a pleasure to meet a child with proper manners.

'You thanked Mr Poulson very nicely,' said Nell, as she and Beth went up to their room.

'It'll be pretty good making Bakewell tarts,' said Beth. 'And I don't s'pose that woman could get in here at all, do you?'

Her voice wavered slightly on this, and Nell said cheerfully, 'Not a hope in the world. And tonight we'll lock our door, and tomorrow you'll be with Mrs Poulson.'

'Can I read a bit of Malory Towers in bed? It's still in my pocket.'

It was half-past nine. Nell said, 'You can have twenty minutes.'

The helpful Mrs Poulson had found washing things for them, and there was even a spare toothbrush and a tube of toothpaste set out in the bathroom next door. Beth washed and undressed and dived under the covers. She looked young and clean and fresh, and Nell was rather horrified to find herself wanting to use extreme violence against the woman who had frightened Beth so much earlier on. Instead, she washed and got undressed, and slid into the second bed. Beth was already absorbed in the cavortings of the Lower Fourth, and Nell felt slightly lost without something of her own to read. Should she get dressed again and go downstairs to see if there were any newspapers or magazines? Something light and even trivial would certainly help to drive away that nightmare image of the woman stalking them through the darkness, holding out that macabre-looking piece of iron. *This is for you . . .*

I ought to be able to identify that thing, she thought. Because I'm sure it's something I've seen before somewhere. She waited for the half-memory to come into focus, but it did not, and she returned to the matter of something to read. She had thrust the wodge of old papers into her bag before they made their hasty exit from Stilter House. Samuel Burlap's statement had been among them, and she might have snatched up a few other letters or reports, as well. They would not exactly make for escapism, but maybe it would give her thoughts a new direction. She retrieved them from her bag, and got back into bed.

She had got to the part where Burlap had broken down into incoherency, babbling about the music. Music where no music could exist . . .

Nell considered this. She had heard music inside Stilter House, as well. Esmond's music, she thought, remembering the yellowing Chopin Nocturne, and the blurred figure of the boy who had been playing it. He had had Beth's colour hair – Brad's hair – and he had seemed simply to melt into the rain-drenched gardens.

She frowned and looked down at the pages again, seeing the note from Dr Brodworthy about administering a bromide. The next page began with the continuation of the statement, and the date was two days later.

NINE

Report in re: Mr Samuel Burlap.
Continuation of statement made by Mr Burlap to Dr Brodworthy, on 25th April 1900

You'll say seeing that woman trapped in the old game larder was my imagination. But I saw her. And what made me sick and ill with revulsion was that I knew who it was. There was only one person it could be. Isobel Acton. And you may tell me Isobel Acton is long since dead – you may tell me that until hell freezes – but I know different. She's still there.

What Isobel did all those years ago is seared into my mind – as if my father heated one of the white-hot irons in his forge and burned it straight down into my soul.

He was a blacksmith, my father, and in those days that was a good thing to be, well, it still is. But I've heard it said that it's a skill that will dwindle in the future, because one day folk will travel around by means of motor cars. I see you smile, Doctor, and I agree with you, for they're dirty noisy things, those motor cars and as for unreliable . . . Well, you might count yourself lucky to reach your journey's end, from what I hear. But I know they're part of what they call progress. Didn't our fathers and mothers say electricity was dangerous, and yet how many people now have the electricity in their houses? And didn't our grandparents scoff at the thought of lighting a house with gas, or travelling in steam-powered machines?

I learned a fair amount about my father's work when I was young. But he was what you might call forward-looking, and when I was ten or eleven, he said, 'Samuel, I won't have you taught the smithy trade properly, not but what a bit of knowledge mightn't be a good idea. But for all we can tell it might be a dying art when you're a man. So it's in my mind that you'll be a builder, for you've an eye for a fine house, and it's what I'd like for you. How about it?'

I said I thought I should like it.

'Good. Even so, it won't harm you to know a bit about smithing, so you'll come along to the forge on Saturday afternoon and between us we'll fashion that new wheel for Simeon Acton's carriage.'

So I learned a fair bit about the art of the smith and my father was right to say it would be useful at times. But I learned my trade as a builder and I think I can say with truth that I've done well with it. I've built many a fine, strong house hereabouts. I've travelled a bit to one or two cities, as well. Manchester and Chester – a fine old place, Chester. And I built the new extension for Mr Ralph West's factory in Derby, where he deals with the grand china he brings into the country from Holland and France. Mr West was so pleased with my work that a couple of years afterwards he gave me the job of building Stilter House.

(And I'm sorry if I'm talking too much, but if you're wanting to make a proper record – and since I'm wanting you to know I'm not afflicted with a moonstruck madness – it's important for you to know it and understand.)

So I knew, early on, that I wasn't going to be a

blacksmith, but I always liked going into my father's forge. Sometimes it would be cold, the hearth just an ordinary hearth, clinkered and pitted, the welding hammers and irons stacked against the wall. But when the fires were glowing and there was the ring of the hammer on the anvil, something seemed to wake and you could believe you'd stepped into an enchanted land. I'd see it as peopled with fiery steeds wearing bridles of melted gold and harnesses of chalcedony like in the Bible, (not that I ever knew what chalcedony was). Or maybe the Beast from the Book of Revelation that was thrown into the blazing furnace for its wickednesses. Really, the Beast would only be Sir Beecham Bondley's old piebald standing near the open forge waiting for a new shoe on account of having thrown one across Goose Green, but firelight changes things, so I'd see stallions shod with fire or the Four Horsemen of the Apocalypse, chained and caged at last. The imagination of a child plays these tricks. Not that I ever had much imagination, not really, and now – well, dealing with hods of bricks and tubs of mortar drives out all thoughts of fiery-shod steeds.

The forge was alive on the day I'm speaking of. My father was hammering out a pair of spurs for Sir Beecham Bondley and I was helping. Sir Beecham himself had gone off to The Pheasant while it was being done, telling my father, with a sly wink, that there was a new serving wench there. I remember, as well, my father saying he knew all about the new serving wench, and I remember having the feeling that the two men had shared a joke I did not understand.

My mother came to fetch me just after my father and I had eaten our dinner. I had been looking forward to getting the spurs finished, but mother said I was to go along with her to Acton House, so I put on my scarf and cap and made ready to set off along the lanes. I could help with spurs any time, but I had never been to Acton House. It would be quite an adventure; something to tell the other children at school. I wouldn't boast, but I would certainly talk about it.

It seemed there was to be a weekend party, and there were turkey poults to be plucked for a big dinner and none too much time to do them, so mother wanted an extra pair of hands. She often did this kind of work. House parties, there'd be, with tennis on the lawn or picnics in the orchard in summer, and lavish dinners at night.

I knew the lanes around Acton House of course. A few of us would go blackberrying there in autumn and hunting for horse chestnuts. We'd pick elderflowers and rose hips in spring for jam. But I had only seen the house itself through the trees and hedges that grew thickly round it.

'Nice enough,' mother said once, when I asked about the house. 'If you care for grandeur and a lot of frippery. She likes her comforts, that Isobel Acton.'

My mother did not approve of Mrs Acton. 'Light-minded,' she said of her. 'More interested in wearing silk gowns from London, or playing that rubbishing music on her piano, than in running her house.'

But she did approve of Simeon Acton, which was why she always accepted any work at the house. Simeon Acton had paid for the church roof to be mended and built six almshouses for elderly people in the area who found themselves in difficult circumstances or people who had suffered hardship and were unable to work. Once it would have been Sir Beecham Bondley's task to donate money for the church roof and build almshouses, him being the squire and living in the big house, but the Bondleys had done what was called squander their substance years since.

Simeon Acton did not squander anything on anyone, unless it might have been his wife. People said he was besotted with her and that there was no fool like an old fool, but they said it quite affectionately.

I had seen Isobel Acton once, and I had never forgotten it. Her carriage had stopped outside the forge while Mr Acton came in to arrange for some job he wanted my father to do. I went out to ask if she would step inside for it was a bitterly cold January day. She said something – I forget now what – but her voice was like no voice I had ever heard. It made me think of deep dark midnight skies and cats' fur. I dreamed about that voice for weeks afterwards and in the dreams it was always saying all manner of nice things to me.

But I think that even within the dreams I was always a bit afraid of Isobel. Because, you see, it did not take much of a stretch to make *Isobel* into *Jezebel*. And I knew my Bible: I was a diligent attendee of Sunday School, and I knew Jezebel had been a Hebrew princess, guilty of all kinds of wickedness, and that just before she was executed by Jehu, she dressed herself up in a fine gown and painted her face. What kind of abandoned creature, demanded our Sunday school teacher, would do that half an hour before being thrown to wild dogs to be eaten?

Anyway, there I was, walking through an English spring day, to the house where a lady who was also called Jezebel (or very nearly) lived. But a lady who had that marvellous silken voice that reminded you of evening birdsong or thin spring water with sunlight shining through it. I wanted to meet her properly. I wanted her to smile at me and think good things of me.

I remember that walk vividly. The trees hummed with birdsong and the meadows were splashed with buttercups, and it was a day when marvellous things might happen.

Acton House had big elaborate iron gates, and on that day the tips glinted in the sunlight. As we pushed them open (silken smooth and silent they were, no screeching hinges for the Actons), I remember thinking – at last I'm going to see her properly. I might even speak to her again. She's inside this house, wearing a silk gown, lying on one of the velvet couches or sitting on a cushion to sew a fine seam, like the ladies in the old rhyme. Even at twelve years of age it gave me a very strange feeling to visualize that, partly pleasurable, partly guiltily uncomfortable – and *that's* something I've never told a living soul, not even Mrs Burlap, in fact, especially not

Mrs Burlap, so I'll be grateful if you'll treat it with discretion, Doctor and miss.

We didn't go the front door, of course. My mother would have been shocked to think of doing such a thing, and we went along a side path and around to the kitchens. But no one came in answer to her knock, and that was when I began to feel uneasy. Not frightened, exactly, but as if something was tapping against my mind – something that said, *Beware* . . . They say that once upon a time human beings had an extra sense that warned them of danger approaching, but that we've become so civilized we've lost that sense, whatever it might have been. I don't know about that, but I do know that on that afternoon I was very uneasy.

'This is strange,' said my mother. 'No one seems to be here. But I'm expected, that I do know.' She frowned, then reached for the door latch and turned it, calling out to Miss Stump, who was the person who sent a message when mother was needed to help out.

But there was still no response. My mother was clearly puzzled, but in a brisk voice, she said, 'Well, they can't be far away, because the kitchen door was unlocked. I dare say that Eliza Stump is off somewhere with young Poulson from The Pheasant again, though, the giddy creature.' She made a tutting sound, which meant she disapproved. 'We'll try the front.'

We retraced our steps along the side garden path and through the gardens. The front of the house was framed by trees and bushes, and to me it seemed like a palace. It was a large building – there were what I now know to be gables with painted trims. The walls were red brick, which was unusual in itself. Most houses in Caudle Moor were – still are – built of the local stone. I remember I stared up at those walls entranced, and I thought: I'd like to make houses like this.

We had to walk past two windows to get to the front door. Small windows they were, with thick, slightly wavy glass, criss-crossed with lead strips. I knew, of course, that you did not look through people's windows. Very ill mannered, mother always said. But this was Acton House – it was a big, grand place, not as big or as grand as Bondley Manor, but nearly so. And it was where *she* lived. So, greatly daring, I looked through one of the windows.

At first the room seemed entirely ordinary and the two people in it seemed to be doing ordinary things. The only thing unfamiliar to me was the piano – a glossily black instrument standing at the far end. I had never seen a house that had a piano.

Isobel Acton was sitting on a button-back sofa, very upright, very composed. She was wearing a soft fine gown, pale green silk, exactly as I had pictured her, and her hair, which was dark and glossy, was scooped on top of her head. I wanted to stay there and watch her for ever.

She was embroidering, which I knew was what ladies did. People like my mother hadn't the time for such frippery stuff; if they sewed anything it was mending of socks and shirts.

A tray of cups and saucers stood on a low table in front of Isobel, together with what I took to be a thin, tall teapot. I know now that it was a coffee pot, but I had never seen one then.

Simeon Acton was seated on the other side of the fireplace. He had been reading, but he had put the book down, and he was watching his wife with a look of deep love and pride – I had never seen anyone look like that, but I knew the expression for what it was.

Neither of them saw me, but after a moment Isobel put down her sewing, and leaned over the small table to pour coffee into a cup. She glanced over her shoulder, then tipped something into the cup – white powder it looked like and it could have been sugar. She stirred it in, then carried the cup to her husband. He smiled up at her as he took it, and drank. Then he stopped and frowned. His hand went to his throat as if something had clutched it, and he started up from his chair, his face turning a dull ugly crimson.

Isobel had stepped back and she was standing on the pale rug, watching her husband. She stood very still, not speaking and I waited for her to call for help, to go to him, but she did not. As God is my judge, Isobel Acton, that beautiful silken creature with that midnight velvet voice that had spun an enchantment through my nights, turned her back on the man writhing in agony on the floor. With apparent unconcern, she walked to the piano standing in the big bay window, sat down and began to play. Light, cool music, cold and fragile as icicles, drifted across the room, and whether or not she was doing it to mask the sounds of her husband's struggles, or for some other cause altogether, I have no more idea now than I had then. But it was as if white painful light was spiking into my mind.

Acton had fallen to the floor and he was writhing and gasping, clutching his stomach. His lips had taken on a bluish tinge, and his eyes were almost starting from his head. He made a dreadful bubbling sound in his throat, and then vomited wetly on the pale rug. I felt my own stomach lift in nausea and for a moment I thought I, too, would be sick, there against the beautiful red-brick wall. I bent over, but nothing came up, and after a moment I was able to straighten up again and look back into the room.

I thought: surely she will have gone to him now, but she had not. Simeon twisted and turned on the ground, arching his back as if trying to escape the pain, and horridly and incredibly his gasps were in exact time with the soft chords coming from the piano. As if the pianist was playing her music to coincide with his agony.

I didn't think that then, of course, but I've thought it since, and I've heard that grim rhythm and those gasping moans over and over in my mind. And it's one of the memories that's stayed with me so strongly. That image of her coolly making that beautiful music, in which the waves of pain and terror from the struggling man seemed so tangled. (And that dreadful light still slicing through my mind, piercing my brain . . .)

It seemed as if Simeon Acton's struggles went on for
a very long time, but I don't suppose it was more than a
few minutes. I wonder, even now, what would have
happened if Isobel Acton had not turned her head and
caught sight of me at the window.

Between one heartbeat and the next she changed. In
place of the cold detachment there was a panic-stricken,
distressed woman. She sprang up from the piano and ran
to the window, flinging it wide.

My mother, who had been in the deep old porch, turned
at the sound, and at once Isobel called out to her.

'Help me! Please!' She stepped back from the window,
and seconds later there was the sound of the porch door
opening.

My mother paused only long enough to bid me remain
outside – 'On no account are you to come into the house,
Samuel,' – and I obeyed. I was too frightened to do
anything else and I was still feeling slightly sick and my
head was aching. But I don't believe anything could have
stopped me looking through that window.

It was like watching a play – I had seen a play when
a troupe of actors came to Caudle Moor to the church
hall. Mother said play-acting was sinful and play-actors
were painted whores and libertines, and I was not to go.
But father winked at me, and said we would go along
together, he and I, and if there was any sin then the vicar
would be there to deal with it anyway. So we braved
mother's disapproval and went to see the actors. I
remember the piece was called *Maria Marten in the Red
Barn,* and very gruesome it was.

But what I saw through that window that fine spring
afternoon was far more vivid than any play-acting on a
lit stage.

My mother bent over Simeon Acton for a moment,
then said, quite sharply, 'Where is Eliza Stump? The
other servants?'

'They have the afternoon off. Please help me. I don't
know what to do.' Isobel's voice sounded shrill and
frightened, but I heard the false note, like a cracked bell,

and the dreams splintered deep inside my mind. I thought: you cheating bitch. And *bitch* was not a word I was ever allowed to use, even in my mind.

My mother strode to the window and opened it, calling out to me.

'Samuel, you're to go along to Dr Brodworthy's house directly, and tell him he's to come to Acton House at once. You understand.'

'Yes. But—'

'At once, Samuel.' She was already turning back into the room, saying, 'An emetic. Warm water and a good dessertspoon of mustard.'

The window closed with a snap and I ran for all I was worth, back down Gorsty Lane, and into the village. It's a fair distance and running so hard made my head feel as if it might be splitting in two, but I didn't stop until I reached the doctor's house and was hammering on his door. That was your father, of course, Doctor. Old Dr Brodworthy we call him nowadays, meaning no disrespect, for a very good man he was. He lived in this very house we're in now, although it was a sight different then, for he hadn't the electricity and he still used wooden instruments for sounding people's chests, and gave all the children brimstone and treacle for regular habits.

His man harnessed up the donkey cart, and we drove back down Gorsty Lane at a fair old lick. A storm was blowing down from the Pennines and there were huge purple bruises in the sky where there had been cotton-wool clouds earlier. Flurries of huge rain spots dashed against our faces.

The storm broke as we turned in through the gates, forked lightning splitting open the skies, so you'd think the heavens were being ripped open and something – God or the devil – was about to reach down and snatch you up. Rain lashed down, drenching the gardens, but it was cooling, and it seemed to quench the lights inside my mind a little.

With Dr Brodworthy there was no nonsense about me staying outside. He strode into the house and I followed,

even in those confused moments noticing how beautiful
Acton House was. I thought: if ever this house is
destroyed, there should be another in its place as nearly
like it as possible.

It was too late to save Simeon Acton, of course. I
learned later that mother had tried the mustard emetic,
but I think he was already dead by then.

You know what happened afterwards, Doctor, for
everyone hereabouts knows, even after all these years.
Your father, who was a conscientious man, sent for the
local police constable to enquire into Simeon Acton's
death and the machinery of the law ground into action.

And the nightmare that was to stay with me all my
life began in earnest.

Nell came briefly out of the world of Samuel Burlap to the
warm safe bedroom of The Pheasant, and shivered, drawing
the covers around her. It was extraordinary how vivid the
account of Simeon Acton's death was, and how the young
Samuel's reactions leapt off the page.

She glanced across at the other bed where Beth slept soundly,
apparently untroubled by any bad dreams of the evening's
macabre terrors.

There were only a few more pages of the statement, and
Nell knew she would not be able to sleep unless she read to
the end. With the feeling that she was stepping deeper into a
macabre pocket of the past, she picked up the final pages.

TEN

Continuation of Samuel Burlap's statement:
    Simeon Acton's sister came to Caudle Moor two days
after his death, and she treated the village to a fine display
of high drama, wailing and carrying-on, publicly calling
Isobel several names I had never heard until then and
haven't often heard since. She was a tall thin lady and my

father said she had a face like sour milk. My mother said Miss Acton should think shame to make such a public exhibition of her feelings, but that was after Miss Acton had walked into The Pheasant, bold as a brass farthing, and denounced Isobel as a Messalina and a creature in whose blood ran the juices of the Black Widow spider. Some versions accredited Miss Acton with flinging an entire tankard of cider over Nehemiah Goodbody who happened to be the nearest person and had been peaceably supping his evening potation, which he had done every night for the last fifty years.

None of it was behaviour anyone in Caudle Moor had ever witnessed, and no one quite knew how to deal with it, apart from helping Nehemiah Goodbody to mop the spilt cider off his jacket. But then young Mr Poulson, who walked out with Eliza Stump and was a kind-hearted soul, took charge and persuaded Miss Acton into one of the private rooms, after which he called out Dr Brodworthy who drove her back to her lodgings in the pony cart.

Everyone was shocked. Folk reminded one another that no decent woman would have dreamed of entering the tap room under any circumstances whatsoever, in fact few woman would have entered The Pheasant at all, except it might be for a meeting of the Ladies' Sewing Circle or the Girls' Friendly Society if the church hall was not available. But, as my father pointed out, Miss Acton was in a distraught frame of mind, so allowances should be made.

Then it became known that Simeon Acton had been poisoned, and people immediately pointed out to one another that poison was a woman's weapon.

Isobel paid none of this any attention. She remained inside Acton House, the curtains drawn, as befitted a house of mourning, receiving no one and going nowhere. I imagined her in that room with the piano, sitting in the shadows, weaving her plans. Had she killed her husband because she wanted his money? Or because she loved someone else?

She would wear black of course, a widow's weeds,

but it would be black silk or velvet and her skin would be like polished porcelain against the black, and she would be beautiful. But it would be the deceiving beauty of a fruit that was velvety and tempting on the surface, but rotten and pulpy within. She was no longer that magical creature I had thought her; she was Jezebel, a murderess who had cared so little for her victim she played music while he writhed in his death throes, just as Jezebel in the Bible had cared nothing for the prophets she had slaughtered.

Isobel did not attend Simeon's funeral. This shocked the village to its marrow, although, as my father remarked, it was surprising her absence was noticed at all, since the whole of Caudle Moor, along with Caudle Magna and several other neighbouring villages attended, and the congregation was packed tight with only those at the front able to see or hear the actual service. My mother was forced to have a back pew, which annoyed her very much.

Isobel Acton's housekeeper, Eliza Stump, was there, of course. 'And very overdressed, too,' said Mother, but when Miss Stump came along to our cottage two days later she accorded her a very cordial welcome. It's probable that she was more pleased to see Miss Stump than was the wolf when Red Riding Hood skipped up to his cottage. My father was pleased to see Miss Stump, as well; he liked a lady with a bit of liveliness, he said.

So Miss Stump, who was lively enough for three, and had hair as golden as a copper warming pan, was ushered into the parlour and offered tea from the best cups.

'Such a fortunate chance I had baked this morning,' said Mother, who had baked every day in the hope that someone – anyone – would call to discuss the terrible happenings. Several had, of course; Caudle Moor was a gossipy place in those days, well, it still is.

Miss Stump partook of tea and cake, praised the lightness of the baking, and settled down to be every bit as indiscreet as Mother could have wished.

It isn't something I'm proud of, but I crouched on the

stairs just outside and listened avidly. It was rather dark
on our stairs, and there was a faint smell of baking soda
and borax from the cupboard where Mother kept her
cleaning rags and scouring powders. I didn't hear
everything, but I heard most of it and it's been printed
on my memory ever since.

The servants at Acton House had been given the
afternoon off, which Miss Stump said was 'not unknown
and generally meant madam was going to be up to a bit
of no good with some gentleman, pardon my frankness,
Mrs Burlap, but you'll understand my meaning.'

There was a vague murmur of assent from my mother.

'I'm not one for gossip,' said Miss Stump righteously,
'but all manner of gentlemen visit the house when the
master's away – some of them London gentlemen and
ones you'd think above that kind of carrying-on. In quite
high walks in life, they are. And they come into the house
as stealthy and slinky as if they were tomcats going on
the randy.'

My mother said something about all men being beasts,
and added she had always known Isobel Acton to be a
trollop for all her famous beauty.

'Many a pretty face hides a wicked heart, Miss Stump.'

Eliza Stump said this was very true indeed, but
howsoever, she and the two girls had gone off as instructed
that afternoon.

'And a very nice afternoon we had over to Caudle
Magna. Tea and scones at a very genteel teashop in
Magna, and I found some silk ribbon at the draper's to
trim a bonnet.'

There was a rustle of bombazine as Miss Stump leaned
forward to impart further confidence. 'When we got home
. . . Well, Mrs Burlap, you know what we found when
we got home, for you were there already, and that's why
I wanted to come and tell you what has happened.'

The springs of my mother's chair creaked as she
nodded and leaned forward. She said, 'I know well
enough what you found, Miss Stump. Poor good Mr
Acton dead as last week, his innards all eaten up with

poison, and Dr Brodworthy not able to do a thing about it. I mixed a draught of mustard and hot water, as you know, but we couldn't get it down him, for he was writhing and struggling. And the sickness that overcame him – well, that was something terrible to witness.'

'It quite spoilt the Persian rug,' nodded Miss Stump. 'I set the girls to scrub it with white vinegar and soda, but it'll never be the same.'

'Then the doctor came and said the poor man had gone,' went on my mother, who thought Persian rugs frivolous. 'He gave me a powder for Mrs Acton to take – a bromide or some such he called it – and she retired to her bed.'

'And still there the next day, calling for cologne to bathe her head, and wailing and sobbing fit to wake the dead – meaning no disrespect – and asking us all what she should do without her beloved Simeon.' There followed a snort of disgust. 'Beloved indeed! Beloved of his money, more like,' said Miss Stump, 'and wanting to have the freedom to entertain her gentlemen callers, and to hold the reins of Mr Acton's fortune, that's my view, and . . . Well, yes, I will have another cup of tea, thanking you kindly, and perhaps just a small slice of your delicious cake. I'm very partial to seed cake.' A pause. 'I dare say you knew Miss Acton, the master's sister, is here?'

'I did hear,' said my mother. 'Staying with the Gilfillans, so they say.'

'That she is, for Madam won't have her in the house. I never cared much for the Gilfillans,' said Miss Stump. 'Always a bit above themselves in my opinion – although not above taking a paying guest in that cold house of theirs, and forever reminding folk how saintly they are. And that boy of theirs – no older than your Samuel he isn't, but walks around with a Bible, telling everyone how Jesus is our saviour. Well, Mrs Burlap, Jesus may well be the saviour of us all, but what I say is, it ain't natural for a twelve year old to go about saying it.'

'I suppose,' said my mother, who frequently held up Edgar Gilfillan to me as an example, 'it was only right that Miss Acton should come here after her brother died. And she'd want to stay a while to know the findings of the medical gentlemen.'

'I'll grant that,' said Miss Stump. 'And I'll grant, as well, that she's sorrowful at his death – yes, and the manner of it. But her behaviour . . . Well, Mrs Burlap, it's scarcely sane at times. Why, she comes to Acton House every single day demanding to see madam, never caring that madam has given orders not to let her in. She bangs on the doors, and if we don't open them she taps on the windows. Positively eerie it is to go to a window of a night, perhaps to close it against the twilight, and see that sour face peering in.'

'I expect,' said my mother, 'that there's money at the root of it. There so often is. Tell me – is there a will?'

'Oh, a will there'll be, sure as eggs is eggs, the master not being one to leave his affairs in a disarray. I'd lay you a year's wages that everything is left to that young madam. That'll be why she wanted to get rid of him,' said Miss Stump. 'And she thought as she'd got away with it, I'd say. But because of what happened this morning she'll be thinking differently.'

'What happened this morning?' said my mother, and even from my precarious hiding place I could hear she had to fight with herself before asking the question.

'Early today,' said Miss Stump, thrillingly, 'the police came to Acton House.'

'No!'

'Oh yes. Bold as you like, and arrested Isobel Acton for the murder of poor dear Mr Acton. So now, what do you think of that!'

What anyone in Caudle Moor thought of Isobel Acton's arrest was soon known when people crowded into the police house claiming to have seen her in various compromising situations. These ranged from seeing her buy poison at the apothecary's shop in Abbots Caudle – 'Brazen as you like, asking how long the stuff would take to kill a man,' – to declarations that the lady had been witnessed gathering hemlock at the full moon. Nehemiah Goodbody told the tap room in The Pheasant that Mrs Acton was not the daughter of a respectable Ashbourne merchant at all, but had been a lady of pleasure with whom Nehemiah himself had once had dealings, but since Nehemiah was eighty-two and apt to confuse past and present after his third tankard of ale, I don't think anyone paid this much attention.

Mr Poulson was heard to tell how Isobel entertained many a gentleman while the servants were out of the way, and, with a sly wink or two, said some of the identities of those gentlemen would surprise everyone. Asked how he knew that, he said, Ask no questions and I'll tell no lies, adding that some of the gentlemen in question paused at The Pheasant before going back to their homes.

'For refreshment?' asked a timid soul.

'Refreshment? Never! In need of reviving, more like.'

The trial took place at The Pheasant four weeks later. A courtroom was arranged in an upstairs room, and the Poulsons were in high glee with all the bustle and flurry, and people wanting tankards of ale and the ladies taking port and lemon or a glass of stout.

I didn't go to the trial, of course. My mother went because she had been at Acton House when Simeon died, and she had to give evidence. My father said he could not spare the time. Work did not stop just because someone might have committed murder.

People crowded into The Pheasant each day, sitting on wooden benches or jam-packed in corners and even perched on window-ledges. The legal gentlemen wanted to exclude them, but could not on account of it being the law that such proceedings are heard in public

'A nasty smoke-filled place,' said my mother, who had never before set foot in a public house, and hoped never to do so again. 'Almost the whole of Caudle Moor there and the women dressed in their Sunday best as if it was a church outing. And,' said my mother, clearly much annoyed, 'who do you suppose is foreman of the jury?'

'Who?'

'Why, that young George Poulson who walks out with Eliza Stump. Standing up and taking the oath, fine as fivepence. Pushy, that's what those Poulsons are, pushy.'

'There'll be no holding Eliza Stump after this,' said my father.

I never told anyone that I knew exactly what had happened the day Simeon Acton died. If I had been asked, I don't know what I would have said.

I no longer had the image of Isobel as a creature of perfection. I understood by then that she would smile in a way that would warm a man's soul, and behind his back stir poison into his cup. But I couldn't bear the thought of her being hanged – of being led to the gallows like a tethered animal – of her neck broken so that her head lolled to one side, and her eyes bulged from their sockets and her tongue protruded from her mouth . . .

I couldn't bear it. So I said nothing to anyone.

ELEVEN

Continuation of Samuel Burlap's statement:

The children of Caudle Moor didn't know everything that happened at the Acton trial, but details reached us in fragments and shreds, like bloodied strings snaking outwards. Children don't always find out what goes on in the adult world, but they overhear bits of talk and they pick up fear and suspicion from their elders. There was plenty of that in Caudle in those weeks.

There was no suspicion on the night a group of us children went up to Acton House, though. That was sheer downright curiosity. And perhaps there was a wish to prove how brave we were.

The servants had all left Acton House after Isobel's arrest, and the house was closed up. Sergeant Neale was supposed to be keeping watch on it in case of vagrants and gypsies and suchlike, but he wasn't there that night we went, and even if he had been, we knew all the tricks for dodging policemen.

There were five of us and Edgar Gilfillan was one of the five – of course he was; catch that one missing out on a bit of local excitement. He said God was with us on this journey, but Matt McCardle, whose father farmed several hundred acres over to Caudle Magna, said if that was so, it was to be hoped the Almighty wouldn't want a share of the liquorice sticks we had bought from Mr Billock's sweet shop, because there were only just enough to go round.

We had chosen our time carefully. It was the hour after school, but not yet supper time, which meant most of our mothers would be busy and most of our fathers still working. My father was in the forge, I knew that, for it was just starting to grow dark and I could see the glow against the sky. You could sometimes see it across the whole of Caudle Village at dusk.

As we went along, we boasted about what we would do when we got to the house – how we would get into the Murder Room, and play Isobel Acton's piano and dance around the room. Edgar Gilfillan was against this. He said if we disturbed Simeon Acton's soul, we should hear it screaming, because the souls of the murdered never lay quiet in their graves. He talked about this all the way along Gorsty Lane until Matt McCardle threw him in a nettle bed. After that Edgar was too busy searching for dock leaves to worry about the screaming souls of the murdered dead.

There oughtn't to be anything particularly fearsome about an empty old house standing by itself, but Acton House was very frightening indeed. I think secretly we all wanted to say, 'Let's go home,' but no one did for fear of appearing a coward. We went along the path with the thick shrubs and listening trees, and the crouching stones that in the twilight almost had leering faces like the stones on churches. I remember somebody stumbled on an uneven bit of path, and the sound of stones skittering across the ground made us all jump.

We stood in front of the house, staring at it, trying to pluck up courage to approach it. Once I thought something nearby sighed, and once a figure seemed to move across one of the windows, but when I pointed to it, the others said it was only the reflection of the clouds.

Then Edgar grabbed my arm, making me yelp. 'Don't do that,' I said, jerking my arm free.

'But listen. I can hear something.'

'Well, nobody else can, and if you're starting on about screaming souls again you can shut up or go back in the nettle patch,' Matt said, crossly.

'No, really listen,' said Edgar, sounding genuinely scared.

'I can't hear anything,' I said. 'You're just being—' Then I stopped, because I could hear it as well.

'I can hear it, too,' said one of the others, in a shaky voice. 'What is it?'

'It's piano music, you ignorant peasant, don't you know music when you hear it?'

'And there's someone sobbing,' said a voice from the back of the group.

'It can't be inside the house,' I said firmly. 'Isobel Acton's at the police station, locked away, and the servants have all gone.'

'Edgar's right, though. There is someone in there,' said Matt, very quietly, as if fearing to be overheard.

I don't know what the others were thinking, but for several moments I believed Isobel had escaped from the police cell and returned to her house. For an even wilder moment, I wondered if we had stumbled into some kind of evil magic, like something from a storybook, and that the murder was about to happen all over again – even that it would keep on happening for years and years. I didn't say that, of course. Nor did I tell them I recognized the chill music as the music Isobel Acton had played the day she killed her husband.

Then, as if an unspoken decision had been made, we all crept towards the latticed windows, which were wreathed in shadows. We went on tiptoe, glancing over our shoulders as we did so – it was dreadfully easy to believe someone tiptoed after us, dodging behind a tree or a shrub if we turned to look. And so we reached the window of the music room.

A woman was seated at the piano. She had a ravaged face, drained of all colour by the moonlight and she was bowed over the keys, playing that cold light music with what I can only call an intensity – although I didn't know that word then. As she played, she sobbed in a way I had never heard anyone sob before. It did not need Edgar's whisper of, 'Anne-Marie Acton,' to tell us who this was. I think we all felt a shiver of fear, because the sobbing was so wretched and so wild and uncontrolled. It was as if thick choking grief filled up the room, like clotted grey fog.

She paused, and we cowered down, thinking she had heard us, but she had not. When we dared look again she had turned towards a glass door behind her, and she was staring into the garden so eagerly I thought she had heard someone, and was waiting to welcome whoever it was. Then I knew that was not right. She had not heard anyone, but she was waiting to do so. She wanted to hear or see someone with such fierce longing – such hunger and such need – it was thrumming through her, stretching and straining her muscles and the tendons of her neck and hands. If you've ever seen someone waiting to see a loved one – longing to see them with every nerve in their body, after a long absence, perhaps – you'll know what I mean.

Then her shoulders slumped and she turned back to the piano and began playing again, still sobbing. Again she broke off and turned to the window. Her lips moved, and by leaning forward I was able to make out what she said.

'Please . . .' Then again, '*Oh, please . . . Let him come to me . . . Let the music have called him here . . .*'

And the incredible thing was that with the words,

something seemed to move across the open glass door – something that was not quite formed, but that seemed to be trying to take human shape . . . As if the music had spun the figure out of strings of moonlight and shreds of melody. (I do *know* how absurd that sounds, but it's what I believed that night).

At the sight of this misshapen figure, Anne-Marie's whole body tensed even more. She said, 'Simeon? Is it you? Let it be you – I will give my soul to the devil and all his minions if it can be you . . . I will never leave here until you come back . . . *Never.*'

For a few seconds the outline that might have been nothing more than a glimmer of moonlight seemed to take more definite shape. It was as if it was trying to be human – trying to do what she wanted – but we didn't stay to see. We moved as one, half falling back from the window, and running helter-skelter through the dark gardens of Acton House, along the uneven paths, and out onto Gorsty Lane. Even when we reached the lane we kept running, heedless of the thickening dusk, and we didn't stop until we could see the village square and the flaring sconces outside The Pheasant and the lights in the windows of several of the houses. Safe . . . I could feel the word form in all our minds, and we slowed to a walk, trembling and sweating with having run so far and so hard, still deeply scared.

Edgar got his breath back first. He said, 'She was calling him. Miss Acton was calling her dead brother. She thought he could come back to her – she thought she could call him back to life.' He sounded horrified but also fascinated.

'She thought old Simeon could come back through the music?' said Matt, half disbelieving, but also clearly remembering that not-quite-formed shape in the doorway and the queer urgency of the music.

'Yes,' said Edgar, although even he did not sound sure.

'You can't call back the dead, not by music or anything else,' I said.

'People in the Bible did. Saul did.'

'Saul tried to do it. Nothing to say he managed it.'

Edgar shrugged in a way that meant he knew better. 'We all saw what we saw,' he said. 'Whether it works or not, Miss Acton was trying to reach the spirit of Simeon Acton. Even if we don't believe it, she did.'

'And,' said one of the others, 'she said she would never leave Acton House until Simeon came back.' We all shivered again and Matt ducked his head as if frightened to look anyone in the eye. Straight afterwards we all went off to our homes, and none of us spoke about what we had seen ever again.

And now, Doctor, I see you and your young lady looking at me as if you think I'm talking like something out of a penny novelette. But grief takes folk strangely. Sometimes they'll try anything to reach those who've died. I know it isn't sane, but I believe Anne-Marie Acton was mad with grief that night. Even now I can remember the scalding torrent of pain that came from her – wave upon wave of it, so vicious and so strong it seemed to bubble like acid into the walls and the bricks and the timbers, then trickle down into the ground and soak into the very earth.

You may discount everything I've said, but there's one thing you can't discount, and that's the music. Anne-Marie Acton's music. Believe me, that's what I heard three nights ago on the old Acton land. That same music Anne-Marie played that long-ago evening when she tried to call back her dead brother. And I'm not the only one to have heard it – you know that. There's plenty of others.

Anne-Marie said she would never leave that house until Simeon came back and she never has. The old house – Acton House – has gone, but the land's still there. Land stays, it can't be burned or broken. It holds secrets. The Acton land holds the secrets and the fears and the madnesses.

That boy knows about the secrets. Esmond, that's his name. Esmond West. I've seen him looking about him when he comes to the site with his father. I've seen the look in his eyes and I can tell that he knows.'

Nell laid the last page down and leaned back on the pillows, her mind gradually returning to the twenty-first century and the warm bedroom with its shaded bedside light and Beth sleeping nearby.

How much of Samuel Burlap's narrative was true? The murder of Simeon Acton was presumably fact and could be checked in court or police records. As for the rest, Nell was still inclined to believe that over-indulgence in The Pheasant's ale lay at the heart of most of it. That youthful escapade when the local children had seen Anne-Marie Acton could simply be a case of children egging one another on, almost a form of mass-hypnosis.

But what about the music? *Music where no music could exist,* Burlap had called it. Anne-Marie Acton's music, he had said, and had added that others had heard it. I heard it as well, thought Nell. On two occasions it could have been Beth who was playing it, but not on the third.

Clipped to the last page of the statement was a newspaper cutting, yellowed with age, and so brittle and dry that when Nell touched it, tiny flakes shedded over the bed. But the print was clear, and although the date was not displayed, across the top someone (Dr Brodworthy?) had written: *A local newspaper report of the Acton Trial, which is referred to in Samuel Burlap's statement [attached], and which may be required by the Mutual & Benefit Society as corroboration of it.*

Caudle and East Derby Gazette
SCENES IN COURTROOM
  A verdict of Not Guilty was yesterday pronounced on Isobel Acton, who has been standing trial for the murder of her husband, Mr Simeon Acton.
  Readers will recall that Mr Acton died earlier this year, from arsenical poisoning. Mrs Acton was charged and arrested shortly afterwards.
  Local feeling had run high over the murder and Mrs Acton had been subjected to abuse and threats. Simeon Acton, whose family had lived in Caudle Moor for several generations, was greatly respected and revered, being a noted philanthropist and having built and endowed the

almshouses on the outskirts of Caudle Village. [Editor's note: see photos and article about Caudle Almshouses on page 6].

Mrs Acton stood very quietly in the dock throughout, [editor's note: a temporary structure built by the local carpenter, and set just beneath the plaque commemorating the names of local men from the 95th Derbyshire, who had fallen in the Crimean War], and, when called on to give her evidence, did so in a low, subdued voice. Several times our reporter had to edge nearer to the dock in order to hear her. It was noticeable that the judge, Mr Justice Marplot, also found it necessary to lean forward to hear her.

She testified to having no idea how the arsenic could have got into her husband's coffee, but openly admitted that there was a small supply of arsenic in the house, which she occasionally used in a weak solution for whitening her hands. Asked if she knew the substance to be dangerous, she said she did know, she supposed everyone knew, and added that she had always taken the greatest care to keep the packet locked in her dressing table.

Each day Mrs Acton appeared wearing a different set of garments, always in black according to her widowed state, but (your reporter is assured) always very stylish as to cut and cloth. There was much speculation among the female members of the public as to what she would wear on the final day, when the verdict would be given, and Mrs Acton did not disappoint them, donning a black silk grosgrain skirt and jacket, with a cloche hat and veil. [Editor's note: see our fashion correspondent's sketch on page 4].

The jury had been in conclave for more than twenty-four hours, using an upper room in The Pheasant. Our reporter was told by a confidential source, that there was much discussion and strong differences of opinion between them before an agreement was eventually reached.

Mrs Acton faced them with composure when they

came in, but as she stood up, she gripped her hands tightly together.

The foreman, Mr George Poulson, son of The Pheasant's landlord, gave the verdict clearly and firmly, but with the pronouncing of the words, "Not Guilty", there was an outcry from the public benches. Many of the locals leapt to their feet, shouting their anger and contempt, and waving their fists at the prisoner. One of them, Miss Anne-Marie Acton, sister of the deceased Simeon Acton, went so far as to run to the centre of the court and vow vengeance on Mrs Acton for her brother's death, calling her by several derogatory names, which this paper is not permitted to print. Mrs Acton appeared unmoved, but Miss Acton, having reached the end of her tirade, collapsed in sobbing distress, and had to be taken into custody. However, the magistrates were sympathetic to her bereaved state, and merely bound her over to keep the peace for a token term of three months. Others who had been part of the fracas were not so fortunate; three gentlemen were given a probationary sentence of one year, two ladies were fined the sum of half a guinea for contempt of court, and an elderly resident of the village, Mr Nehemiah Goodbody, suffered two bruised toes from having a bandaged foot stamped on in the fracas by Sergeant Neale. He later told our reporter it was a crying shame when folk could not sit to enjoy a murder trial without being trod on by a flatfoot policeman. (We should add here that Sergeant Neale later apologized most profusely to Mr Goodbody).

It is understood that Madame Acton, released from her ordeal, will remain in Acton House for a short time only, after which the house will be closed and she will travel abroad for an indefinite period.

Nell put the sheaf of papers on the bedside table, switched off the light, and lay down.

The Not Guilty verdict was surprising. She had assumed that Isobel's place on the gallows was assured. But Samuel Burlap had only been twelve when it happened, and he might have misunderstood what he had seen. Also he had been relating the story many years after it happened. He had not given evidence at the trial, so no one had realized he had seen anything of any significance. It had probably not occurred to anyone to even question him.

How much of the truth had Mrs Burlap known though? Had she simply not seen what had really happened that afternoon, or was she too intimated by the Acton family to speak out against Isobel? Nell did not think Mrs Burlap had sounded a person who could be intimated by anything, but people did not always act as you expected.

And how did all of this tie up with Esmond, who, according to Burlap, had known the secrets?

TWELVE

Michael's journey to Caudle Moor had turned out to be fairly straightforward.

He played some tapes which the Music Director had loaned him after their discussion about the book on poets and music. Berlioz's Second Symphony, apparently inspired by Byron's epic poem, *Childe Harold*, took him as far as Coventry, and he followed this with an overture which Berlioz had written after seeing a performance of *The Tempest*. By this time he was at Bakewell, and he remembered that Nell had phoned from here yesterday morning. With this in mind he pulled into a roadside service station and tried her number again. Still nothing.

Berlioz had wound himself down to the splendid finale of his overture, and Michael switched to the car radio for the last lap of the journey. He was rather pleased that he had not taken any wrong turnings, although he suspected he might have to ask for directions to Stilter House when he reached Caudle itself. If he reached Caudle.

But he did reach it. It was half-past ten when he got there, but there was a fairly well-lit road, with a scattering of small houses and a sign saying this was Caudle Moor, visitors were welcome and please to drive carefully. There was no one about and Michael thought if he could not find Gorsty Lane, he would pull in at The Pheasant, a little further along and ask for directions.

But he found the lane almost at once. The sign was partly hidden by overhanging trees and greenery, but it was readable in the car headlights. Michael swung the car over.

Gorsty Lane was narrow and winding, but there did not seem to be any houses anywhere. Michael drove on, seeing only fields and trees, beginning to feel as if he had fallen into a dark half-world in which there were only the unlit roads and sodden trees, and the rippling rain on the windscreen.

Then without warning the house was there, a dark silent shape rearing out of the sodden twilight, silhouetted blackly against the night sky. The legend *Stilter House* was on the gate, but everywhere was dark. Michael glanced at the dash-board clock. Twenty minutes to eleven. Beth would have been in bed long since, but it was a bit early for Nell, although if there was no electricity on she might have gone to bed with a book and be reading by candlelight. He drove through the gate, and parked near the house. Nell's car was not in sight, but perhaps it was around the other side, or there might be a garage somewhere.

Now he was closer to it, he did not like the house very much. There was a sullen greyness that was not entirely due to the recent rain or the stone walls. And yet this, reportedly, was the place to which Brad West had come for several summers, loving spending his holidays here, always keen to return. Because of Esmond, had that been? Michael reminded himself that Stilter House would have looked very different twenty-five years ago, and that Charlotte West might have filled it with local children, with whom Brad had formed friendships.

Only the one friendship in this place, only ever the one . . . The words whispered on the air like ragged cobwebs, wistful and lonely, and Michael spun round, peering into the dark garden. But there was only the patter of the rain and the blurred breath of the night wind.

He turned up his coat collar and crossed to the front door, then paused. Planning this journey, he had visualized a house with signs of life, and Nell hearing his car and coming out to meet him. But if she was in bed – maybe even asleep – it would certainly alarm her to hear someone knocking on the door.

He walked cautiously round the side of the house, hoping there might be lights at the back. The gravel crunched under his feet with faint wet squelches. If you wanted to be fanciful, you might even think there was an echo – that someone trod in the wet gravel after you. Michael spun round, but there was nothing to see. It was simply that the gravel was sodden and it was displacing as he walked on it, then settling back into place.

The back of the house was in pitch darkness. Michael stood on what seemed to be the remains of a terrace with steps leading down to an overgrown lawn, and stared up at the blank windows. He was just making up his mind to go back to the front door and knock after all, when there was a movement within the shadowy garden. A figure ran across the grass and vanished between the trees. An animal? No, it had been human-shaped.

The sensible action, if you happened to find yourself in a dark old garden with the ghost-tales of former occupants threading through your mind and vague shapes flitting across the terrain, was to make sure the house's occupants were safe, then go for help, after which a search for possible intruders could be made. If said intruder got away during these preliminaries, that was your bad luck and the intruder's good, but it was still the sensible course of action.

What you did not do – what no one in his right mind would do – was go in instant pursuit of the amorphous figure.

Michael cast a glance at the unlit bulk of Stilter House again, gave the equivalent of a mental shrug, and went in pursuit of the amorphous figure.

It had vanished somewhere within the trees and it was towards them that Michael ran, skidding slightly on the wet grass. The damp scents of moss clung everywhere, and the garden, leeched of colour by the night, was a grey-green mistiness. Beyond the trees was a small block of outbuildings, low roofed and half covered with thick mats of ivy.

This is starting to be unreal, thought Michael, pausing to consider his next move. It's as if I've fallen backwards into somebody's elegy, because this is the grey, glimmering landscape with the ivy-mantled tower if ever there was one. But who – or even what? – did I see a few minutes ago? Was it the beckoning ghost in the gloaming light, luring me to God-knows what fate? Or was it Shelley's pard-like spirit, beautiful and swift? Never on your life, he thought, kicking his mind back to reality. Those kind of apparitions don't exist outside the gothic imagination of the romantic poets. Anything supernatural I see out here, will more likely be a cartoon ghost swathed in a bunch of laundry sheets, and if it's clanking chains as well, it'll have purloined them from an old lavatory cistern.

This skewed logic made him feel so much better it occurred to him that he had probably seen nothing more macabre than a local on the way back from The Pheasant, taking a short cut and not realizing anyone was in Stilter House's grounds. Michael banished all thoughts of draggled wraiths or laundry-sheet winos, and resolved to check the ivy-mantled tower for down-to-earth trespassers before going back to the house to wake Nell. A stray trespasser would long since have fled, and even if he had not, he was not likely to be violent. In any case Michael could pelt back to the house or his car if anything menacing came boiling out of the shrubbery.

He had just stepped out of the sketchy protection of the pear tree when through the moss-scented night, came the sound of piano music, light and fragile, but unmistakable. In the same breath-space, a thin smeary light flared at the far end of the outbuildings.

It was an extraordinary moment; it was almost as if the music had ignited something deep within the dark old stones. Michael stopped dead. Should he go back to the house to trace the music to its source or should he go on, and investigate the glimmering light? But music was a normal, unthreatening thing and it might be coming from anywhere. The light was different; it looked as if it might be the start of a fire and those old buildings could go up like matchwood. Michael thought he would take a quick look and if it was a fire he would dash back to the car for his mobile and hope there was a signal. If not he would bang on the doors of Stilter House, get Nell and Beth out, and drive hell-for-leather to the village to summon the fire brigade.

The ramshackle outbuildings looked considerably older than Stilter House. Even in the dimness he could see that the bricks were crumbling, and the roofline sagged. He could still make out the thin light, but there was no ominous smell of smoke or warning crackle of flames, just the scent of wet leaves and grass. The only sound was the cool clear music tapping against the darkness. A corner of his mind registered vague surprise that he was still hearing it, this far from the house.

There were two – no, three – doors on the front of the outbuildings, as if there might be three separate structures. Two doors were shut and half hidden by the ivy, but the third had swung inward a little way. Scaled-down version of Bluebeard's chamber, thought Michael, wryly. Let's hope that room isn't the one with the stored-away corpses of discarded wives. Oh, for heaven's sake, it's a coal house or an ancient earth closet, that's all! But it's where the light's coming from, so I'd better make sure the trespasser didn't drop a lit cigarette or that no wailing shades caught their shirt-tails in the smouldering embers.

Reducing the slightly sinister situation to these vaguely comic proportions reassured him again, and he went up to the half-open door, and called out.

'Hello? Is anyone here?' His voice echoed in the emptiness, and bounced mockingly back at him.

Anyone here . . . anyone here . . .?

And what would I do, thought Michael, if a clotted voice came trickling out of the shadows, and a hoarse whisper said, 'Yes, I'm here – push the door wider and step inside, my dear . . .' Don't be melodramatic, said his mind crossly.

He stepped inside, and sour dead air gusted into his face. It would be animal droppings and decaying vegetation, but it was repulsive, nonetheless. Directly ahead was an inner door which was closed, but the light was coming from beyond it – Michael could see the glow through a small aperture near the top. If it was a fire, at least it seemed to be contained in the inner room, and it looked so small it could probably be doused with a bucket of water.

He turned to go back out, intending to wake Nell and get water from the house, but as he did so, the outer door swung forward and closed with a rusty finality.

Michael dived to it at once, not panicking, because there was nothing to panic about. The door had simply swung closed because of its sagging hinges, that was all, or a gust of wind had blown it. He had only to open the door and step outside . . .

The door opened inwards – it had to be pulled not pushed. That merely meant he had to find the handle. It was not completely dark in here, but the door was in deep shadow, and Michael felt all the way round the frame. It took sixty seconds for him to realize there was no handle on this side. The inside of the door was smooth, virtually seamless, and it was wedged tight into its frame.

He swore and felt round it again, this time searching for a knot-hole or a warped piece of wood he could use to pull the door open. Nothing. He was still not panicking, but he was becoming worried. He would get out, of course, even if he had to smash his way through the door. It was an old one anyway and the hinges were rusting – he had felt the rough edges of them on the frame. It would not take much to snap them off and get the door open. And even if that failed, there would be a window somewhere, or another way out.

Another way out . . .

He turned to look at the inner door. The light still glowed behind it, and the aperture was actually a small grille – a square window with thin vertical bars. Halfway down the door frame was an immense iron bolt, and near the top was a second one. Both were drawn across so that anything on the other side would be shut in. As if the thought gave substance to something that waited in the darkness, thin hands with impossible, bone-pale fingers, curled around the bars of the grille. A face looked out at him between the bars.

Michael fell back, banging his shoulder hard against the outer door, but hardly noticing the jab of pain. His mind was filled with horror, because there was someone in there – someone who had been shut in there, and the fearsome bolt drawn. A woman – yes, the eyes were a woman's eyes, large and dark, and there was the impression of dark hair, unkempt and stringy. But there was something wrong about the woman's face, something dreadfully wrong, only he could not make out what it was, because the clotted shadows were obscuring part of the features, and thick cobwebs clung everywhere – they dripped from the woman's fingers like sticky strings. But it was her eyes that held him – terrible, beseeching eyes, eyes that said, *Let me out, please, oh please, let me out . . .*

He scrambled to his feet and went forward, intending to draw back the bolts, calling out to her as he moved. But even as his words echoed in the enclosed space, there was a blurred movement from beyond the grille. The uncertain light shut off, and thick, bad-smelling darkness rushed at him like a blow.

For several minutes Michael was completely disoriented. He had been facing the inner door, but the sudden loss of sight – the silent quality of the darkness – threw him. He stood very still, then turned his head and managed to make out the thread of light coming from beyond the main door. He was just trying to decide whether he should try to get to the bolted door, or whether he should make a renewed attempt to get outside, when he became aware that someone was standing very close to him. Someone who was breathing very quietly and lightly. Something brushed against him – hands? The edge of a garment? His heart bumped with panic, because there was someone in here with him. Was it the hollow-eyed creature shut away in the inner room? Could she have got out after all and be standing close to him?

Whoever this was seemed to be standing between Michael and the outer door – he could just make out a dark blurred shadow. Male? Female? The thought of a tussle in the pitch dark was so daunting that Michael backed away to the bolted door with the grille and, tying to keep his eyes on the shadowy shape, he fumbled for the nearer of the two bolts. It resisted at first, then slid back with a screech of sound, and his hands felt for the second one. That, too, stuck, then yielded.

The shadow seemed to flinch at the sounds and Michael pushed the inner door open. He had no idea what would happen, but surely the freed woman would be on his side if it came to a fight.

The inner room was empty. Faint threads of light slanted down from where the roof had partly fallen in – more than sufficient light to see that there was no one here. Or was there? Michael looked uneasily into the corners. Did the crouching shadows hide something? But his eyes were adjusting to the dimness now, and he could see that there was nowhere for anyone to hide. But I saw her, he thought, puzzled.

This room was somewhat larger than the outer one. It had stone walls, and it was just possible to see a rotting table and chair pushed against the far wall. A length of old chain lay beneath the table, thickly covered with dust and grime. Could that be used as a weapon in the event of an attack?

It might be possible to break out through the damaged roof, but not without a noisy struggle. And Michael was not going to stay in a room where the door could be slammed and bolted from the outside. Moving as quickly as he could in the dimness, he went back to the outer room. And this time he knew, in the indefinable way the human brain does know, that there was no one here except himself. Whoever or whatever had stood watching from the door had gone. He drew in a sigh of relief, and turned his attention to getting out. The door was still a seamless slab of wood, but he found the hinges and tried to snap them off. At the first attempt the rusty edges cut into his palm, so he wrapped the edge of his jacket around his hand and tried again. To begin with he thought he was not going to manage it, then quite suddenly the old metal broke away from the frame and the door sagged slightly. Encouraged, Michael attacked the second hinge which, loosened by the fracture of the other one, came off almost at once. The door fell outwards, crashing onto the ground. The sound reverberated through the gardens, splinters of rubble flew upwards, and scatterings of earth showered everywhere.

Michael dived out of the noisome stone room, and ran across the gardens towards the house. He expected to see or hear signs of life – they would surely have heard the crash – and he was getting ready to call out that there was nothing to worry about, but the house remained dark and still. A prickle of new anxiety jabbed at his mind, because whatever he had seen, or thought he had seen in that bolted and barred inner room, he had certainly seen someone run across the garden, and someone had shut him in that stone building.

He walked around the house, intending to knock loudly on the front door – always supposing he could find it. The rain had stopped and a watery moon was shedding enough light for him to find his way around the side. Halfway along was a wrought-iron gate, and Michael realized he was on the side furthest from the drive. It was then he saw, just before the gate, a window, wide open, and jutting out at right angles to the wall. No one would leave a ground floor window open at this time of night, not when it was pelting down with rain. Nell certainly would not, particularly not in someone else's house.

There were footprints in the wet ground directly underneath the window. Did they indicate that someone had got in or that someone had got out? Michael could not tell, but when he looked into the room, he could see two or three pieces of heavy-looking furniture pushed up against the door. Barricades? His mind instantly saw Nell and Beth taking refuge in this room, (from who? from what?), piling up the cupboard and the settle to stop someone getting in. And then climbing out of the window and fleeing for safety?

His first instinct was to run back to his car and phone the police, but he remembered the lack of a signal. He would have to investigate on his own: he could not risk any delay. Abandoning the original idea of openly knocking on the door, he grasped the window sill and swung himself over it. As he dropped down into the room, Stilter House's darkness and its scents closed around him. But woven into the darkness was the thin fragile music he had heard earlier. Michael stood still, listening. The music might actually mean Nell or Beth had a radio on, in which case there was nothing to worry about. But it's not a radio, said his mind. It's someone playing the piano.

Crossing to the door, he called out, 'Nell? Beth? It's me – Michael.'

His voice did not echo as it had done in the stone building, but there was a hollow ring to it, as if he was calling into an empty house. Only it could not be empty, because of the music. He began dragging the cupboard and the settle clear of the door. When he paused once to listen, he could hear the music still playing. But surely the pianist must have heard him? Wouldn't whoever it was come in here to investigate? He focused on getting the settle clear of the door, and opened it.

Beyond the room was a wide dim hall, with several doors opening off it and a narrow passage leading to the back. There was a stairway, winding up into darkness. Michael called out again, willing Nell to answer, but the only sound was the music. It was coming from a room near the front; the door was slightly open. He went towards it, trying not to think the soft sound of creeping footsteps followed him or that the faint rustlings were anything other than the ordinary sounds of an old house.

To chase these sounds away, he called out again. 'Hello? Someone here?' This struck him as an outstandingly stupid thing to say, because of course there was someone here. 'I got in through the window,' said Michael, which sounded even more absurd, and before he could succumb to real fear, pushed the door of the room wide and stepped inside.

It was filled with swirling shadows, but he could see the piano clearly enough at the far end, near a curtained window. What he could also see clearly was the small figure seated at it. He started to say, 'Beth?' then stopped, because even through the dimness he could see this was not Beth. It was a boy of about Beth's age, and whoever he was, he did not, at first, seem to have heard Michael come in; he continued to play, leaning forward to read the music, frowning with the effort of concentration. Michael stayed where he was, watching, and the boy played a few more bars, then faltered and looked up. His eyes widened – disconcertingly they were Beth's eyes – then he darted across the room towards the curtained windows behind the piano. The folds of the fabric stirred slightly and he was gone.

Michael went after him at once, banging into things in the dark, knocking over a small table, but reaching the window within seconds. He dragged at the heavy curtains, pulling them back, revealing an old-fashioned French window. Then the boy had gone out through that, although he had done it so silently and swiftly . . .

Except that he could not have done. There was a key in the lock of the French window and it was not just locked, it was also bolted at the top. Michael looked at the two panes of glass flanking the French window; they were long and narrow, with heavy leaded lights criss-crossing the entire panes. Neither had any kind of opening hinge or handle and certainly no one could have got through them. It was a version of the old conundrum in a whodunnit – the room with the murder victim and the door locked from the inside.

He peered through the glass, shading the reflection with his hand, trying to see into the gardens, but if any more spectral figures flitted across the gloaming, he could not see them.

Well, Great-Aunt Charlotte West, thought Michael, turning back to look round the room, your house certainly has some surprises. I suppose I ought to be thoroughly spooked – in fact I think I ought to be downright terrified, because at the latest count I've seen three figures, two of whom could certainly be called wraithlike, and one small boy who poured ethereal music into the house, then disappeared.

Esmond. The name was already in his mind, of course. Was it Esmond he had just seen? *Esmond never left Stilter House,* Emily West had said on the phone. *And Beth is so very like Brad was at that age.*

If Michael was going to be spooked by anything in this house, he thought it would be Esmond. Was Esmond here now, hiding somewhere in this dark silent house? Oh for pity's sake, said his mind crossly, and on this heartening note of anger he went back into the hall. There was just enough light to make a brief check everywhere, but the moonlight drained the colour from the rooms, and Michael felt as if he had stepped backwards into an old black-and-white film – something from the 1930s, perhaps. Charlotte West's youth, would that be?

Whether the elusive boy had been Esmond or not, he did not seem to be around, but Michael did not have the sense of a completely empty house. He took a deep breath and went determinedly into all the rooms, making as much noise as he could. But there was only the gentle imprint left by an old lady's long occupation and the faint mustiness of a closed-up house, here and there overlaid with a drift of old-fashioned polish and the scent of stored apples in the kitchen. But there *is* something more, thought Michael. Is it Esmond, after all?

In the room with the barricade he found several sheets with Nell's writing on. Clearly she had sat in here to make out a draft inventory of the house's contents. But then what had happened?

By now he was as sure as he could be that Nell and Beth were not here – Nell's car had not been outside and there was that open window. If they had seen the boy in the music room, or the nightmare figure in the stone outbuilding it was no wonder they had made a hasty retreat. But he had to make absolutely certain, and without pausing to think too much, he went upstairs. The bedrooms were all empty, most of them furnished with rather heavy old-fashioned wardrobes and tallboys. In a big bedroom overlooking the side garden with the wrought-iron gate were signs of occupancy: a sleeping bag on the two beds, and a sweater Michael recognized as Nell's over a chair. In a smaller bedroom were shelves of old books and neatly stacked games and jigsaw puzzles. Had this been Brad West's room when he stayed here? Had he sat at the desk by the window and written that extraordinary composition which Emily had sent to Nell?

Esmond always waits for me in the piano room, Brad had written. *He doesn't like being around when the grown-ups are there.*

With the memory of those words something seemed to brush past Michael in the quiet room – something that was unbearably sad and heartbreakingly lonely. In a soft questioning voice, he said, 'Esmond?' and waited. For a moment he thought the silence was faintly disturbed by a faraway bar of music, so tenuous it barely thrummed on the air. Then there was nothing, and he thought after all it had only been the old house creaking in the cool night air.

He glanced into the large, slightly old-fashioned bathroom, and into a linen cupboard, and found nothing. Attics? But he could not see any stairs that might lead upwards, and any attics that might crouch under the roof would be as dark as the Stygian rivers.

He went back downstairs. There *was* something here, but it was keeping out of sight. As if drawn by an invisible thread, Michael went back to the music room. He would not have been surprised to see that small figure again, intent on the keys, but there was nothing, although the piano lid was open, and a tapestry-covered stool was drawn up to it. Michael saw now that a music score was propped on the stand, which he had not noticed earlier. He hesitated, then picked it up. Even in this light it was yellow with age, but at the top were the words 'Chopin's Nocturnes for Piano' in thick bold italics, with the name of the publisher beneath. Above this, in faded writing, was the name 'Esmond'. Then you really are still here, thought Michael, and putting the music score into his pocket he closed the door on the room. He made sure the open window was shut, then let himself out through the main front door which had a standard Yale lock, and slammed it firmly closed behind him.

As he got into his car and drove back along Gorsty Lane to Caudle village, he was trying to remember if he had seen a police sign in Caudle village, because if Nell and Beth were not at The Pheasant, Michael would call out the whole of the Derbyshire County Police Force to find them. But surely they would be at The Pheasant, surely if they had fled Stilter House, for whatever reason, they would have taken a room there, rather than drive home at this hour? And if anything had happened to them there would have been signs of a struggle in the house.

Here was the turn onto the main street, and a little way along the street were the sign and lights of The Pheasant. Would it still be open? Would they let him in? It was only just on half past eleven; he realized with incredulity that he had only been inside Stilter House for forty minutes or so.

But when he turned onto The Pheasant's small car park he saw, with overwhelming relief, Nell's car at the far end, parked neatly and tidily, not as if she had been in a particular hurry or in a panic or injured. Michael sent up a prayer of thanks to whatever god might be most appropriate, parked alongside, and went up to the door.

It was locked, but lights showed at the downstairs windows, and when he rang the bell a plump, pleasant-faced gentleman opened up and enquired, in an amiable tone, how he could help.

Michael said, 'I'm sorry it's so late, but – is Mrs West staying here? And her daughter?'

'Indeed they are here, sir,' said the man.

Michael just managed not to sag against the door frame with relief. He said, 'You have no idea how glad I am to hear you say that.'

'Did you want a room for yourself?'

'If it isn't too late. And if you've got one. If you haven't,' said Michael, 'I'll happily sleep on a sofa or in a linen cupboard.'

THIRTEEN

The Pheasant was able to do considerably better than a sofa or a linen cupboard. Michael was shown to a room, whose smallness the landlord apologized for.

'All we have at present,' he said.

But the sliver of a room was comfortably furnished, and with it came the offer of coffee or brandy and sandwiches. 'For,' said the landlord, who had introduced himself as Joe Poulson, 'you'll have had a long drive if you've come all the way from Oxford, and if you've been out to Stilter House – well, that's a chilling place of a night these days.'

'Chilling is one word for it,' said Michael, a part of his mind noting that Stilter House seemed to have something of a reputation locally. He accepted the coffee and sandwiches gratefully, followed them up with a brandy for warmth, and wrote a quick note to Nell, saying he was here and would explain over breakfast. Tiptoeing along the bedroom corridor to slide it under her door without waking her or anyone else who might be staying here, it amused him to realize he had switched from behaving like a character in a Gothic ghost tale, to someone out of a French farce or an Edwardian house party. It was a pity he was not wearing a lush smoking jacket, and dodging itinerant husbands or wives engaged on various priapic errands. Back in his room, he devoured the sandwiches, downed the brandy, and fell thankfully into a sleep which was only briefly troubled by disturbing dreams.

The dreams had dissolved by morning, however, and seated in The Pheasant's small dining room, with Nell and Beth opposite, eating Mrs Poulson's idea of a nourishing breakfast which Michael thought was almost Victorian in its variety and quantity, the world seemed a normal place once more.

Beth was full of the adventure they had had last night; Michael thought she had been considerably frightened by the woman who had come into the house, but it was clear Nell had played down any possible threat, and Beth was now more interested in describing the dramatic aspect for Michael's benefit.

'We pushed the furniture against the door so's she couldn't get in, and then we climbed through the window,' she said, eating sausages and tomatoes with industrious pleasure. 'Then mum drove away at about a hundred miles an hour, and we left the woman there, and we came here and we were safe.' She looked at Nell, suddenly doubtful, and Nell said, 'Couldn't be safer. And whoever that woman was, she was probably just a bit muddled in the head, which is actually a very sad thing. I explained that, didn't I?' she said to Beth. 'About people sometimes getting their minds in a muddle and not realizing what they're doing? I know it was horrible at the time, but she wouldn't have known how peculiar she seemed to us.'

Beth nodded, considering the concept of people whose minds were muddled. 'I 'spect a doctor can unmuddle her, though?'

'Certainly. That's why Sergeant Howe is going to look for her this morning, so he can make sure someone helps her. Is that honey in that jar? Well, stop hogging it, Michael, and pass it over.'

Michael passed her the honey and the topic switched to The Pheasant and Beth's forthcoming session in the kitchen. Beth was buoyantly explaining about helping Mrs Poulson make Bakewell tart.

'She thought it'd be a pretty good idea for me to know how to do that,' she confided. 'I think it would be pretty good as well, on account of we can make some when we get home. It's extra-double good, Bakewell tart.'

'If you make it, we'll have a tea party in my rooms,' promised Michael. 'You can invite some of your friends and we'll shut Wilberforce in the kitchen.' He buttered a piece of toast, topped up his coffee cup, then said, offhandedly, 'Nell, do you have to go back to Stilter House this morning?'

'Yes,' said Nell and, as Beth looked up, she said, 'Only for an hour or two, to finish the inventory. I told you Sergeant Howe is coming with me. We should be able to go home soon after lunch.'

'If I came with you as well,' said Michael, deliberately casually, 'I could help with the inventory and . . . Why is Beth giggling, do you suppose?' He winked at Beth, who said, gleefully, 'Last time you helped with an invent'ry you got it all wrong, and you lost the bit with Mum's prices on it. Mum was furious with you, and she said she'd never let you within a mile of an invent'ry again.'

'I'd forgotten that,' said Michael, who hadn't, but was glad he had achieved his aim of making Beth laugh.

'I hadn't forgotten,' said Nell. 'But you can come with me this time. I'll let him hold the pen and paper,' she said to Beth. 'He can't get that wrong.'

'I bet he can,' said Beth.

'I'll make sure he doesn't. How about you going up to your room to tidy up and brush your teeth before we find Mrs Poulson? Here's the key. I'll follow you up in a minute. You know how to unlock the door, don't you?'

'Oh yes.' Beth, pleased to be allowed to walk through the grown-up hotel on her own, took the key, scrambled down from her seat, and vanished.

'She's all right?' said Michael. 'I mean – really all right?' Nell's account of how the woman had got in and followed them through the grounds had been a rather hasty story while Beth was in the shower, and Michael had the impression that there were other details still to come.

'I think she's almost completely recovered,' said Nell. 'She's astonishingly resilient. And it was so fantastic – literally like something out of a fantasy, that I think she's accepted it as an adventure. I told her we would get away from the house and be safe, and she trusted me. In fact she's probably already half written the whole thing as an essay for school or an email for Ellie in her mind.'

'I have a terrible feeling she might grow up to be a writer,' said Michael. He set down his coffee cup and said, 'Nell, did anything else happen at Stilter House?'

'It's an eerie house,' said Nell, non-committally. 'It's a bit too easy to imagine you see things that aren't there. Or,' she said, not looking at him, 'that you hear things that can't be happening.'

'Such as piano music?'

Her eyes flew up to meet his. 'You heard it as well,' she said, half questioning, half making a statement.

'Yes. I saw the pianist, too. Just for a moment, but it was unmistakable.'

'You can't imagine how glad I am to hear you say that,' said Nell. 'I saw him, but I thought I was imagining it. I kept telling myself it was a trick of the light, or I was half asleep over the inventory notes.'

'We might be well attuned, but I don't think we're attuned to the extent of seeing the same hallucination.'

'When I heard the music the first time,' said Nell, 'I thought it was Beth trying out Charlotte's piano. But then I heard it again, and I saw the boy, and I thought—'

'That it might be Brad you were seeing?'

'I . . . yes, I did. Thanks for understanding. I thought it might be a fragment of memory projected onto the room, or wish-fulfilment, or something,' said Nell, in a mumble.

'It's an obvious conclusion for you to make,' said Michael. 'You were in the house where he had stayed so often as a child, you'd be feeling close to him.' He reached for her hand. 'Listen, my dear love, I wish you wouldn't have this block about talking to me about Brad. I want you to have those memories of him – they're all good ones. Beth should have them, too.'

'I know. But what I don't want,' said Nell, almost angrily, 'is to think I'm seeing the ghost of him as a child in that horrible house. Apart from anything else, I'm the one who doesn't believe in ghosts, remember?'

'I do remember.' He smiled at her.

'I found some odd things in the paperwork Margery sent about the house,' she said. 'A really peculiar account from the original builder – a man called Samuel Burlap. It's all capable of logical explanation, although if you saw that boy as well—'

'I did see him.' He enclosed her hand in both of his. 'He looked a bit like Beth, didn't he? A masculine version, I mean.'

'Yes.'

'But I don't think it was Brad.'

'I know that now.' She was frowning at the table, avoiding his eyes again. 'I didn't know it to start with, but now I do. Michael, I think it was a boy called Esmond.'

Michael said, very deliberately, 'So do I.' He waited for her response, which came instantly.

'You know about Esmond?' She looked up at him, startled.

'Yes. There're a few things I haven't had chance to tell you,' said Michael, knowing that he would show her Emily's letter and Brad's composition, but not wanting to swamp her with it yet. He reached into his jacket pocket. 'Let's get Esmond dealt with first. I found his music,' he said, and placed it on the table between them.

'I found that as well. On the piano stand. It was after I heard him playing, and after I saw him. Esmond,' said Nell softly, and traced a fingertip over the faded ink of the name on the music score. 'Who is he, Michael? Because I found a note as well – something Brad wrote when he was a child at Stilter House; he left it in Esmond's favourite book for Esmond to find.'

'Brad wrote a school essay about Esmond, as well,' said Michael. 'Emily West found it and sent it to the shop for you to see. She left a voicemail message for you – Henry Jessel picked that up and called me. We both listened to it, and it sounded important. Actually, it sounded as if Emily thought you and Beth might be in some kind of danger. But I couldn't reach her to find out any more and I couldn't reach you, either. So in the end I opened her letter. Nell, it felt like the worst kind of invasion on your privacy to do that, but I needed to know if you really were in any danger – that it wasn't just a nice, slightly scatty old lady's fantasies.'

'I'd have done the same,' said Nell, at once.

'Thank goodness.' Michael was relieved to have got over this hurdle. 'There are several things in the letter that made me decide to come hotfoot up here. I can't tell you how glad I am that you're both all right. I can't lose you, Nell. I can't lose either of you.'

'Nine lives,' said Nell, smiling at him. 'You won't lose me.'

They looked at one another, then Michael said, 'Well, good.'

'Let's save the intense romantic stuff for later,' said Nell briskly. 'Did you bring Emily's letter with you?'

'Yes. I'll let you have it before we leave.'

'Good. I'll let you see Samuel Burlap's stuff, as well.'

'It does sound,' said Michael, hoping he was giving her the information in sufficiently small doses, 'as if Charlotte met Esmond, too.'

'Charlotte did? But look here,' said Nell, frowning, 'if Brad knew Esmond when he was here as a child, and if Charlotte also knew him—'

'And if you and I both saw him,' said Michael, continuing her thought, 'it means Esmond hasn't grown any older for at least thirty years.'

Nell considered this, then said, 'That's impossible. I don't believe it.'

'I know you don't. But let's just go out to the house, finish the inventory, and get the hell out of here.'

'Leaving the ghosts to their own devices.'

'You don't believe in ghosts,' pointed out Michael.

'I don't,' she said again, and grinned. 'But I don't think I want to stay at Stilter House to prove or disprove that.' She stood up. 'It'll be easier if we take my car, I think. Then I can pack up my stuff and Beth's and sling it all in the boot while we're there. I'll get Beth installed with Mrs Poulson, and meet you here.'

Left to himself, Michael wandered around The Pheasant's ground-floor rooms, which had the pleasing, early morning scents of fresh coffee. In the oak-panelled hall he found a potted history of The Pheasant. Apparently D. H. Lawrence had occasionally called here while he was living in Derbyshire and writing some of his short stories, and Michael instantly wondered if he could set up a holiday study tour for post-graduate students who would probably like the idea of a pub crawl tracing the paths of writers and poets. He sat down in a window seat to write this down in the notebook without which he never travelled and whose pages were somewhat imperfectly contained by a thick rubber band. He put Esmond's music on the seat beside him so it would not become mixed up with the pages, and wrote down a few preliminary ideas for the holiday tour, adding some details of The Pheasant's background which might come in useful. In addition to D.H. Lawrence's habit of nipping in for a couple of drinks, the pub's genealogy appeared to include hosting a local murder trial, the giving of shelter to a highwayman fleeing the Bow Street Runners, and the existence of a first-floor room occasionally rented by a lady known as Threepenny Meg who had been prodigious with her favours to the gentlemen of the 95th Derbyshire regiment when they returned from the Crimean War.

He was just closing the notebook when Nell returned to report that Beth was safely ensconced with Mrs Poulson, and would probably end up covered in flour and jam from head to foot and it was anybody's guess what the resultant Bakewell tart would taste like.

'Oh, and Sergeant Howe rang to say it'd be easier if he went out to check on Stilter House after lunch because somebody set fire to a hayrick somewhere and he has to lock the culprit up. I said after lunch would be fine, because you were here and we were going out to the house together,' said Nell. 'What have you been up to?'

Michael explained his idea for a literary pub-crawl for postgrads.

'That's a good idea.'

'Yes, except that faculty budgets being what they are, I'd probably start out aiming for Lake Geneva with Byron and Shelley, or Robert Browning and Elizabeth Barrett in Florence—'

'Making use of all those lyric wine shops and tavernas, of course.'

'Yes, but then I'd find there'd be only enough funds to get as far as Arnold Bennett in Stoke-on-Trent.'

'Nothing wrong with Stoke-on-Trent,' said Nell, practically. 'All that gorgeous porcelain and china. Wedgwood and Royal Doulton and Minton.'

'True. And we could certainly do a lot worse than this place for starters,' said Michael, glancing about him. 'I've been reading about its history.' He indicated the printed details on the wall. 'I love the sound of Threepenny Meg, don't you?'

'She probably gave half the 95th regiment a severe dose of clap,' said Nell, reading the framed history and grinning.

'You're such a romantic.'

'One of us has to be. Is that Esmond's music? I'll put it in my briefcase so you don't lose it, shall I?' As she picked up the music score, the title page fluttered open slightly, and Nell gave a small gasp.

'What's the matter?'

'Well, nothing much, except . . . There's another name written inside the music. There, on the first of the inner pages.'

'Isobel Acton,' said Michael, leaning over her shoulder to read it. 'Do we know who Isobel Acton was?'

'A lady who poisoned her husband and watched him die while she played Chopin,' said Nell, rather brusquely. 'I found an account of it at the house. It's a bit macabre. She was tried here in The Pheasant, actually, in fact that's probably the murder trial referred to in that text.'

'I wonder if this is the music she played while she watched him die,' said Michael, picking up the Chopin score to examine it in more detail.

'You're making romantic connections again.' Nell put the music into her briefcase, and closed it with a determined snap. 'Not to mention stretching the coincidences.'

'Well, whatever it is, it looks as if Esmond appropriated the music,' said Michael. 'And he put his name on it. Or somebody did. Did Brad ever play Chopin?'

'I can't remember,' said Nell. 'Don't forget your notebook.'

During the short drive, Michael was annoyed to realize he was feeling apprehensive about going inside Stilter House again. But Nell did not appear particularly worried or, if she was, she was not showing it. She said she would let Michael see the material she had found about Isobel Acton, 'Mostly written by its builder,' she said. 'It sounded as if he'd had a bit of a strict upbringing, and I think Isobel was the local vamp and she intrigued him. He thought her house – the original house on the site – was beautiful and hoped he could emulate it.'

'I wouldn't call Stilter beautiful, precisely,' said Michael, as they went down Gorsty Lane, and the house came into frowning view. 'At least, not from what I saw of it last night, although I'd have to admit it wouldn't look its best in that rain. But I should think it's a good example of Edwardian design. What happened to Isobel's house?'

'No idea. It looked as if there were remnants of it in the grounds, though,' said Nell, and Michael was just wondering whether to tell her what had happened in the outbuildings which presumably were the remnants, when they reached the house and the moment passed.

And after all there was nothing so very sinister. This was merely an old house, with parts of its facade slightly crumbling and one chimney a bit lopsided. Even the gardens no longer looked as if ghosts might prowl their grey-green depths: they were simply a tanglewood mass of rose bay willow and thrusting weeds, and if anything lurked there it would be rabbits and grass snakes rather than wraiths abandoning their ivy-mantled tower for a night's revelry among the humans.

The ivy-mantled tower was still there, of course, but in the morning sunlight it was only a ramshackle straggle of dilapidated outbuildings, each one looking as if it was propping its neighbour up. Still, he could make out the gaping hole where he had smashed the door from its hinges to get out, which proved he had not imagined the entire episode. He would mention the unhinged door to Nell at some suitable moment, in case they needed to arrange a repair.

Nell stood for a moment in the hall, and Michael waited, unable to gauge her feelings. But she only said, 'I'll head upstairs to see how accessible the attics are. I didn't really explore them yesterday and I'd better check them properly.'

'I'll have a look round while you do that,' said Michael. 'Everywhere's perfectly ordinary by daylight, isn't it? How remarkable.'

Nell went up the stairs, armed with a torch, and Michael went towards the music room. A film of dust covered the piano and there were one or two framed photographs on the high, narrow mantelpiece – posed, black-and-white shots, the hairstyles and clothes mostly from the 1930s and 1940s.

He was just wondering whether to replace Esmond's music on the stand or to leave it on the shelf by the fireplace, when he saw that the tapestry seat of the piano stool was hinged. To store music? If so, the Chopin score, brittle and fragile as it was, would be better in there. He put it on the piano's surface, and lifted the lid of the stool. It had the stiffness of long disuse, but it came up fairly easily, displacing quantities of dust, but revealing a thick stack of more music scores. They looked quite old, and Michael, momentarily interested, lifted out the top pieces.

They all seemed to be piano scores, dog-eared and brittle, and he was about to replace them when he realized that interleaved with them was a letter in a familiar hand. Emily, he thought, with a kind of affectionate exasperation, and took the letter over to the window seat to read.

It was dated five years earlier, and Michael thought the address was the Aberdeen one that had been on the letter sent to Nell's shop.

Dear Charlotte,

Here, as promised, is the musical score, which you always call Esmond's music. It was good of you to let me borrow it – I know you treasure everything linked to him. I'm sending it back by registered post as you'll see, because it's quite fragile and whatever we all believe or don't believe about Esmond, the music is still a little piece of family history.

I've had it examined by a very helpful young man who knows about these things – he has a most charming shop in the village and is thought quite an expert, in fact he sold me some delightful glassware at Christmas, and he was as upset as I was when it turned out not to be actual Limoges. But it looks very nice in the glass cabinet, and of course he was unable to refund the money on account of my having bought it in the previous financial year, or something like that.

He says the score isn't worth so very much, although if the signature of Isobel Acton is genuine – and can be proved – there might be some curiosity value to be got from that, what with the murder trial. If she had been convicted and hanged, the signature might be worth considerably more, he says, what with people today being just as ghoulish as the crowds that stood outside Newgate to see a hanging, or the French harridans who took their knitting to guillotining sessions.

But – and here's the real reason I'm writing – tucked inside the music, right at the back, were some papers written by Ralph West – Great-uncle Ralph that would be, I think, or perhaps one more great, or maybe even not an actual uncle, but still . . .

I don't know if you ever saw these, but they make interesting reading, and all I can say is I hope none of our parents ever read them, because they raise a very worrying possibility. Still, they say there are one or two skeletons in all families' closets.

I've made copies of Ralph's papers in case the originals are lost or damaged, but do take care of them, won't you? It's dangerously easy to throw out old papers thinking they're worthless, and before you know it a whole section of local history has vanished beyond recall. Imagine if the Paston family had never sent all those letters, we'd have lost such a valuable bit of the past. Our book club read the Paston Letters as a project last

year. I found some of them a bit boring (I didn't tell
anyone in the book club that), but I did enjoy the way
the Pastons used to sandwich enquiries as to each other's
health and grumbles about who was entitled to inherit
lands, in between comments on the progress of the Wars
of the Roses. And think of Pepys' diaries telling about
his work at the Admiralty and Charles II's court, but also
how he chased his wife round the bedroom, and how
they buried the cheeses and saucepans in the garden
during the Fire of London and he took Mr Holliards'
pills for his constipation. So I keep *all* old papers and
letters, just in case.

Thank you for your enquiry about my indigestion. It's
a little better. I'm taking a preparation of peppermint and
rhubarb. Charles Darwin apparently underwent
hydrotherapy for the same thing, but I shouldn't think one
would be able to find a practitioner of hydrotherapy these
days, should you? Apparently in New Zealand there's
something called Manuka Honey which is supposed to
be very good for dyspepsia, but I haven't been able
to track any down, and New Zealand is such a very long
way to travel for honey, although a beautiful country, I
believe, and the people most interesting.

Look after yourself, my dear, and let me know when
you feel able to travel up to bonnie Scotland to stay with
me. I would make you very welcome.

Fondest love,
   Emily.

Oh, Emily, thought Michael, I simply must meet you one of
these days.

He considered the letter's main contents. If the unknown
Ralph's papers were not in the music stool, he would feel like
tearing down the whole of Stilter House to find them. Failing
that, he would wait for Emily to emerge from her health farm
and try to get a sight of the photocopies. First, though, he
went up to the bedroom floor and found a flight of narrow
stairs which clearly led to the attics.

'Nell? How are you getting on? Is there enough light?'

'Yes, but I don't think there's much here.'

'No undiscovered Turners?'

'Not even a first-folio Shakespeare manuscript.'

'Shall I come up to give you a hand?'

'No, the roof pitch is so steep there isn't much room for one, let alone two. I won't be long, then you could help put the notes together. Oh, and I've got to throw my stuff and Beth's into the cases. It won't take long – we only brought the basics.'

'All right. Shall I make some coffee and bring you some?'

'The stove's a bit Heath Robinson,' said Nell. 'It took me ages to fathom it. Wait till I come down.'

Michael assented, and went back to the music room to search for Ralph.

To begin with he thought he was not going to find anything. He went carefully through all the music in the tapestry stool, then without much optimism checked the shelves. The books were a dry, dusty collection, and the music mostly duplications of what was stored in the stool.

But he did find it. Sandwiched between a book of sermons written by a local vicar in 1935, and a dry-looking history of the Great War, was a sheaf of handwritten pages, all fairly good-quality notepaper which bore the printed heading, *Ralph West, Importers of Fine China and Porcelain,* and a Derby address. Most of the sheets were curling at the corners, but the writing was perfectly readable.

There was no heading, although 1900 was written in the top right-hand corner. But clearly these were the papers Emily had written about.

Michael took the pages to the window seat, sat down and began to read.

FOURTEEN

1900

Being of a methodical nature it seems sensible to keep an account of the details relating to the building of my new house. So I shall record all developments and preserve all documents relating to its construction – from the initial architect's plans to the estimates and invoices from builders and workmen. I shall also include the documentation from the Gas and Coke Company, which is becoming extensive since the gas supply is, to put it kindly, erratic. I have had to remonstrate with the company several times and have insisted on their workmen returning to address several problems. To be plunged into sudden darkness without warning midway through an evening because the gas supply has developed what they are pleased to call a hiccough, is not what I am accustomed to, nor prepared to tolerate. If I could electrify Stilter House I would, but I am told it would mean electrifying the whole of Caudle Moor and several adjoining villages, thus making the cost prohibitive.

This file is my private (and readily available) record of the house's construction, and the Title Deeds will be held by my solicitors in Derby. I have insisted they reduce their fees for the house's purchase, and paid no heed to their bleats about how complex it was to trace any member of the Acton family to effect the purchase of the land. Vague excuses were made and apologies for the delays laid at the door of the land's erratic ownership. 'The inheritance was passed down and around like a parcel, going from cousin to nephew and then to other cousins,' my solicitor said, which I thought a somewhat specious excuse for inefficiency.

However, the purchase of the land was eventually effected in January 1900 – a new century and a new house and a new beginning – and the land is now properly and legally registered in my name. I feel it important to record here the Land Registration Title number, which is 912 40085. In addition, I am noting down that the ownership was finally traced to a person by the name of Nathaniel Acton, living in Cheshire. He was found by a curious and somewhat circuitous route, starting with six local almshouses which it seems a Simeon Acton built and endowed some forty or fifty years ago. They are administered by the National & Provincial Bank, and it was they who communicated with Nathaniel on my behalf. There appears to be some kind of trust for the almshouses which Simeon Acton created to maintain them and to pay a tiny sum each quarter to the residents, so clearly he was a philanthropically inclined gentleman. I have made a separate note of the arrangement, since it is not something I have previously encountered (the import and export of china and high-quality pottery not being such as to bring one into contact with philanthropy), but it is clearly the kind of thing expected of people of means. I think I may see if I can continue the arrangement.

Once reached, Nathaniel Acton – an elderly gentleman – expressed himself as only too glad to get rid of the land, which he said had sad associations for his family. As an apparent afterthought, he said it had also become something of a liability, which I take to mean a complete eyesore since, when I first saw it, it was strewn with the burnt-out ruins of the original Acton House, and was nothing less than a blemish on the surrounding countryside.

However, my title to and ownership of "The Toft, originally known as Acton Field" are now assured. I am told that Toft means a piece of ground where a house formerly stood, but is decayed or burnt. This certainly applies here, and my builder, who is a local man, tells me the former house did indeed burn down. Samuel Burlap seems a man to be trusted; I employed him two years ago to extend my offices in Derby. He spent some considerable time on this work, and I was pleased with the results and also with Burlap's demeanour and manner, so when I made the decision to move to Caudle Moor, I had no hesitation in commissioning him to build a house for me.

I have already heard the local rumours that the land is cursed, and I have also received representations from a Prebendary Gilfillan to have it exorcized. I shall take no notice of that whatsoever. Mr Gilfillan is plainly a fanatic, if not a fantasist and I intend to make sure Esmond does not hear such nonsense, in fact I have already told the Prebendary that if I find he has been filling Esmond's ears with his absurdities I shall complain to his bishop.

Note to self: necessary to find out exactly where a prebendary stands in the hierarchy of the church, and which bishop has authority over this diocese. I dare say it will do my standing no harm to send a polite letter to His Lordship (further note to self: make sure this is correct form of address to a bishop), and although I should be sorry to blight any man's career, I am determined that Esmond shall not be disturbed by Mr Gilfillan's tales. Children can be so impressionable, and Esmond has had quite enough disturbances in his short life already . . .

The next sentence was heavily crossed out, but because the ink was so faded, by dint of holding it up to the daylight Michael managed to read it. In a much more erratic script, Ralph West had written, 'Bringing Esmond to this isolated place *must* be the right thing to do. No one here can possibly suspect what is in his past and mine . . .'

The straggling, indistinct sentence broke off there, but Michael had the sense of Ralph having allowed some strong emotion to escape from his pen onto the paper, and then of regaining control of his feelings and trying to delete the words. And since the notes were evidently a private record, instead of tearing up the paper and starting afresh he had simply scored the words out and continued.

The facts of my house, which I am setting down against future need are these:

In October 1899, following the death of my dear wife six months earlier, I commissioned plans for a residence from a Derby architect, Mr Archibald Filbert. Working to those plans, Mr Burlap began construction in the spring of 1900.

The house is to be called Stilter House and its address will be Gorsty Lane, Caudle Moor, in the county of Derbyshire.

And then again the writing suddenly became less careful, although not as erratic as earlier. This time Michael had the impression that Ralph West had suddenly felt the need to set down more than the dry facts, but that he had his emotions in check. Had the document become a kind of therapy for him? But therapy for what? 'No one here can possibly suspect what is in his past and mine,' he had written about Esmond. Esmond, thought Michael, remembering yet again how Emily had said Esmond never left Stilter House. He glanced at the piano, but no small, mop-headed figure sat there, and the room was silent and placid. From overhead came faint bumps and dragging sounds as Nell explored the attics. It was a reassuringly normal sound.

Work on Stilter House was slightly delayed due to Mr Burlap's having suffered a brief illness. I did not, of course, ask what it was. There should be a seemly reticence about ailments. So I merely record that I am glad Mr Burlap recovered from his affliction in good time, and that during his absence Mr Filbert was able to oversee the work.

Do I deserve this wonderful new house, this "gentleman's residence"? Dammit, I do. If I am not precisely a gentleman born and bred, I've worked hard and I've saved hard and I *do* deserve this. I denied myself things as a young man in order to save my money – things most young men regard as their right. Clothes, the occasional drink, a modest supper with friends. Even an evening at a music hall.

Esmond's mother, of course, came from a different stratum of society; her family said she married beneath her. "Trade" they said about me, disparagingly, and were very cool and distant to her after our marriage. She was never bitter, though, at least I never saw any signs of it. She retained her gentility and her refinement until her death. I was pleased about that, and it did me no harm with business friends. Often, after a dinner party, she would play the piano to them, and they were always appreciative and admiring.

After she died her family would have nothing to do with me at all, and I, in retaliation, swore they should have nothing to do with Esmond. And wasn't it better that way anyway? Isn't it better that Esmond is kept safe and kept close, in this isolated rural pocket of the countryside? Isn't that my whole plan, for pity's sake! He must be kept in silence, in *silence, in SILENCE* . . . In Holland the word for silence is *stilte*. I know that – I have acquired a smattering of Dutch – also German – from my dealings with both countries. That's why I'm calling my house Stilter House. No one here will know what that word, *Stilter,* means, but I shall know. It means Silence. This house is really Silence House.

Yet again, these last three sentences were heavily crossed out, but again Michael was able to read them, and to see how the writing suddenly deteriorated. Esmond must be kept in silence, Ralph had said, and he had even called the house 'Silence', using the Dutch word to mask the real meaning. Michael felt a chill brush against his skin. Had Ralph West been a little mad?

Friday 24th: Today I commissioned Carter Paterson to pack all the furniture and belongings in this house, and transport it all to Caudle Moor in two weeks' time. The house is completed and Burlap has done a good job. Stilter House is sound and sturdy and filled with the scents of new timber.

The landlord of the local inn – Mr Poulson of The Pheasant – has undertaken to see to the engaging of domestic staff – that is to say his wife has agreed to do so. They are both Caudle people, born and bred, and have family and friends in the area. I do not think they will cheat me, or hire unsuitable servants.

I have written to the local sawbones – a Dr Brodworthy who apparently inherited the practice from his father, and is said to be well regarded. I received a courteous response from him, which I shall include in this file.

As Michael reached for the next page, paper of a different colour and texture met his hand, and he saw it was the letter from Dr Brodworthy that Ralph had referred to. It was typewritten and was headed:

Doctor Brodworthy, The Surgery, Caudle Magna. Consulting Rooms open 10.00 to 12.30 each weekday. Members of Mutual, Benefit or Friendly Organizations, and Oddfellows Societies, seen on Wednesday afternoons by appointment.

My dear Sir,

I am in receipt of your esteemed communication of 10th inst., and beg to inform you that I should be very happy to add your good self and your young son to my list of patients.

I am today in receipt of the medical notes sent to me by your erstwhile physician in Derby, and have studied the details of Master Esmond West's case. It seems to be a curious condition, and although it is outside my field of expertise I shall do all I can to help. In your place I would certainly continue to encourage the boy's affinity with and to music, since this could be something that will help us to reach him and to bring him back to what I could perhaps term normality.

At your request, I am communicating with a colleague who specializes in the care of children and is on the governing board of St Mary's Hospital in Manchester, which, as you may know, has an excellent reputation. I shall request a consultation for you and your son and shall let you know when and if this can be arranged.

I do not know of any piano teachers in the immediate area, but with your permission will make suitable enquiries with the village schoolmistress and also the local vicar.

Once you are in residence at Caudle Moor, I hope I may call to introduce myself, and, of course, to meet Esmond.

Kind regards,

I am, dear sir, respectfully yours,

E Brodworthy. M.D.

Attached to this was what seemed to be a draft of a further letter, in Ralph West's hand. There were one or two crossings-out

and insertions, and Michael guessed that West had later made
a fair copy from it, which had then been sent.

> My Dear Mr Bundy
>   Your name and direction have been passed to me as
> being a qualified teacher of the piano, and as currently
> living some eight or ten miles from Caudle Moor where
> I shall shortly be residing. My son, Esmond, aged nine
> years, has received piano lessons in Derby and I am
> keen for him to continue with these. His mother was a
> gifted pianist, and I believe him to have inherited some-
> thing of her talent and love of music. Esmond's present
> teacher assures me the boy has a considerable gift. He
> has so far achieved Grade IV in the exam syllabus set
> by the Associated Board of the Royal School of Music,
> which I am told is a very good achievement for a boy
> of his age.
>   A note of your fees and qualifications would oblige,
> together with some intimation as to whether you could
> undertake Esmond's musical education for the next year
> or two.

The next sentence was so heavily crossed through that Michael
could only read a few words. Whatever Ralph had written,
included *tragedy* and *terror.* But in the end, he had merely
closed his letter saying that Esmond was rather an unusual
child, although apparently intelligent and sensitive.

The next page was in a different coloured ink; again there
was no date, but it seemed to have been written some little
while later.

> I had closed and put away this file, but have reopened it
> this evening to add other papers. Recent events are, after
> all, as much a part of the house's history as the registering
> of the land and the building of the walls.
>   The copies of the three statements made to the police
> describe the events of last Tuesday evening – the 10th.
> It seems prudent to keep a private account – one day I
> may be glad to reread the statements, my own in

particular, which I set down while my mind was clear. Or do the mad believe themselves clear in mind . . .?

The main facts are plain enough, though. I had just finished dinner, that is the first solid fact. I remember thinking that the two servants found by Mrs Poulson were proving excellent. I had had a half bottle of Chablis with my dinner – I am a fairly abstemious man, but even the Bible allows a little wine for the stomach's sake. I am not sure if the Bible also allows a modest measure of brandy to follow, but that is what I had, regardless of Biblical approval. I was not, however, in the least affected by either the wine or the brandy.

Esmond was in bed. He had gone to his room apparently quiet and contented – probably because he had had a music lesson with Mr John Bundy. Esmond has taken to Bundy who, for his part, appears in accord with the boy and unworried by him. (This is a great relief to me, although in the privacy of these notes, I confess it occasionally disturbs me very much to see him seated at the piano in the way his mother used to be, and to hear his attempts at pieces she used to play with such ease.)

The piano lessons seem to have progressed amicably, although to pursue my afternoon's tasks to repeated scales and arpeggios is not what I should have chosen. Happily, however, Mr Bundy generally ends the lessons with a selection of simplified light pieces, including, I believe, some Chopin, which Esmond particularly likes playing and which is certainly very pleasing to the ear. I appreciated Bundy's care in finding out Esmond's preferences, and have said so to the man. Indeed, we have discussed the possibility of Bundy undertaking more of Esmond's education, since he has several years' experience of teaching in a boys' school.

After dinner I wrote a few business letters, the outcome of perusing the quarterly accounts sent me that very day. The company I founded all those years ago is in healthy shape, and although since my wife's death I have taken a less active part in the day-to-day management, I have retained my place on the Board.

Those, too, are sound facts and they reassure me, for I do not believe I could have studied columns of figures and understood them if I had been suffering any kind of brain seizure.

The copies had to be sworn before a Notary Public, but Sergeant Kiddimore raised no objections, and a suitable local solicitor was easily found.

FIFTEEN

Statement made by Mr Ralph West of Stilter House, Gorsty Lane, Caudle Moor.
Statement taken by Sergeant Kiddimore.
Copy attested and sworn by Mr J Hurst, solicitor and Notary Public

On the evening of Tuesday 10th I was in my drawing room after dinner, writing letters. My son, Esmond, was in bed and my two servants were in their own quarters at the rear of the house.

At about nine o'clock I heard what seemed to be a tapping on the window. It was very light and soft, and at first I thought it was merely a tree branch, disturbed by the wind.

But the tapping came again. It was not loud enough to be someone wanting to attract my attention; rather it was the soft furtive sound of someone wanting to see if there was anyone in the room before breaking in. In case an intruder was prowling around, I opened the curtains to look out. The gas supply had flickered during the evening as it so often does, making the light rather poor, but I assured myself no one was outside and returned to my letters.

The tapping ceased, but I had the strong impression that I was being watched and I could not dismiss the suspicion that someone might be standing outside the window, just beyond my sight. I was making up my mind to investigate further, when the floorboards outside the drawing room creaked.

This ought not to have been alarming. The logical explanation was that the parlourmaid was making a round of the house to close curtains and make sure all doors were locked. Perhaps she was even putting out candles against a complete failure of the gas, which was still dipping and flickering. But there was a soft, stealthy sound to the steps, as if someone did not want to be heard. I was uncomfortably aware that I was in the house with only two female servants – one not young – and my nine-year-old son in bed upstairs.

As I crossed the room to the door, another sound broke the silence – a sound that was so unexpected, but so familiar I ceased to be alarmed. Someone was playing the piano.

I immediately assumed Esmond had crept downstairs and into the music room, and that the footsteps I heard earlier were his. However, half past nine of an evening is not the proper time for a child to be practising the piano, so I accordingly went along to remonstrate with him.

The flickering gas mantles in the hall made the shadows creep and shiver, and the hall seemed unnervingly filled with stealthy movement. Earlier I had felt reassured by the music, but I was starting to be increasingly uneasy, because it was being played with far more skill than Esmond could manage. I was not overly concerned about burglars though, for the average housebreaker was unlikely to sit down at the piano and play Chopin.

The gas mantles in the music room were turned low, and the curtains were open to the garden. The light was strange – the smoky blue twilight was edged with red from the gas jets, but I was able to see the silhouette of the pianist framed in the windows. I could not see the features, but it certainly was not Esmond. It was a woman, and she was so deeply absorbed in her playing she was unaware of me.

I admit that at this point I was prepared to defend my

home against this, or any other, intruder. But I could not use violence against a woman. Also, I could not believe any sane person would come into a strange house and start playing a piano, and, if this was some poor witless creature, I was chary of doing anything that might spark her into madness. I believe the insane have their own strength.

So I went quietly up to the piano, and put out my hand, thinking to take her arm and bring her to her senses – that is to say, to what senses she might possess. But as my fingers closed on her arm, I felt the most extraordinary sense of revulsion. Her skin was so cold and strange – like no flesh I ever touched – that I recoiled. And *still* she seemed unaware of me, *still* she continued to pour out her music.

I backed away to the door, intending to call to my servants, and to telephone to the local police for help. Then I saw that a second woman was standing outside the French windows, looking in. I could not make out her features, but I could see she was thin and from the way she moved I think she was not very young, although not old. A lady in her late thirties or early forties, perhaps. What I can be sure of is that she was watching the pianist with the most extreme intensity I have ever seen.

Before I could decide what best to do, the woman in the garden pushed open the French door and stepped inside. She held some kind of weapon – I cannot describe it, for it was not like anything I have ever seen. I could not sketch it, either. I can only say it looked as if it was made of iron and that it was not very large and appeared to be a semicircular shape. Perhaps it was the size of two handspans. I assumed it was some sort of restraining device, although I cannot imagine how it would work.

The woman crept forward, clearly not wanting to alert the pianist to her presence, and there was such menace about her that I drew breath to call out a warning. But I was too late. Her entry into the room brought a gust of wind from outside, and the curtains framing the French window, which hitherto had hung down limply, billowed out, obscuring both women. The gas jets flickered and went out.

It was barely two minutes before I found candles and the tinder box, but it was sufficient time for the pianist to escape and the woman with the iron contraption to go after her. I did not see them go, but they must have darted into the garden – that is the only possible explanation.

I certainly went after them, but I did not explore the gardens very thoroughly. I hope I am as courageous as any man, but I was convinced that the pianist had been some poor mad creature, perhaps escaped from a local institution. If so, the woman outside the house would be her keeper or even someone from her family, trying to recapture her. My first duty, as I saw it, was to ensure that my son and the two servants were safe. I went into my son's room, then to the scullery where the two women were making their evening cocoa, and then telephoned to the police station.

I should liked it placed on record that Sergeant Kiddimore arrived promptly at the house, in company with a constable, and they made a thorough search of the house and gardens, finding nothing, but arranging for a constable to remain in the grounds overnight. They were courteous and efficient to me and my household, and considerate towards my son.

Signed: Ralph West

Statement made by Mrs Martha Hatfull, Cook and Housekeeper at Stilter House, Gorsty Lane, Caudle Moor.
Statement taken by Sergeant Kiddimore.
Copy attested and sworn by Mr J Hurst, solicitor and Notary Public

I was sat in the scullery with Vi – that is Violet Needle – and the steak and kidney for tomorrow's dinner had just simmered down nicely, which I was making on account of the master having two business friends coming to the house, and him asking particular for steak and kidney pudding, since one of them is a foreign gentleman the master has business dealings with as I understand it, and wanting to give them a real English dinner.

The kitchen clock had just chimed the quarter before ten and those pesky gaslights were going as they're always doing. Violet and me was thinking it was time for our cocoa, when the master came in to tell us there had been an intruder.

'Oh sir,' I said, all alarmed, 'is Master Esmond all right?'

But the master said everything was all right, so we went to the drawing room, and Sergeant Kiddimore come up to the house, which the master had telephoned him. We had to tell how we had been in the scullery all evening and say if we had heard any intruder, which we had not, for we had both been there ever since clearing away the master's dinner at half past eight.

I was took all of a tremble afterwards, particularly when the master said a policeman would be in the grounds all night. Police in the house is not what I am accustomed to, having always worked in well-run, godly houses, and I had to have a nip of gin and a hot water bottle to my feet in bed or I should not have slept a wink.

I would like it wrote down that I am very happy with my position at Stilter House, having come from my previous place in Ashbourne where I was cook to Sir Gervais Warrenby, who died at Christmas, and now with Mr West since March.

Signed: Martha Hatfull, Cook

Statement made by Violet Needle, parlourmaid at Stilter House, Gorsty Lane, Caudle Moor.
Statement taken by Sergeant Kiddimore.
Copy attested and sworn by Mr J Hurst, solicitor and Notary Public

I am house parlourmaid at Stilter House, and I was in the scullery all evening, having cleared away and washed up after the master's dinner.

Me and cook – Mrs Hatfull, that is – had been making the steak and kidney pudding for tomorrow's guests. I was just chopping the suet so as to have everything well forward, when the master told us somebody had broken in, but he had seen them off. He said the police was coming to the house and would want to talk to us.

Me and cook hadn't seen nor heard nothing at all, save it might be the steak and kidney bubbling over on the stove once on account of the heat being too high, but we wouldn't have heard anything going on at the front of the house, even if the entire 95th Derbyshire regiment had broke in, not that I would have minded that, on account of my young man being a lance corporal and off to fight the Boers any day.

I have been house parlourmaid here since the master moved in. It is a very nice place and the house lovely, saving it being built on the old Acton land. Everyone hereabouts knows about the wicked Isobel Acton who killed her husband. My mother, who was born in Caudle Moor says Isobel walks the land to this day, and folk sometimes hear her playing her piano music like she did after she poisoned her husband, the heartless hussy.

My mother says I'm to give my notice to the master, for if Isobel Acton is getting into the house of a night I won't be safe in my bed, and better I should work as a skivvy in a house where the dead don't walk, than be a parlourmaid with a frilly cap and apron in a place where the ghosts of murderers climb in through locked windows and play pianos.

Signed: Violet Needle, house parlourmaid

The next letters were typed, and were in very smudged blue ink, which left marks on Michael's fingers when he picked them up. It took him several moments to realize that they must be early carbon copies; he had a half memory of someone in Oxford writing a rather tedious paper on late-nineteenth- and early-twentieth-century office procedures, and citing the use of early copying techniques, including carbon paper which had recently come into circulation. Michael's crony in the history faculty, Owen Bracegirdle, who believed research did not need to be dull, had composed an unofficial riposte, painting a lively picture of several of the great diarists wrestling with carbon paper and photocopiers and fax machines. The article had unaccountably found its way to one of the more satirical student newspapers, incurring the wrath of the proctor, and Owen had been reproved, although the proctor had privately admitted to enjoying the descriptions of Samuel Pepys swearing when a copier chewed up his description of the Fire of London.

Michael grinned at the memory, and turned to Ralph West's carbons, which were faded and blurred, but readable.

To: Farthing's Domestic Agency, Derby
    Dear Sir or Madam,
    I should be obliged if you would arrange to provide me with a good, properly trained house parlourmaid at the earliest possible opportunity.
    The household is small and consists of myself and my young son. I employ a cook, and local help three times a week for heavier cleaning. There is a little entertaining, mostly small luncheon or dinner parties, seldom more than six or eight persons, and occasional weekend guests, usually no more than three persons at a time.
    Salary is £20 a year, all found, with every Sunday off and every Wednesday afternoon.
    Your early reply would oblige.
    Yours faithfully,
    Ralph West Esq.

To: Mr John Bundy
    Dear Mr Bundy,
    Pursuant to our discussion of yesterday's date, I am happy to confirm that as discussed you will undertake my son Esmond's education in the area of literature, history, geography, and arithmetic. As you suggest, a suitable tutor for French and possibly German can be found in a year or two, when matters can be reviewed.
    The salary agreed (£50 a year) will be paid to you each Quarter Day, and your hours in the schoolroom will be nine in the morning until three in the afternoon, with an hour for luncheon at midday, which will be served in

the morning room. Esmond will be set suitable homework tasks for weekends and other holiday times.

Your written acceptance of this will oblige.

I am, sir, yours truly,

  Ralph West Esq.

From: Mr J Bundy

To: Mr R West,

Dear Sir,

I am very happy to accept the supervision of Esmond's education for the next two years, and your terms are agreeable to me.

Despite his affliction, Esmond is a bright, intelligent and sensitive boy, and I have high hopes that a suitable path in life can be forged for him. In particular, his music develops apace, and I believe he has a rare gift, the nurturing of which is affording me great pleasure and satisfaction.

Yours truly,

  John Bundy

From: Farthing's Domestic Agency, Derby

To: Ralph West Esq.

Sir,

In the past three months we have supplied four parlour-maids for employment in your house. As you know, all have given their notice and left after only a very short time. We give below a summary:

Mary Pod: In your service for one month. Left because could not be doing with caterwauling music at all hours of the night and gloomy rooms where the gaslight never properly worked so you couldn't hardly see your hand in front of your face.

Eliza Littledyke: In your service for three weeks. Left because it was ever such a scary place, with folk wandering around the gardens of a night, and Master Esmond not like any natural child a person ever met before.

Rosie Hannaford: In your service for one week. Left

because it was a long way to the village and not so much
as an omnibus to take a girl anywhere, nor shops. (Note
from Farthing's: Miss Hannaford has since obtained
employment in Kendals Department Store in Manchester,
selling bath salts and face creams, and clearly was not
intended by nature to be a parlourmaid. We have removed
her from our books).

Polly Waterside: In your service for two weeks. Left
because bits of music paper got scattered around never
mind how many times you tidied them away, and a piano
playing by itself, as well as the gas suddenly dying and
plunging a person into darkness, which isn't something
a person likes.

I am sorry to tell you I do not feel we can provide
you with any more domestic help. Indeed, perhaps you
may be better served by employing local girls.

Have you ever considered having the electricity
brought to your house?

I remain, sir, your obedient servant,

S Mackling

(For and on behalf of Farthing's Domestic Agency,
est 1880)

To: Derby Gas, Coke and Light Company

Sir,

I write to protest in the strongest possible terms about
the gas supply to my house. It is erratic and weak, and
on a number of occasions has plunged my household into
a Stygian darkness, which is both inconvenient and
dangerous. I have employed a person knowledgeable in
gas fittings to inspect all the gas mantles and cooking
facilities, and he reports that all are in excellent working
order.

At a time when you are trumpeting your expansion
into other areas, it is sad to find that you cannot provide
a reliable gas source to your existing customers.

If the situation does not improve within one month I
shall be forced to transfer my custom to an electricity
company, which, I venture to suggest, may result in loss

of business to yourselves, since it would make electricity power available to a great many people in this area.

I await your comments with interest.

Yours truly,

Ralph West Esq.

To: Mr Alfred Frinton,
Piano Tuner of Ashbourne.

Sir,

I should be obliged if you would arrange to call on me at your earliest opportunity to tune a piano, which is, I believe, of a size termed a boudoir grand. It has developed a disconcerting habit of emitting sounds – actual musical chords and notes – when no one is playing it. This is upsetting to my servants, and I should wish to remedy matters as soon as possible.

The piano is a Broadwood, and has been carefully looked after. It was brought from my previous home in Derby and had belonged to my late wife. It was, of course, tuned after being moved to Caudle Moor, but I suspect the tuning may not have been sufficiently thorough. I am advised by my son's music teacher that the *equal temperament* may be misaligned, and that the interaction among the notes of the chromatic scale may need adjusting. I hope I have these technical terms correctly.

Your early attention would be appreciated.

Yours truly,

Ralph West Esq.

To: Prebendary, the Rt Reverend Edgar Gilfillan.

My Dear Prebendary Gilfillan,

I am in receipt of your most recent missive, and wish to thank you for your concern. However, I feel myself perfectly able to deal with problems on my own land, and can give no real credence to the various legends attached to the place – interesting though they may be.

Perhaps, therefore, you will do me the courtesy of refraining from further approaches of this nature.

With kind regards,

I am, sir,
Yours truly,
   Ralph West, Esq.

Michael laid these pages down thoughtfully, and leaned back against the windowpane, staring unseeingly at the gardens beyond.

It was a curious tale that had unfolded – although it was surely only a portion of the whole. Even though the police statements were couched in flat, official police language, the characters of the main players came over vividly. The young Violet Needle's account of Isobel Acton walking the land could be put down to the credulous mind of a village girl. Subsequent reports from her replacements could have been influenced by local gossip. But Ralph West was neither credulous nor village-bred and was unlikely to have heard or listened to local gossip. Michael, rereading Ralph's statement, had the impression that Ralph, while conscientiously telling the truth, had been striving to keep the incident within the boundaries of normality.

The description of the woman who had tapped at the window and had carried some kind of iron weapon almost exactly matched Nell's account of what she and Beth had seen. Michael was able to dismiss the possibility that Nell had read Ralph's statement or been told of it. If Nell had known about Ralph's encounter, she would have said so.

But they all heard the music, thought Michael, uneasily. I heard it, too. He picked up Violet's statement again. Violet had said that Isobel walked the land and that people sometimes heard her playing piano music. *Like she did after she poisoned her husband*, Violet had asserted. It sounded like a typical old country ghost tale, part truth, part legend, part embroidery of facts by succeeding generations.

Yes, but Isobel had existed, and Nell had said she had been tried for her husband's murder at The Pheasant. The Pheasant said so, too; they had seemed rather proud of that fragment of the building's history. Would records of the trial still exist?

There was one more letter left in Ralph's file, and it bore the heading of Dr Brodworthy's surgery.

My Dear Sir,

I beg to enclose the report from Sir William Minching whose consulting rooms you attended last week, in company with Master Esmond. You will see Sir William has addressed the report directly to you.

I do not know if you will find it of help, but it is certainly interesting.

With kind regards,

I am yours faithfully,

E. Brodworthy. M.D.

SIXTEEN

Report on Master Esmond West.

I find Esmond West a perceptive and sensitive child. He appears to be of slightly above average intelligence for his age.

The usual methods of approach to a child are through games, school, school friends, and hobbies – but because of Esmond's affliction none of these were possible. He is, however, devoted to his music, and is also quite widely read. I was able to elicit that a particularly favourite book is *The Water Babies* by Charles Kingsley. Having the book on my own shelves, left during a nephew's visit to my house, I used this to try to reach him. After some initial suspicion, he seemed – albeit cautiously – to accept me as someone he might trust.

The book's concept of a child who finds itself in an alien environment (i.e. below the water, having drowned), but later earns the right to return to the world of humans, seems to exert a fascination on Esmond. The description of the humans who 'do as they like' in the story, but who consequently lose the power of speech, also appears to have a strong hold on his imagination.

Having studied the book's illustrations with him, I then suggested he might try his hand at drawing some of his own illustrations – not of *The Water Babies*, but of his own life. At first he seemed unsure what was required of him, so I explained he might draw anything he liked, but I should very much like to see a picture of the house where he lived, and also the things he liked to do. For example, I had been told he enjoyed his piano lessons. This found favour, and my nurse provided drawing paper and a selection of the coloured chalks and crayons I keep for my young patients, then we left him alone, with a glass of lemonade and some sweet biscuits.

I returned to the room after three quarters of an hour.

The drawings Esmond did during that time are a salutary indication of his state of mind.

There are four sketches. Superficially they are mere childish scribbles – although he may have a latent gift for drawing which you might care to allow to develop, for he has the trick of conveying life and movement in his figures.

The drawings seem to form a definite sequence, which is unusual in a boy of this age. The first is of a lady seated at a piano. A child – clearly intended to represent Esmond – is standing with her, either singing to the piano music or just listening to it. It is not a very good drawing, but the main details are easy enough to discern.

The second picture is better, and is of the same lady lying prone – either on a bed or sofa. Scarlet marks disfigure her face and neck, and two figures, a man and a child, stand over her. The lady in both these drawings I believe to be Esmond's mother, who I understand passed away some eighteen months ago. It seems reasonable to assume the two figures are Esmond and yourself.

The third picture is of the same child sitting at the same piano, but the room in this sketch is very different, and I think it may be your new residence in Caudle Moor. There are open windows behind him, and Esmond has sketched in trees and bushes. However, when I examined this drawing more closely, I saw that woven into the trees was the unmistakable figure of a woman – a thin lady, only partly formed, so that it was hard to make out where the trees ended and her outline began.

The fourth picture is the one that seems to me to provide the key to Esmond's affliction, for, in this one, the amorphous female has taken definite shape and is standing in the open doorway of the room, with the child at the piano. Even in the childish sketch it is possible to see the fierce concentration the boy is bringing to bear on his playing, and also the fact that his head is tilted towards the open window in an unmistakable attitude of the most intense longing.

It is my conclusion that Esmond is in some way convinced he can bring his mother back to life through music – perhaps music she used to play. I have no notion as to where he could have acquired this idea; bringing the dead back to life through music is not, as far as I know, a legend or a myth that appears anywhere in children's fiction or, indeed, in any other fiction.

I do not, of course, know the circumstances of your wife's passing, but the second drawing suggests Esmond was there when she died. That is something that would have a very great effect on a sensitive child of seven or eight (as he was at the time). It may help to talk to him about his mother's death – to emphasize the happier side of death, if you can possibly do so. If you find that too distressing, perhaps there is a family friend, doctor or clergyman who could do so. The Christian side – for instance the certain belief that she will be reunited with others who have passed over – could be stressed to him.

Before Esmond left, I examined what I will call the death sketch more closely. What I found disturbs me greatly. Esmond had managed to draw several pieces of furniture fairly recognizably – table, chairs, and so on. On the wall behind the dying or dead woman, is what I take to be a tapestry or a large framed piece of embroidery, not depicting an actual scene, but simply a pattern made up of scrolls and curlicues. Within the scrolls Esmond has drawn, in heavy black pencil, two narrow, slanting slits. Through those slits, quite unmistakably, eyes look out.

I drew his attention to this, saying I found it quite unusual, and asking why he had shown eyes there. Surely there had been no eyes in the tapestry, I said.

He stared at the sketch for a long time, as if puzzled as to how they had got there. Then he reached for the pencil again. Carefully and deliberately he wrote this:

The Eyes told me I must never speak.

I believe this is why Esmond never speaks. There is no physical defect to prevent him talking, and by your admission, he possessed normal speech until his mother's death. You have told me that your previous doctor in Derby suggested the shock of her death could have caused the condition, which is known as mutism. However, I would take that a step further, and say it is directly attributable to his having seen something connected with her death. Whatever he saw, someone told him very forcibly that he must never speak of it. I cannot dismiss the idea that someone was in the room when she died, and if the evidence of Esmond's drawings and his written statement that 'The Eyes' told him he must never speak, can be trusted, it might be that someone was hiding behind a screen, watching. Whoever it was, that person told him he must never speak of what he had seen, and Esmond was so terrified he has never spoken since.

There will, I am sure, be a normal explanation. Perhaps a nurse was measuring medication behind a screen, or perhaps a clergyman was preparing for the Last Rites. However, I hope, sir, you will forgive my asking a question which may be of vital help in reaching Esmond. The question is simply this: how, and in what circumstances, did Mrs West die?

I would be happy to arrange another session with Esmond if you should wish. Perhaps you will communicate with me if you decide in favour of that.

'I didn't expect,' said Nell, laying down the last page of William Minching's report which Michael had given her along with the rest of his discoveries and which she had read curled up in the window seat, 'to find that Beth might have a wife-killer in her ancestry.'

'You think that's what happened?'

'Don't you?'

'It's certainly one's initial reaction,' said Michael, carefully. 'Ralph killed his wife, Esmond saw it all by accident—'

'And Ralph told him he must never speak of it.'

'Ye-e-s. But let's not leap to any conclusions. That stuff about eyes watching Esmond and telling him he mustn't speak – that could be interpreted several ways, in fact Minching came up with a couple of sensible possibilities. A nurse or a doctor might have been preparing some unpleasant procedure and not wanting to give prior warning—'

'Like leeches? An enema?'

'Yes. Or maybe a priest was sloshing around holy water and anointed oil.'

'That's a good thought,' said Nell, eagerly. 'Esmond's mother might have been a Catholic, and they wouldn't want her knowing she was on the way out.'

'They might not even have wanted Ralph to know. Say he was a rabid Quaker or Baptist and didn't approve of Catholicism, and a servant or the doctor smuggled in a priest at her request. She might have been Irish and—'

'Oh God, not Irish, not after that mad outing last year,' said Nell.

'I'd rather we were facing a closet Irish Catholic or a jar of leeches than a ghost.'

'We aren't facing a ghost,' said Nell, firmly.

'You still don't believe in them, do you?'

'What I believe,' said Nell, speaking slowly as if she was assembling her thoughts, 'is that there might be things in the world – phenomena – that have an explanation we haven't yet stumbled on. After all, we don't understand how birds in flight can suddenly form themselves into wonderful patterns and fly in those beautiful formations. At least I don't understand it. So maybe there's a power of some kind we haven't yet discovered – something we don't know exists – that could explain paranormal activity.'

'Well, yes—'

'Imagine,' said Nell, pursuing her line of thought, 'just imagine trying to demonstrate electricity to a medieval man or woman. Or phones or television. They simply wouldn't understand. But there's a rational, scientific explanation of how television works. So there could be a rational explanation for paranormal activity. Something to do with light – sound – even telepathy. I'll give you telepathy,' she said. 'I will give you that.'

'Always the pragmatist,' said Michael, smiling.

'Yes, but here's another thing about Esmond,' said Nell. 'Have you thought that his grisly remark about The Eyes might have been pure fantasy? He sounds rather an imaginative child, doesn't he?'

'Minching had his share of imagination, as well. That suggestion that Esmond had got hold of some curious belief that he could bring his mother back through the music . . . That's really odd. I've never heard of anything like that, and I've heard of some peculiar things.'

'Ralph doesn't seem to have replied to Minching's question about how his wife died,' said Nell. 'Or if he did, he didn't keep a copy.'

'Or it's been lost.'

'Yes. I wish we could find Esmond's sketches,' said Nell. 'But I think that's too much to ask for. And Minching probably filed them with patient records and they've long since been destroyed.'

'I thought you didn't believe in Esmond.'

'I believe in Esmond as a person, because clearly he once lived here. But Esmond as a ghost, yes, I do find that difficult to accept.'

'You saw him though,' said Michael. 'So did I. And I think Beth saw him, as well.' He briefly considered whether to tell Nell about the email Beth had sent him. *We played a kind of duet*, Beth had said of Esmond. No, it was better not to mention that yet. And there was the figure he had himself glimpsed in the outbuildings. Had it been one of the women Ralph had seen? And what about that hunched shape that had stood between him and the door for those nightmare, trapped, moments? Had the closing of the door been merely due to an errant gust of wind?

He was trying to decide whether to tell Nell about this when Nell said, 'Brad wrote about seeing Esmond, as well.'

'He did, didn't he? He said they played a duet. And the letter you found – the letter Brad left for Esmond – was inside *The Water Babies*. Brad knew it was Esmond's favourite book.'

'That doesn't prove anything. Charlotte could have talked to Brad about Esmond – in fact she might have shown him the book.'

'And from that Brad created an imaginary friend for his holidays here? And made him a boy from the house's past?'

'Yes,' said Nell, rather defiantly. 'He might have spun his encounter with Esmond from Charlotte's stories.'

'To the extent of writing letters to that friend?' said Michael, doubtfully. 'Was Brad that kind of person?'

'Well, no, not when I met him, but he might have been different as a child. Things happened to him while he was growing up – quite traumatic things. He lived abroad for a few years – his father was attached to the Foreign Office so Brad was uprooted from everything he knew when he was about nine – quite abruptly, I think. He had to leave his friends, school, the house he had lived in, all in one fell swoop. It couldn't be helped, but it happened. And then his parents both died when he was sixteen. That's something that could change you quite radically,' said Nell.

'It might create an armour,' said Michael, thoughtfully. 'You'd set up a guard against emotions, and you'd force your-self to focus only on the practical things in your life. You'd blot out anything else.' He hesitated, not wanting to take that line of thought any deeper, then said, 'But let's suppose Esmond really is still around – no, I don't pretend to under-stand how that could be any more than you – but just suppose. What would be his motive?'

'Do ghosts need a motive?' said Nell, her expression relaxing into a near-smile for the first time for an hour.

'Of course they do.' Michael was relieved at the lighter note they had struck. 'They don't just turn up because there's a vacant slot at the moated grange, or the grey lady at the old rectory wants someone to make up a fourth at bridge. The classic thing is that they've been cheated out of something.

Or punished or defrauded of an inheritance. Or,' he said, warming to his theme, 'they might be charming gentlemen in Elizabethan outfits, hinting slyly that they know where an undiscovered Shakespearean folio is buried.'

'You do get carried away, don't you?' said Nell, smiling properly this time. 'You're missing out murdered Tudor queens or spectral bridegrooms or walled-up nuns.'

'I was coming to that.'

'You're also missing out that ghosts can be murder victims.'

They looked at one another. 'You think that?' said Michael at last. 'You think Esmond was murdered?'

'I don't know.' She hesitated. 'Michael, I keep getting an image of Ralph killing Esmond's mother, and Esmond seeing it happen. And – and that it was Ralph behind the screen, who told him never to speak of it. Then later, Ralph having to shut Esmond up. They're dreadful images, and I can't get rid of them – I wish I could, because—'

'Because you keep seeing Brad in Esmond's place?' said Michael, carefully.

'Brad – or Beth,' said Nell, and Michael felt the barriers that occasionally reared up between them snap into place.

But, speaking in an ordinary voice, he said, 'How about that builder's statement you found? Didn't he see some odd things?'

'Samuel Burlap,' said Nell, eagerly. 'Yes, he did – you haven't read it yet, have you? But it sounded as if he had some kind of mental breakdown, so everything he saw could be hallucination.' She said decisively, 'I *don't* believe Esmond is haunting this house, I really don't. But I'd like to know what happened to him. If we find he lived to a ripe old age and died in his bed at ninety-five, you owe me a lush dinner at Il Forno's.'

'Fair enough. It should be easy enough to track down a death certificate. But if we find Esmond vanished one dark and stormy night, and there's a local legend that he walks the lanes when there's a full moon, you're the one buying dinner.'

'OK.' Nell hopped down from the window seat. 'Where shall we start?'

'How about the estimable Poulsons and their useful family

connections stretching back for God knows how many generations?' said Michael. 'We can have lunch while we talk to
them.'

'Good idea. You can read Burlap's stuff as well – oh, and
the newspaper account of Isobel Acton's trial,' said Nell,
scooping up Ralph West's various papers. 'She's someone else
I could bear knowing about. She rather intrigues me. She might
have been a murderess – if Samuel Burlap can be believed,
she certainly was. But she sounds like a complete
temptress.'

'If anyone's going to be chasing temptresses, it should be
me,' said Michael. 'But thinking about it, I'm not sure if could
cope with another temptress in my life.' He held her against
him. 'I wonder if The Pheasant has a double room free for
tonight?'

'I thought we were leaving after lunch?'

'You don't fancy the idea of a double bed in a seventeenth-
century inn? You heartless wench,' said Michael. 'What
happened to "all my fortunes at thy feet I'll lay and follow
thee throughout the world"? Why are you smiling like that?'

'I can't help it. I do love you when you suddenly wax
poetical.' Nell stopped and turned abruptly away.

Michael grabbed her hand. 'Say it again.'

'That you wax poetical?'

'The other part. You've never said it before.'

'You've never said it, either. In fact,' pointed out Nell, 'you
haven't said it now.'

She had not turned back to look at him, and Michael released
her hand, knowing the sudden moment of emotion had passed
and the barriers were still there. Was that because Brad's ghost
still lingered in this house? He said, lightly, 'Oh, that's because
I need the scenery and the props. A moonlit garden, roses,
music, wine . . . Even a seventeenth-century inn. Which
reminds me, it's already one o'clock and The Pheasant doesn't
serve food after two.'

'So much for romance and moonlit rose gardens,' said Nell,
more cheerfully. 'But now you mention it, lunch is a good
idea. I'm starving.'

*   *   *

The ever-helpful Mr Poulson was charmed to be approached for information about the old Acton trial. He was not sure whether the official police records would be obtainable; what he did know was that his great-grandfather – maybe another couple of 'greats' – had been foreman of the jury at that trial. And his own grandfather used to say there were jury notes of the trial. If so, the likeliest place to find them would be the attics.

'Attics, always attics,' said Nell, sighing half humorously.

'Could we possibly have a look?' asked Michael. 'We'd do the searching ourselves, so as not to put you to any trouble.'

'And put everything back afterwards,' said Nell, with a sideways glance at Michael.

'Yes, of course we would. It's only to make some notes – to find out a bit more about the history of Stilter House.'

Mr Poulson said bless them and save them all, Dr Flint and Mrs West could make notes until the Last Trump if they wanted.

'It's an offer we can't refuse,' said Michael, rather apologetically, as they ate their lunch.

'If you're going to accept, I think I will refuse, though,' said Nell. 'For one thing I think you'll be better on your own, and for another it's not really fair to coop Beth up in an attic. I can't expect Mrs Poulson to watch her again. And I'd quite like to have a look round the village.'

'All right. Shall I book us in for another night here?'

'Probably not, but see how far you get with the search,' said Nell. 'If you think there's more to unearth, we can stay until tomorrow. If not, we could set off around five – it'll still be light, and we can drive in convoy and stop off somewhere to eat.'

'That sounds fine. Let's meet in the bar around four,' said Michael.

Beth was gleefully pleased at the success of her morning's cookery, and had carefully written out the recipe for the Bakewell tart, promising Mrs Poulson that they would bake it in Oxford, and tell everyone where it came from. Asked by Nell if she would like to take a look round the village after lunch, she said that would be super-double-cool, especially if they took some photos.

'Michael might want some for the Wilberforce book,' she explained. 'On account of Wilberforce visiting Egg-nog Village. It'd be good if he could – um – consult photographs to describe it, wouldn't it?'

They set off with Beth wearing the scarlet wellingtons, which were her current pride, and happily jumping in all the puddles that lay everywhere after the heavy rain. Nell watched her, wanting to wrap the moment up and keep it safe, because Beth would not be a child like this for ever; before long she would be trying out outrageous make-up and listening to whatever music was in vogue, and giggling maddeningly with her girlfriends over boys. Would Brad have been tolerant of that? Would Michael? It was suddenly and seductively easy to see a future where Beth was growing up and Michael was still part of the picture. They might buy a house in Oxford – Nell could keep the shop, Michael could remain at Oriel . . . No, better not to let those daydreams take too much substance. She turned her attention to the village square, which was a serene sight in the afternoon sunshine. There was a war memorial, a village green, a well that was probably ceremoniously dressed at the appropriate season, and a massive old oak tree with a circular bench around it. There was also a doctor's surgery with a brass plate. Was a Dr Brodworthy still here? The police station was nearby – a low, stone-clad building, with an old-fashioned blue lamp outside.

Beth had dashed across to the oak tree, which might be a good place for Wilberforce to have an adventure, and was enthusiastically taking shots of it with the small, but quite sophisticated camera, which Ellie's parents had sent her from Maryland.

'Pretty good,' she said, when Nell enquired as to the shots. 'Can we load them onto the laptop for Michael to see?'

'Yes, of course. And let's get a couple of those almshouses at the far end. That's a nice bit of the old village.'

The almshouses were low, stone-built houses, with mullioned windows, and neatly tended gardens. There was a square tablet, inset into the centre house, saying the properties had been built and endowed by Mr Simeon Acton in 1852, for the shelter, succour and sustenance of the old or the frail.'

'See if you can get a close-up of that as well,' said Nell, indicating the tablet. 'It's a bit of a link to Stilter House. Don't go too near though – people live in there, remember.'

Beth hopped onto a fence, took several shots, and reported moderate success. 'It might be a bit smudgy, but it's pretty good.'

'Well done. I think we'll head back to The Pheasant, shall we? We said we'd meet Michael at four and it's nearly three already.'

They were retracing their steps, when Beth said, 'Will we have time to go back to Stilter House?'

The question took Nell off balance, but she said, 'If we have to we can, but I packed everything up this morning, and it's all in our room at The Pheasant. There's no need to go back.'

'It's just that I'd sort of like to take – well, borrow – some of the music, if that would be all right,' said Beth. She was not looking at Nell.

Nell said, 'Esmond's music?' and Beth look up, startled. 'It's all right, Bethie. I know about Esmond. At least, I know as much as anyone knows about him.'

'I thought you mightn't like it, on account of him coming into the house when we didn't know him,' said Beth, clearly relieved. 'I don't s'pose I ought to have let him come in, but he was really pleased to be there, and he was extra pleased to play the piano. He didn't say anything, but I thought p'raps there isn't a piano where he lives.'

It's all right, thought Nell. She thinks he was a local child who wandered in. She didn't think there was anything unreal about him – any more than her father thought it all those years ago. She did not examine the logic of this against her own beliefs and disbeliefs, but listened to Beth, who was still talking about Esmond.

'He's a really good pianist,' Beth was saying. 'So I thought if I had some of his music, I might practice it and get as good. The aunts wouldn't mind if I took a few bits of it, would they? I mean those aunts whose house it is?'

'I'll tell them about it,' said Nell, 'but I shouldn't think they'd mind in the least. In fact they mentioned you having one or two keepsakes from the house, so I'm sure a few sheets of music would be fine.' She hesitated, then said, 'You wouldn't mind going out there? After last evening?'

'I wouldn't want to go back at *night*,' said Beth, earnestly. 'But everywhere's sunshiney now and the house will be all sparkly, so it'd be pretty OK. And that policeman—'

'Sergeant Howe?'

'He said he'd be there this afternoon,' said Beth. 'So he'd chase away any muddly people, wouldn't he?'

'Yes, he would. I'd forgotten he was going to be there.' Nell thought there was no reason not to make one quick final visit to Stilter House, and it might even be good for Beth to see it by daylight; to see it as an ordinary, unthreatening house, and take away with her a happy, normal memory of the place her father had loved.

'Plus,' said Beth, avoiding Nell's eyes again, 'you know that photo of Dad at the piano? The one I told you about?'

'Yes.'

'Well, I wondered if I could have a photo of me at the piano like that. Then I could have both photos in a frame. It'd be me and Dad at the same piano, when we were both nine. I'd really like that. Dad would like it, as well, wouldn't he?'

'Oh Beth,' said Nell, suddenly having to fight back tears. 'Of course he would. It's a terrific idea. Let's do it right away. We'll get the car from the pub and whizz out there at once, and we'll pick out some of the music and I'll get some shots of you at the piano. We can easily be back to meet Michael at four.'

SEVENTEEN

The Pheasant's attics were lit by a single, unshaded electric light bulb hanging from the rafters, but even in its glare the attics had a mysterious atmosphere. As Michael stepped through the narrow door he had the feeling of being invisibly beckoned to come deeper into this quiet storehouse of the past; invited to pick, uninterrupted, through the squirrelled-away flotsam and jetsam of ordinary everyday life. Was this how Nell felt when she foraged through attics? He would ask her later, and she would probably grin and say what she usually felt in attics was irritation at the sheer untidiness, because people just dumped their cast-offs anywhere and closed the door, so you got a hotchpotch of ill-assorted junk. Then Michael would tell her she was being unromantic again and quote that line (was it Shelley or Keats?) about the past being like an inspired rhapsodist filling the future with harmony. Upon which Nell would most likely laugh and say trust him to dredge up the metaphysical poets at any opportunity.

But there appeared to be a fair degree of tidiness in The Pheasant's attics. In fact it almost looked as if the cast-offs had been arranged in order like the earth's strata or Neapolitan ice-cream, although this was probably because everything brought up here had simply been heaped on top of the last layer. How deep into these layers was Isobel Acton, the temptress poisoner? Was she even here?

Michael began to move the miscellany of items, trying to identify the different eras as he did so. Working his way through the broken bits of furniture and abandoned curtains and three-legged dining chairs, he wondered if there was a scene for Wilberforce to be gleaned from this. Perhaps Wilberforce, during his visit to Great Aunt Tabitha, would investigate the attics of her house for some reason – that would allow for a lively illustration of him in a nightcap, tiptoeing furrily and furtively up the stairs, carrying an old-fashioned candle.

He cleared away the most recent layer – the topsoil – which was mostly of out-of-date kitchen appliances and vinyl discs from the fifties, along with some sixties remnants including purple and green linoleum flowers from the flower power days. Beneath that lay memorabilia of WWII – black and white photographs of young men standing next to Spitfires, a tea-chest containing an old RAF uniform, and framed photographs of a Caudle street party commemorating VE-Day.

He stacked all this in one corner, and embarked on an older group of items, piled neatly against one wall, seeing with a beat of excitement that he was approaching the era he was looking for. Here were fragments from the Great War: sepia photographs of clear-eyed boys, heartbreakingly young. I'm getting closer, thought Michael. But I haven't reached Isobel yet. Would she be here? Had Joe Poulson's great-great-whoever really left notes of her trial?

But Joe Poulson's ancestor had. Michael found the notes in an enamelled box beneath dusty folds of a chenille table-cover and a set of cast-metal figurines depicting the Muses. The box had protected the notes from the worst of time's ravages – also from the mice that certainly raided the attic from time to time.

The top sheet was headed, *Trial of Isobel Acton*, and the writing was careful and clear. Michael glanced at his watch, saw that he had almost two hours before meeting Nell and Beth, and sat down on an old horsehair sofa to read.

Monday 1st July
The Pheasant

I am George Poulson, residing at The Pheasant Public House in Caudle Moor, which my father is landlord of, and I am foreman of the jury for the trial of Mrs Isobel Acton, which duty I take seriously and according to the Queen.

All of us were given these books to make notes during the trial. I would like to state I shall be helping two jurymen in that, since they can't barely read, never mind write, not having had the benefit of much education, although both good honest men as will pronounce sentence according to their true beliefs, and not be swayed by any trumpery buying of drinks in the public bar, nor fluttering of eyelids from fancy ladies pretending to be sorrow-struck.

We took the Oath, speaking out very solemn and correct, although the judge had to rebuke Nehemiah Goodbody afterwards for saying he could not hear and asking folk to speak up and not mumble. My young lady, Miss Eliza Stump that is, was asked to remove her bonnet or take a seat in the benches against the wall, on account of folk not being able to see over the feathered trimmings, which was a pity for she had bought the bonnet special for the trial and is a young lady as likes to look her best, not to mention her position as housekeeper at Acton House making her an object of folks' interest.

The indictment was read by a man who was called the clerk of the court, and very impressive it was. I copy it here.

'The Crown, for our lady, the Queen, by the Grace of God, presents and charges that the defendant, Isobel Mary Acton, *née* Susskind, did kill and murder her husband, Simeon John Acton at their house, Acton House, Caudle Moor, in the county of Derbyshire.'

(The dates and times were included, but I couldn't write fast enough for those, and also Albert Coppin, who was sitting next to me, sneezed, so I missed some of the details).

Mrs Acton stood in the dock. (It wasn't a dock like in a proper court: it was some of the rostra from the room where the Ancient Order of Buffalos meet the first Thursday of the month, and Davy Higgins, the joiner, had hammered together some oak staves as an enclosure. They'd put the Queen's photograph on the wall behind it, to remind everyone of the solemnity).

I'm not a great one for describing ladies' garments, but Miss Stump said afterwards that Mrs Acton was wearing a black watered silk gown, and that while black was perfectly proper for the occasion, not to mention her being a widow, watered silk was a bit showy if one was standing trial for murder. Also, said Eliza, she had heard as how Mrs Acton had dabbed rice powder on her face (which was quite proper, and something many ladies did nowadays), but had also reddened her lips. She had it from the policewoman who was guarding her, said Eliza, and she knew it would be true, for Mrs Acton had an array of powders and creams on her bedroom table, and often wore powder and even, on occasions, rouge.

As a matter of fact, it wouldn't have mattered if Isobel

Acton had painted her face with blue and crimson like a heathen, for she wore a veil over her face most days, and none of us could see her expression at all.

The gentleman who spoke against Mrs Acton – prosecutor they told us he was styled – next called Mrs Burlap.

She told what she had seen the afternoon Mr Simeon Acton died, and you could see that everyone listening found it shocking and terrible. The judge wrote things down in his book, although he didn't seem to find it particularly shocking, and I dare say he's used to hearing suchlike as murder every day. But Caudle Moor is a law-abiding place, and we all found it dreadful.

Mrs Acton did not seem shocked. Nehemiah Goodbody said afterwards she hadn't even listened to it, and was as proud and haughty as if she believed the devil had her in his care. But Nehemiah believes the devil has a lot of folk in his care, and he talks about Lucifer as familiarly as if he had his dinner in hell's fiery caverns every Saturday, so nobody paid him much heed.

Asked had she tried to help Mr Acton, Mrs Burlap said indeed she had, as any Christian soul would. She had gone along to the scullery and mixed a draught of mustard and water, and she and Mrs Acton had tried to get the poor man to drink it down.

The man who spoke for Mrs Acton – defence, they call him – pounced on this.

'So Mrs Acton tried to revive him?' he said.

'You might think so,' said Mrs Burlap glaring. She's a holy terror, Mrs Burlap, and terrorizes her young son, Samuel, into an unnatural obedience, and the general opinion is that it's no wonder Jack Burlap looks for his comfort in other places than his own cottage.

'But the jury will see that as the action of a loving wife anxious to save her husband's life, rather than a cold-blooded killer,' said the defence, and sat down, smirking at the prosecutor as if thought he had scored a point. From the back of the courtroom came Nehemiah Goodbody's muttered voice, saying something about folk who darkeneth counsel by words without knowledge, and for a moment we thought the judge was going to order Nehemiah to be removed, but the prosecutor intervened asking Mrs Burlap to continue her story and the moment passed.

Mrs Burlap was clearly not going to be put down by smart young men from London, or judges in wigs. She said loudly, 'It might look as if Isobel Acton wanted to revive her husband, but it's my opinion she'd planned all along to be rid of him, and—'

'Thank you, Mrs – Mrs Burlap,' said the judge, 'but we are not able to take your opinion as evidence. Please do not sniff at me like that, unless you are suffering from a head cold.'

'Did you,' asked the prosecutor hastily, 'actually see Mrs Acton administer any kind of liquid – anything at all – to her husband?'

'No, I did not, but—'

'Thank you, Mrs Burlap.'

Dr Brodworthy next told how he was called to Acton House and how Mr Simeon Acton was already on the brink of death. He had tried to get him to drink something to make him sick or have a purging.

'That'd be to rid Mr Acton's body of any poison?' asked the prosecuting gentleman, all polite like, and Dr Brodworthy agreed, and told what had been in the stuff, although I never heard of any of it and neither had anyone else, and none of us knew how to spell the words anyway. But the judge wrote it down, and Dr Brodworthy said it was powerful effective if taken soon enough.

'But on this occasion it was not effective at all?'

'No, for the poison was too long in the system, and already working its ills,' said Dr Brodworthy. 'Organ failure had already begun.'

Here, the doctor became very medical in his explanation, and I dare say not more than two people listening really understood the exact details, but his meaning was clear enough to us all. Mr Simeon Acton, good and kindly soul, had been given poison and it had killed him.

The last person to be called on was my young lady, Miss Eliza Stump. There seemed to be some question as to whether she ought to have been let to sit on the benches to hear what had gone beforehand, but somebody pointed out that The Pheasant did not have enough space for folks to sit anywhere else, and they wrangled for a bit and most of us got bored, but in the end, Eliza was let to tell her story.

Very smart and pert she looked (in the new bonnet), and she spoke up well about how Isobel Acton had sent the servants out of the house on the afternoon Simeon Acton died.

'Very fishy I thought it at the time,' she said. 'A fair at Caudle Magna, she said, and we could all go along that afternoon. But I never heard tell of a fair at Caudle Magna, nor anywhere else hereabouts.'

The prosecutor here intervened to assure the jury that there had been no fair at Caudle Magna that day, which was not a thing he needed do, for we all knew it.

'We got home about five o'clock,' said Eliza. 'And there was Dr Brodworthy trying to help poor Mr Acton, but able to do nothing for the man.'

'And so you – all the servants – were out of the house the whole afternoon?'

'Straight after our dinner, which we take at midday so as to serve up the dining room lunch,' affirmed Eliza. 'We went off soon as we'd cleared away and washed up. I never could abide dirty crockery in my scullery, and I make it a rule to—'

'And you were all out of the house the entire time? You and the two other servants were together all the afternoon?'

'Well, aside of when I went into the draper's to match some feathers for my bonnet, yes.'

'Thank you, Miss Stump.' The prosecutor glanced at the defence, who stood up, and asked about the cleaning routine of Acton Houses. Did Miss Stump oversee the maids? Did she in fact do any of the cleaning herself?

'No, I do not do any of the cleaning,' said Eliza, shocked that anyone should think it. 'I'm the housekeeper. I see to the running of everything and I oversee the maids.'

'You would inspect their work? You would, for instance, make sure things were properly dusted?'

'I would indeed, for I'm most particular about—'

'In the course of that overseeing,' said the defence, 'did you ever see anything odd among the accused's belongings?' Then, as Eliza looked puzzled, he said, 'Did you ever notice any strange jars or bottles? Items you hadn't seen before, or that you couldn't identify?'

'She had a great deal of powders and creams and perfumes,' said Eliza. 'As to knowing them all at a glance, I can't say I did, for she was always buying new ones.'

'But you recognized them for what they were? Creams and lotions for the skin?'

'Yes.'

'And you never saw or found anything that might have suggested the accused had any kind of noxious substance in her possession?'

The word 'noxious' flummoxed Eliza for a moment, then she said, 'If you're asking if I ever saw poison in Mrs Acton's drawers or cupboards, the answer is that I did not.'

'Ah. Thank you, Miss Stump, you may step—'

'But,' said Eliza firmly, 'that ain't to say she hadn't got some, for Acton House is a big old place, and so many nooks and crannies where you might hide a thing, not to mention the outbuildings.'

'We don't need to—'

'And the game larder has a whole array of meat safes and suchlike,' went on Eliza, undaunted. 'You could hide enough poison to kill an army in there, and no one'd be the wiser.' Having delivered this shot, she stepped down, resuming her seat in the public benches, the feathers in her bonnet a-quiver with excitement.

When the trial ended, the judge spoke to us. I'm setting down as near as I can what he said.

'You have listened to all the evidence,' he said. He had a clear voice, but I found it very unpleasant. Cold and hard. A sound you'd hear at times from Jack Burlap's forge when he was hammering out a bit of metal for a wheel rim.

'And,' said the judge, 'I make no doubt you have understood it, for it was told clearly and plainly.' He leaned forward, his voice severe, and the light from one of the gas lamps fell across his face so that I saw he was younger than I'd realized. You think of judges as elderly, but this one wasn't more than forty-five or fifty.

'But there is not a shred of evidence to show that the accused gave her husband poison,' he said. 'Nor is there a shred of evidence to show she has done anything wrong at all. She is a law-abiding lady, who loved her husband and is grief-stricken at his death.' He paused, fiddled with his pen, then said, 'If you pronounce a Guilty verdict, the death sentence would be mandatory. Isobel Acton would hang by the neck until she was dead. Now, that is a very solemn burden for you to bear. And for that reason, if for no other, I will accept nothing other than a unanimous verdict – that is, you must all give the same verdict. I cannot and must not accept anything less. That is all, gentlemen, and may good counsel attend your deliberations.'

EIGHTEEN

George Poulson's notes, cont'd

Well! We were all struck of a heap, as you might say, by the judge's words, for we had it settled in our minds as to what the verdict must be.

We all knew, even without Mrs Burlap's description or Dr Brodworthy's explanation, that Isobel Acton had stirred poison into her husband's coffee. No one had explained where the poison had come from, but any country household – cottage or mansion – has stuff for keeping down vermin.

But here was the judge – and him a gentleman who should know about these things – pretty much telling us that Isobel Acton was innocent.

And this is where I come to the bad part – the part I never spoke about to a soul, not even my dad who's so loyal, not even to Eliza – well, certainly not to Eliza, for she's one for a bit of gossip my Eliza. And we were told, very solemn and stern, that everything that happened and was discussed in the jury room had to remain absolutely secret – even years after the trial. It's a criminal offence to tell any of it, they said.

So I'm not going to speak about it, not ever, but what I am doing is making a proper record while it's still all clear in my mind. If anything were to happen in the future, I might be very glad to show these pages and to say – *this* is the truth of what happened. Please God that won't ever be necessary, but I'm writing it down anyway.

We went off to the jury room, which I should mention was my father's cheese larder, which my mother had swept out for the purpose, and my father had covered up the cheeses and carried in twelve chairs. We were a bit bemused, but we took our seats, determined to deal with the matter as best we could. Only we hadn't got further than sitting down, when the judge came in. Very different he looked without his wig and his robes – a bit frowning around the eyes from glaring at criminals that'd be, but weak around the mouth. It's odd how you can tell a person's character from their mouth   more than the eyes, I think, for all they say the eyes are the windows of the soul. Anyway, the judge had a weak mouth, and it was a bit fleshy as well – what they call sensuous as if he enjoyed the good things in life.

He had a bit of a furtive air to him, as if he didn't want anyone to come in and catch him, although you don't think of judges being furtive.

He stood at the end of the table and, speaking quietly, said, 'Gentlemen, it's slightly unorthodox for me to be here, but this trial is under my authority so in the interests of justice, I've decided I can allow myself a visit to you.'

(One of the others said later that this meant the old boy was bending the rules to suit himself).

'I spoke in court about there being no evidence against

this lady, Isobel Acton,' said the judge. 'Nor is there. I
know the law very well indeed, and I can assure you of
that. That is why I ám exercising my discretion in visiting
the jury room in order to privately direct you to look
favourably on giving a verdict of Not Guilty.'

There was a silence, during which none of us knew
quite what to say. It's not every day you sit in a cheese
larder and are told by a judge that you must let a murderess
go scot free. For murderess she was, I never had any
doubt as to that.

How I had the courage to speak up, I have no idea,
but I said, 'Well, sir, it seems to me that it's for us twelve
to decide among ourselves what we think and what we'll
say. But thanking you kindly for your advice.'

He gave me one of those looks that make you quake
in your boots when you're young, and you've stolen
apples from somebody's orchard and been caught by the
constable. But I managed to meet his look squarely, for
he might be a judge and an important person, but I was
a Poulson and my family had held its head high in Caudle
Moor for a good many generations.

He said, 'Mr . . . Poulson, is it? Well, Mr Poulson,
there are responsibilities in life, and some of us have
greater responsibilities than others.' Then he looked at
us one by one, for all the world like a man inspecting a
collection of insects or butterflies he was about to skewer
with pins. He said, 'Some of you here have particularly
heavy responsibilities – things you would be glad to have
help with.'

That was when I began to get the strong sense of
something going on below the surface. A bit like when
you stand on soggy ground and know there's an
underground river directly below – except that this
wouldn't be a river, it would be a sewage channel, stinking
and rotten.

'You're an interesting set of jurymen,' said the judge.
'I've looked at your different professions and ways of
living.'

(The man who later said the judge was bending the

rules to his own purposes, also said it wasn't right for
the judge to have done this, but I don't know about that.)

'Mr McCardle, you're a farmer, I think,' said the judge,
looking along the table to the man at the far end of it.

'I am, sir,' said McCardle.

'Farming can be a hard life if a man has mortgaged
some of his lands,' said the judge, 'particularly if those
mortgages are held by people who might call them in at
a moment's notice. That'd be a hard thing for his sons,
wouldn't it?'

No one spoke, but McCardle looked a bit sick and I
remembered my father telling me once that McCardle
had indeed mortgaged some of his acres, and was
struggling so much to meet the payments he might lose
the land.

'And Mr Coppin, you own a small chandler's business,
and live on the premises with your elderly father.'

Albert Coppin, as good and decent a man as ever drew
breath, said stoutly that that was right, and belatedly
added, 'sir'.

'I hear it's your great worry that he sometimes wanders
in his wits and strays around the village.'

'Yes, but—'

'I dare say as a dutiful son, you'd employ a help of
some kind to watch him. If,' said the judge, 'you had the
means.'

Albert did not speak, and the judge turned his attention
to the rest of us. I remember I thought, well at least he
won't have anything on *me*. For The Pheasant's prosperous,
and everything in my life is ordinary and honest.

He did look at me, but then his look passed on to Mr
Billock, seated opposite.

'Mr Billock, you have a sweet shop.'

Mr Billock, famed for his humbugs which were like
huge sugary bumble bees and beloved by all the children,
said with nervous pride that he did indeed.

'And a family.'

It was not quite a question, but it was not quite a
statement, either, and it was clear that Billock did not

know how to respond. But he said, begging pardon, sir, your honour, but there must be a mistake. Several of us exchanged puzzled glances at that, for it was well known Billock had no family at all, being a widower these twenty years, and having no sisters or brothers.

The judge said, 'Are you sure there is no family, Billock? No daughter living quietly with her mother? But no matter. And I know you are a pillar of the church and a sidesman at St Mary's.' He looked at each of us again, carefully and slowly, and we waited. But he only said, 'I think that is all, gentlemen. I await your verdict.'

We had a real old brangle after that. Most of us were for a verdict of Guilty, but the three men the judge had singled out – McCardle, Coppin and Billock – stood firm for Not Guilty. Nothing we could say would budge them.

They all insisted they were holding by what the judge had said, and there was nothing else going on. McCardle said it was a question of loyalty and of looking after your own, and Albert Coppin gave this his support, Ned Billock, when pressed, said a man's life was his own, which, as somebody else pointed out, did not get us much further. One or two people would have liked to ask about that sly hint that Billock had a daughter somewhere, but nobody quite had the courage.

Somebody else said the judge oughtn't to have talked to us like that, and it was tampering with the law of the land. Someone said the jury system went back to Magna Carta, but McCardle said he couldn't see what Magna Carta had to do with what was happening in Caudle Moor today, and as far as he was concerned, they could take Magna Carta and hang it on the washing-line.

Albert Coppin said, 'Oh bugger Magna Carta, what's that got to say to anything? I'm staying with Not Guilty – the judge is right. There's no real evidence to prove she did it.' He stuck his lower lip out obstinately, and one or two more, who had been looking thoughtful, said they thought Not Guilty was the fairest verdict as well. You had to look at the thing from all aspects.

'What do you mean?' I said. 'There's only one aspect, isn't there? Whether she killed Simeon Acton or not.'

They seemed unsure of what they meant, then a neighbour of Billock's, a man who kept the draper's shop, and who was known to read poetry in his spare time, said, 'It's very final, hanging. It's a solemn thing to make a judgement on.'

McCardle said this was very true, and we were none of us Solomons, to which Albert Coppin said he couldn't see that Solomon had any more to do with this than Magna Carta.

The draper disregarded this, and went on speaking. 'The thing is that you can't say you've made a mistake after you've sent a person to the gallows. Supposing we found later on – years and years, even – that there was something to prove someone else did the murder.'

There was a vague murmur of agreement and people looked hopeful. I began to suspect there were a few more guilty secrets in the room than was comfortable, and that several people feared the judge might ferret them out. A nasty piece of work, that judge, not someone you'd want to make an enemy of.

Three hours later the original majority of Guilty had dwindled to eleven Not Guilties and one Guilty. And I was the one still holding to Guilty.

I'd have stuck it out. I really would. I don't know what would have happened – whether there would have had to be a second trial or what, but I really would have clung to my belief in Isobel's guilt. I had no guilty secrets for cold-voiced, lecherous-lipped men to uncover.

But later that night I took the others up to the room where we were to sleep. Jurics aren't allowed to go back to their homes while they're considering a verdict – I hadn't known that, but we'd been told it was the law. We weren't even allowed to speak to anyone. So my father had set up truckle beds and mattresses in the big room being used as the courtroom, and we were going to sleep there, like boys in one of those posh schools.

I had gone along to the kitchen to collect a tray of

food to take up for our supper, which my mother was going to leave ready. She had been in a great fluster and flurry all week, baking a ham, stewing tomatoes for chutney, determined that no guest under her roof would go hungry, even if they were under her roof for the macabre purpose of pronouncing the death sentence on that hussy, Isobel Acton. So our supper consisted of fresh-cut ham, sausage patties, home-made chutney, a Cheshire cheese, and a dish of ripe pears. We weren't allowed any strong drink, which Albert Coppin said was a pity, for if you were forced to spend a night in a public house, you'd expect to enjoy a drop of beer. But my father sent in a large flagon of lemonade and a canister of tea, so we foraged very sufficient, as the saying is.

Anyway, I was crossing the landing when the judge came out of his room. He was staying at The Pheasant as well, of course, there being nowhere else in the neighbourhood, and him having to be on hand.

He barred my way and I knew at once he had been listening for me.

'Mr Poulson,' he said, and looked at the tray. 'I see your father is giving the jury a substantial supper.'

'Yes.'

'A very generous host, your father.'

'All in the way of business.' After a moment, I added, 'sir'. I refused to call him Your Honour outside the courtroom.

'And a very lucrative business as well, I believe.'

'We do well enough.'

'There was a time when The Pheasant did not do very well, though,' he said. 'You wouldn't remember that – you'd be very young at the time.'

'I don't—'

'And at that time your father – that good, honest, innkeeper sought a loan.' He stepped nearer, and spoke more softly. 'And do you know where he went for that money?' said the judge in his ugly voice.

'I dare say it'd be the bank.'

'Nothing so conventional. Your father, that respected

innkeeper, went to Mr Simeon Acton. Only it wasn't Mr Acton with all his head-in-the-clouds philanthropy who gave him money. It was his wife, the lady who's standing trial for her life now.'

I stared at him. 'Isobel Acton gave my father money?'

'She did indeed. You may ask your father about it and he'll tell you it's the truth.'

'I don't believe you.'

'You have my word on it. Your father once did Isobel Acton a favour. She repaid it.'

'What favour? Because if you're suggesting my father was up to any no-good nonsense with Mrs Acton—'

'Oh no,' he said, at once. 'At that time, the no-good nonsense, as you call it, was with me.'

'You?' That was when I knew I'd been right about those fleshy sensuous lips.

'Yes. You see, Mr Poulson – George, isn't it? – you see, George, for a few years I bedded Isobel Acton more times than your father served pints of ale downstairs. I'd travel up here and stay at Acton House as a family friend. Only I was a great deal more than a friend to Isobel.' For a moment his lips gleamed with memory, then he went on.

'On the afternoon your father came to the house, to ask Simeon for a loan, he caught me with Isobel in circumstances that could not be misunderstood. Well,' said the judge, with a shrug, 'I wasn't going to have some country yokel talking about that. Linking my name with the Acton bitch – perhaps even causing a divorce. I have considerable standing in legal circles. My wife's father is a baronet. I wasn't going to risk losing any of that.'

I said, slowly, 'So my father got his loan, but it didn't come from Simeon.'

'Simeon never knew anything about it.'

'A bribe,' I said. 'To ensure my father wouldn't tell what he'd seen.'

'Yes. I was the one who actually provided the money. Your father repaid it to Isobel over the next couple of years. She kept it, of course, the acquisitive bitch. Fair payment, I suppose. Still, a fair exchange for what I'd had, and she'd always been very willing.' Again, the memory showed in his eyes. 'But then all that Susskind brood were willing,' he said. 'So now, George, if you stand out for a verdict of Guilty, I swear before God I will let it be known that your father made regular payments to the Acton woman. Quite large sums, they were. And if people hear about those payments, they'll wonder why. They'll wonder if your father had been paying Isobel for certain services. Or perhaps if there was something in his life that he didn't want people knowing about – that he was paying to be kept quiet.'

'But none of that's true!' I said angrily. 'He did nothing wrong.'

'What he did wrong was to see me tupping Isobel Acton,' said the judge. 'But I can spread a story about those payments that will make them seem very suspicious indeed. And the end will be that your father will be shunned by the village. I wonder what your mother would think of it all?'

He waited, and I said, confusedly, 'But why do you want Isobel Acton to go free now? I don't see there's any link.'

'Oh, don't be so stupid. Years ago I was afraid of your father talking about my affair with Isobel. Now I'm afraid of Isobel talking about it.'

'But if they hang her she can't talk. I'd have thought you'd do everything you could to get her convicted.'

'George,' he said, 'there's a gap of three weeks before a condemned man or woman is hanged. In those three weeks, Isobel Acton will talk. She's told me so. Her freedom – her acquittal of murder – is the price of her silence.' He stepped closer. 'And,' he said, 'your agreement to a Not Guilty verdict, is the price of my silence about your father.'

I gave in. I know it was weak, but I couldn't bear to think of my father – also my mother – being damaged like that. The judge would do it, as well, I had no doubts about that. He was a very nasty piece of work indeed. He'd spread his story and he'd make it very damning indeed. So I did what Charles Dickens calls 'shout with the mob'. I shouted with the other jurymen, and I added my vote of Not Guilty.

And Isobel Acton was released as innocent.

Michael put down the notebook and leaned back against the dusty wall of The Pheasant's attic.

It was remarkable how vividly that courtroom and the people in it came alive. Had the present Poulson read this? Michael was inclined to think not; he thought the long-ago George had probably secreted the notebook away in a cupboard or a bureau, and a little legend had grown up about the Poulson who had been part of the famous local trial. But he put the notebook in his jacket pocket, thinking he would ask Joe Poulson if Nell could read it.

It was still only three o'clock. There was time to see if the local police station had any of their old court records and whether he could look at them. It would be interesting to check George Poulson's account against the official report. Then he would come back to The Pheasant and he and Nell and Beth could have a cup of tea and decide whether to stay in Caudle Moor until tomorrow.

The very young constable at the police house was helpful. Yes, they had the old records, he said, a long way back, as well.

'How long back?' asked Michael.

'More'n fifty years. Even a hundred, maybe.' The constable said this with considerable awe, as one to whom even thirty years stretched back to a different era.

Michael said, diffidently, 'I'm doing a little local research – some of it taking in Stilter House. I wonder if I could have a look at the records. I'd be very careful with them – I'm used to archives and old papers.' He remembered he had a business card for this kind of situation, and after emptying his pockets and the contents of his wallet, finally found one. It was a bit dog-eared, but the constable took it with reverence, read it with respect, and said that would be *quite* all right, Dr Flint.

'We do sometimes get people wanting to look at the old case books and records, so I know it's all right to let people see the archives. We can't,' he said, firmly, as one repeating a carefully learned lesson, 'allow sight of the recent stuff, of course.'

'Of course you can't.'

'Nothing for the last fifty years. That's the law.'

'I'm wanting to go back much further than fifty years,' said Michael. 'The 1860s if possible.'

'The Acton trial,' said the constable, nodding solemnly. 'Always a lot of interest in that, well, you might say it's Caudle's main claim to fame. Come through to the office, Dr Flint, and I'll get the screen set up for you. It's all on computer now, you know. Everything scanned in a while back, and didn't it take a lot of work, and the sergeant grumbling about the strain on our budget. But I tell him progress is progress.'

The office referred to was a sliver of a room overlooking a tiny patch of ground at the back of the police house. Michael was given a seat at a small desk, with a monitor and keyboard, provided with a cup of coffee, and given the relevant passwords.

He started with the 1900 thread, thinking he would work his way back to Isobel and the 1860s, and as an initial search request typed in Ralph West and Esmond West. He had been expecting to find the scanned-in statements which Ralph and the two servants had made to the police on the night of the intruder, and those certainly opened up. It was odd to see the faded writing on a modern screen. He scrolled down, not expecting there to be more.

But there was.

The heading was, "*Statement by Mr Ralph West of Stilter House, regarding the disappearance of his son, Esmond.*" The date was the autumn of 1901.

Esmond, thought Michael. *Esmond.*

He reached for his notebook and pen, and began to read.

NINETEEN

Statement by Mr Ralph West of Stilter House, regarding the disappearance of his son, Esmond. Statement taken by Sergeant Kiddimore.

I was in my study on the evening of the 20th when Mrs Hatfull, my cook, tapped at the door to ask if Master Esmond – that is, my son – was with me.

'Why no,' I said. 'He's in bed.' I was surprised at the question, for Esmond is always in bed by quarter past eight of an evening.

'That's just it, sir. He isn't. I went along of his room just now, and he's not there.'

'Bathroom,' I said, speaking a bit shortly, since one does not refer to that room more than is strictly necessary.

'He's not there either,' said Mrs Hatfull. 'And I've looked all over for him, and so has Dora, and there's not hide nor hair nor whisker.'

It was a quarter to nine. I was not actually worried, but I was slightly concerned, so I went up to the bedroom myself. It is not that I distrusted Mrs Hatfull, but I wanted to make sure. Esmond's room was in order, the sheets turned back as if he had been in bed, but had folded them down to get out. Beneath one window was the small desk he uses for the work set him by Mr Bundy, his tutor. I examined this in case Esmond had gone off somewhere and left a note. He is a good, biddable child, not given to wandering off, but it was possible he had read some tale of adventure and wanted to emulate it.

But there was nothing on the desk save his copy of Charles Kingsley's *The Water Babies*, which is his favourite book, some notes for a nature study essay, and several drawings similar to some he had done for Sir William Minching during a consultation last year. The drawings were all on what Sir William had called the same theme. A child seated at a piano, and the shadowy outline of a female framed in the French windows behind him. I had disliked the original drawings when Minching showed them to me, and I was sorry to see Esmond was still drawing in the same way, for they seemed to indicate a preoccupation with his dead mother. My wife was a gifted pianist and Esmond has her talent for music. She would play to him for hours on end and he loved listening. Sir William had propounded the rather fantastical notion

that Esmond was trying to reach his mother and that he
believed he could do so through music. I never paid this
theory much heed – children derive many over-imaginative
ideas from books. However, it may be a factor in his
disappearance, so I record it here for the police to use
as they think fit.

I and my two servants searched the house and the
gardens, but found no trace of my son. Accordingly, I
called the local police, and Sergeant Kiddimore and his
men made a further and very thorough search, helped by
several local people. No trace of Esmond has yet been
found, and he has now been missing for more than
twenty-four hours.

So Esmond really did vanish one dark and stormy night,
thought Michael, sitting back from the screen for a moment.
Nell, my love, it's looking as if you owe me that dinner at Il
Forno's.

But why had Esmond vanished? Was there any link to that
disturbing statement Esmond had made to Sir William
Minching? *The Eyes told me I must never speak . . .* How
much of that was a child's over-imaginative vision? Or was
it possible that Esmond really had seen his mother murdered,
and had been put out of the way before he could incriminate
someone? Was that someone Ralph? Had Ralph engineered
the search for his son, all the time knowing he could not be
found? But where had Esmond gone? And how?

Too many questions, thought Michael, and probably no
means of finding answers to them. He scrolled down to the
next statement.

**Statement made by Mrs Martha Hatfull, Cook and
Housekeeper at Stilter House, Gorsty Lane, Caudle
Moor.**
Statement taken by Sergeant Kiddimore.

I found that Master Esmond was missing just after
half past eight on Tuesday night, when I went along of
his room with his hot milk and biscuit, which he has
every night, generally reading one of his storybooks

while he eats and drinks it, although his father don't know about that, it being a little secret me and Master Esmond have, and me leaving a night light burning under a shade.

The master said most likely Master Esmond had wandered off thinking he was in one of his storybook adventures. So me and Dora went all over the house, then the master fetched the oil lamps so we could look in the gardens. Just as we was putting on our coats Mr Samuel Burlap came to the house, saying the master had asked him to do a job of work on one of the garden walls, and he had brought along his figuring. I answered the door, although it not being my job, but everything so topsy-turvy, and I said, 'Oh, Mr Burlap, there's trouble in the house and the master can't see you.'

But the master heard, and said Mr Burlap should come in, asking if he would help look for the boy, two pairs of eyes being better than one. So we all set off round the gardens with bullseye lamps and candles, calling out as we went. The worrying thing was that Master Esmond don't never speak, so even if was lying somewhere he couldn't call for help. But we shouted anyway.

The master was dreadfully upset, white and sick with worry, and him having lost his poor wife not two year since as I understand it, not that I knew the lady for I only come to work for Mr West after he lived in Caudle Moor. But a very gentle-faced lady she was if her photograph can be trusted, which the master keeps in the dining room.

We got back in the house just after ten o'clock, and the master sent for the police.

Statement by Mr Samuel Burlap, Builder of Caudle Moor.
Statement taken by Sergeant Kiddimore.

I am Samuel Burlap, master builder, and I called at Stilter House with some costings for Mr Ralph West on Tuesday evening, and was told of his son's disappearance. At once I volunteered to help with searching for the boy,

for Mr West was in an extremely anxious state. I was
very pleased to offer my help and Mr West was grateful.

I had seen Master Esmond West while the house was
being built, but only from a distance, for I had told Mr
West that a building site can be a dangerous place for a
child, and had asked him, very respectfully, to keep the
boy away while we were working. However, I was very
happy to offer my services with the search, although,
sadly, I had to tell Mr West and later Sergeant Kiddimore
that I had found no sign of Master Esmond anywhere.

Burlap again, thought Michael, leaning back and considering
the statement. He seems to find his way into every layer of
this story. He read all the statements again, because he had a
vague feeling of something slightly out of kilter. Then he
realized what it was. Martha Hatfull said Ralph West had asked
Burlap to help search, but Burlap stated he had volunteered
of his own accord. It was only a tiny thing, and probably it
was simply that Burlap wanted to appear in a favourable light.
I'm seeing nefarious deeds and hidden purposes where none
exist, thought Michael, and scrolled down to see if there were
any more statements.

There was only one, and that was by Sergeant Kiddimore.
It was dated one week after the report of Esmond's
disappearance, and simply said, 'Stilter House and grounds
searched by Caudle Moor constabulary and several local men
under my direction. All the lanes surrounding Stilter House
also searched, each one several times. Hedges and ditches
carefully inspected, and two duck ponds dragged.

Description and photograph of Esmond West sent to all
police stations in the county and all railway stations. This
description will be sent every two months and a request for a
new search made each time. The case to be kept open until
new information received.'

Several notes were added below this, by way of update. The
dates were at two-month intervals, confirming that the
description had again been sent, and that Caudle Moor and its
neighbouring villages had been searched each time. The last
of these updates was in 1904. After that there was nothing.

Was that because Esmond had turned up, or because the police had simply given up?

It was half past three. Half an hour to make one or two more searches before meeting Nell. What would be most useful? How about Esmond's mother? Had there been something wrong about her death? Might it be connected to Esmond's disappearance? In the papers found in the music stool, Ralph had said something about no one in Caudle Moor suspecting what was in Esmond's past. With that memory came another – that of Ralph writing how the solicitors had had difficulty in tracing the ownership of the land, but that a relative had eventually been found. Did that suggest Ralph had some knowledge of the Acton family? But even if so, was it relevant?

Michael went out to ask if it would be in order for him to access the Internet on the station's computer and received an eager assent.

'Thank you,' said Michael, and returned to the monitor.

He was fairly sure there were registrars' records which could be accessed, and even parish records. He had no idea what these sites were called, and for a moment he considered phoning Owen Bracegirdle, who always knew how to find things and track down old records. But Owen might be anywhere or involved in anything, so Michael, not very optimistically, tried typing in the name of Ralph West, and the words 'marriage'. Then he added import and export of china, which had been Ralph's profession, and Derby as a possible place. This brought forth what looked like several thousand results, but Michael managed to narrow things down, and to discard the more unlikely ones. After exploring some frustrating cul-de-sacs, more by luck than judgement he found a site for HM Registrar's Department, which took him to various marriages and where he could request searches within five-year periods. Ten minutes and several abortive attempts later, he found an entry whose wording seemed almost to leap from the screen and punch him.

'Ralph West, bachelor, importer and exporter of china and porcelain, married Julia Margaret Susskind, spinster, in the county of Derbyshire, 1888.'

Susskind, thought Michael. *Susskind.* He rummaged for his

notebook and the scribbled notes he had made earlier in The
Pheasant's attic. That name had been in the indictment, he
was sure of it. Yes, here it was.

'The Crown, for our lady the Queen, by the Grace of God,
presents and charges that the defendant, Isobel Mary Acton,
née Susskind, did kill and murder her husband.'

The corrupt judge had mentioned the name as well when
he bribed George Poulson. Michael made a further search in
his notes, turning pages, fielding several inserts that fell out,
wondering how other people seemed able to arrange their
research so neatly. Here it was, and he was right. 'All that
Susskind brood were willing,' the judge had said.

Michael closed the notebook thoughtfully. Susskind. It was
the same family. It had to be. Susskind wasn't a name you'd
trip across every day of the week, not in an English village
in the nineteenth century. It sounded foreign, in fact.

So. So Ralph's wife had been related to the alluring
murderess of Caudle Moor. It was a curious link to discover,
but, again, was it a relevant link? Had Julia Susskind, who
became Julia West, also been willing in the same way as
Isobel? Had she been killed by a jealous husband who had
caught her with a lover? I'm straying into the realms of fantasy,
thought Michael, impatiently. It's more likely that Julia was
a respectable Victorian matron, and after her death Ralph
simply wanted to come to a place where she had connections
– even though those connections might be somewhat unsavoury.
But Isobel had been acquitted. There was nothing unsavoury
about being wrongly accused and honourably exonerated. Or
had there been then? That had been a time when people's
outlooks and values had been vastly different.

None of this took Michael any nearer to finding out what
had happened to Esmond. He looked back at the screen where
the Registrar's website was still open, and typed in a search
request for a death entry for Esmond West, between the years
1901 and 1906.

There was nothing. Michael tried the next five years, then
the next, which took him up to the start of the Great War. He
tried again for the final years of it and the years following.
Again nothing.

It was possible that Esmond had lived to a ripe old age, and his death was recorded much later. But if that had been so, Emily West, that diligent chronicler and keeper of family records, would have mentioned it. Charlotte, too, would have known. Which lead to the inescapable conclusion that Esmond had vanished and his body had never been found.

Michael wrote down the details of Isobel and the Susskind connection and folded them firmly into his wallet so they would not become mixed up with the miscellany in the notebook. By now it was four o'clock, so he logged off, went out to thank the helpful constable, and set off back to The Pheasant.

Nell was glad that Beth was keen to return to Stilter House. As they drove down Gorsty Lane, Beth talked about the photograph they were going to take at the piano, exuberantly planning how they would do it.

'I'll sit ezzackerly as Dad sat, and it'll be the same photo, but with me instead of him. And we'll get a really cool silver frame for it.'

'We'll get bankrupted if we aren't careful,' said Nell, smiling. 'But we'll see if Mr Jessel has anything when we get home.'

'I thought I'd ask Sergeant Howe if I could take a photo of him as well,' said Beth. 'He said he'd be at the house this afternoon, and I don't expect he'll mind. Then I'll send it to Ellie. They don't have policemen like ours in Maryland, so it'd be really good.'

But when they reached the house there did not seem to be any sign of Sergeant Howe's reassuring figure. Nell hesitated, but the sergeant was most likely around somewhere. In any case, in the afternoon light Stilter House had emerged from its mysterious and haunted mood and come out into the sunshine like the sunken church in the fabled Island of Ys that was said to rise up from the sea on clear mornings. Even the gate, when Beth opened it, creaked in a friendly way that might almost be saying, *Welcome*. Brad, I can see why you liked it here, thought Nell, parking in front of the house. With the thought she had the sudden comforting sensation of someone quite close to her smiling approvingly. She waited, but nothing happened, and she thought if there were ghosts here they were only ghosts in her own mind.

Nor were there any ghosts in the music room. Sunlight poured in through the French windows, warming the dim old chintzes, and lending colour to the faded wallpaper. Nell suddenly liked the room enormously.

The piano was still open, and the tapestried stool where Michael had found Ralph West's notes was open as well. Nell closed the stool, and Beth handed over the camera, explaining that her mother should stand in a particular corner so as to get the French windows into shot.

'Over there,' said Beth, pointing.

'All right.' Nell obediently squashed into the corner Beth indicated. 'This angle takes in the corner of the fireplace – is that all right?'

'Could you take one with the fireplace and one without?'

'Only if I climb up to the ceiling or swarm up the curtains.'

'I don't s'pose you could do that, could you?'

'Not without bringing the whole ceiling down.'

'You're always making difficulties,' said Beth, grinning. 'Are you ready? I'm going to put my hand on the keys now.'

Nell took several shots with Beth in various poses. She was remarkably unselfconscious in front of the lens. 'The battery's flickering,' she said at last. 'But I think we've got some really good photos.'

'Double good.'

'Ready to set off back?' said Nell.

'Yes, only . . .' Beth got down from the stool and looked round the room. 'Could I go upstairs to look at those old books again? The ones with the schoolgirls who play lacrosse and stuff? Or did you pack them up?'

'I didn't pack them because we don't know yet if the aunts want to actually sell them,' said Nell. 'I just listed them all.'

'I'd really like to have another one to read tonight,' said Beth. 'If I'm extra careful could I take one?'

'I should think so. Let's get one, then we really will have to get back.' Nell did not say she wanted to be out of Stilter House before darkness started to fall. The afternoon sun was still pouring through the windows, but as they went upstairs she felt a flicker of unease. It was no more than a faint ruffle across her mind – like the first warning pinprick of a bad headache – but she was glad that it would only take a few minutes to get one of the books for Beth. Then they would leave Stilter House to the ghosts. Whoever those ghosts might be.

In the bedroom Beth seized eagerly on another Malory Towers book, looked at the first page with a smile, then stood for a moment studying the room.

'All right?' said Nell, softly.

'I was thinking about Dad being here. Sleeping in this room and using that desk.'

'So was I.' Nell reached for Beth's hand, and for a moment they stood together, not speaking. Then Nell said, briskly, 'We'll go back now, shall we?'

'Um, yes, OK.'

Nell glanced round the room as they left. Goodbye, Brad, she thought. If you're still here you aren't the Brad I knew, but you're the Brad I'd like to have known. The small boy with hair and eyes like Beth's, and that eager delight in life. Oh God, I do still miss you.

But these thoughts could not be allowed to take over, and alongside them was the deeply pleasing knowledge of Michael waiting for them. He might suggest again that they stayed for another night, and mention the possibility of The Pheasant's having a double bed. Nell thought she might even accept the suggestion this time. After the ghosts it was a very tempting idea.

They were halfway down the stairs when they heard the music.

TWENTY

The astonishing thing, to Nell, was that Beth was entirely unafraid. She said, happily, 'That'll be Esmond. He said he'd—' She broke off and looked guiltily at Nell. 'Can I go down to say goodbye and explain we're going home?

Esmond gets upset if people leave without saying goodbye.'
Before Nell could even think what to say, she was running
eagerly down the stairs and along the hall.

Esmond, thought Nell, and in the frozen moment before she
followed, she was realizing Beth had known all along that
Esmond would be here. She did not dare think how Beth had
known, but clearly it was why Beth had wanted to come back
– she wanted to say goodbye. Esmond gets upset if people
leave without saying goodbye, Beth had said. And twenty-five
years ago, in a letter to Esmond, Beth's father had written, *I
know you hate it when people go away without saying goodbye
. . .* But there was not time to worry about Beth's small,
understandable lie – Nell would sort that out later.

The music room door was half open, and the music was
still being played. But is it Esmond as Beth believed, thought
Nell? Or is it Anne-Marie who vowed never to leave this
house?

As she reached the hall she heard Beth's voice.

'I don't think it's any good you doing this over and over
again,' Beth was saying. 'Because I don't believe you should
try to – um – call back the dead. I wish I could call my Dad
back and I know Mum does, too, but I wouldn't try to do what
you're doing and she wouldn't, either.'

There was a pause, as if Beth might be listening. Then she
said, as if explaining something very simple, 'Well, because
once they're dead they belong in another place, like I belong
in Oxford now. They're not meant to come back.'

Pity washed over Nell, and she wanted to reach out to the
strange little creature who was so heartbreakingly like Beth,
and who was so clearly trying to call back his dead mother.
She wanted to wrap her arms around Esmond and keep him
safe. But he doesn't exist, said her mind frantically.

Beth was saying, quite briskly, that she did not know where
dead people went. 'Heaven or something, I think. But that
person who said you could bring your mum back through the
music was really bad. I'll bet it doesn't work, either. If it did,
everybody would do it, and there'd be dead people everywhere
and that would be gross. But listen, I'm going home soon, so
I came to say goodbye. And I thought before I go, what we'd

do, we'd play that duet. I'd really like that, only I'm not as good as you, so you mustn't get cross if I go wrong, OK?' She appeared to listen again. 'Well, because I haven't had as many lessons as you, and I've got school and homework and stuff so there isn't as much time to practise. But if we play it now, I'll practise it like mad when I get home, and I'll remember you every time I play it. That's a promise. And I know it's Chopin, but for me it'll always be called Esmond's Nocturne.'

There was the sound of a rustle and a faint creak. She's got onto the tapestry stool next to him, thought Nell. Oh God, I don't believe this is happening. It's a fantasy – she's made up a friend and she's pretending to talk to him. Maybe she found Brad's letter and she's built it on that. But there's the music, said her mind. Both of us heard the music when we were upstairs.

She thought Beth said something else but she did not catch it. Then the music started again, and cold fear swept over Nell because it was being played by two people – there could be no doubt about it. Two pairs of hands were playing this music – one assured and smooth, the other a bit stumbling and hesitant.

He's in there, thought Nell. Esmond is in there with Beth. They're side by side at the piano, playing that duet. And Esmond thinks it will call his dead mother back.

The horror and the unreality of it tightened around her, but this was Beth, her beloved and precious Beth, and moving quietly, Nell stepped into the doorway.

Strong sunshine slanted into the room, lighting up everything it touched, but leaving parts in shadow. Beth was in the light, her bright hair glinting, her small face absorbed. But the pouring radiance only lay across half of the piano, creating a division between her and the boy. Esmond was sitting next to Beth, but he was outside the shaft of light, and his outline was so insubstantial it might have been a tissue-paper cut-out or a reel of threadbare ciné film projected onto old glass. But it was possible to see that he and Beth were so alike they could have been brother and sister – twins, even. He's not real, thought Nell. Or is he?

There was no immediate threat to Beth, though, and Nell did not want to intrude or break the fragility of the moment, or signal to Beth that there might be anything alarming or sinister.

Even as these thoughts tumbled through her mind, the music stopped, and Esmond turned to smile at Beth. A deep pain wrenched at Nell, because it was Brad's smile. Esmond got down from the stool, and went towards the French windows. He paused, silhouetted against the gardens, and looked back at Beth. He made no gesture, but Beth responded as if obeying a command. She went towards him, and for a moment the two children were silhouetted in the doorway, then ran together into the gardens. In those seconds, the sun went in and the gardens tumbled down into mysterious, shadows. The ghosts were reclaiming Stilter House . . . And Esmond was taking Brad's daughter with him.

Nell ran across the room and out onto the moss steps beyond the windows, then paused, trying to see which way Beth and Esmond had gone. But the shrubbery was overgrown and her eyes were still slightly dazzled from the bright sunlight moments earlier. She thought there was a faint laugh from somewhere on the right, and she ran down the steps and through the deep grass with the thrusting weeds, calling to Beth as she went.

The laugh came again, light, brittle, like splintered glass, and Nell jerked round, listening, trying to see. She said, 'Beth?' but there was nothing. Had it been Beth she had heard? She went towards the sound and, as she came in sight of the ramshackle outbuildings, a figure darted across her vision. It was too tall for Beth, and the sight of it sent Nell's mind looping back to the night when the ravaged-faced woman had stalked them through the dripping gardens. Could it be the same woman? Oh God, did she want Beth? Was Esmond a decoy?

The figure paused at the far end of the outbuildings, as if scanning the gardens. Nell could see the two doors into the buildings and a black gaping oblong where a third door might once have been. She ran towards it, aware beneath her panic that she should get help – try to find Sergeant Howe, try to phone Michael. But if the woman had got Beth in that tumble-down place she could not waste a minute. And Esmond? How benevolent was Esmond?

She reached the outbuildings, took a deep breath, and went in. The dimness closed round her and she called to Beth again, but her voice only echoed mockingly and maddeningly. Beth could not be here – she would have called out. But what if she was injured – knocked out? Nell's eyes were adjusting to the darkness now, and she could see an inner door with a grille near the top. This was where Samuel Burlap had been that night; this was what he had seen. There were the bolts he had talked about, one halfway down, the other near the top. Nell glanced back at the garden, then pulled at the door. It was heavy, but it opened with a protesting screech of old hinges, and stale air gusted out.

'Beth? Are you in here? Are you all right? Is Esmond—'

There was a rush of movement behind her, and a pair of hard, bony hands pushed her with such force she fell forwards, into the fetid darkness. Before she could scramble to her feet, the door was slammed hard, and there was the sound of the thick bolts being drawn.

Nell threw herself against the door at once, beating on it with her fists, but aware that the bolts were holding firm. She shouted to be let out, but there was only the fractured laugh she had heard earlier, and then the impression of someone standing on the other side of the grille – someone who was in that outer room, and someone who might have been spun from the shadows and the dusky cobwebs, but who was sufficiently substantial to shut out most of the faint light that trickled in. Mad eyes, with no sanity or humanity in them, stared at her and Nell recoiled.

'Let me out!' shouted Nell, almost hysterical with panic for herself and for Beth to whom anything might be happening. But there was only the sound of the laugh again, this time with a thread of triumph in it. Then the outline vanished – was the figure now turning its attention to Beth? The panic spiralled up but Nell fought it, because panicking would not help Beth. With the vanishing of her captor, a few threads of light had trickled into the terrible room, and Nell inspected it as much as she could. A chair and a table, both clearly very old and both half rotten. Nothing else. And there was no way she could see of getting out of this room, other than through the bolted door. But someone would look for her – of course someone would. Michael would miss her and surely Stilter House would be the first place he would check. And Sergeant Howe was supposed to be around as well. Yes, she would be found sooner or later. But supposing it was later? Supposing it was too late for Beth?

She looked back at the door. The surface bore long gouges in the wood. Exactly as if someone had been imprisoned here and had tried to claw a way out. The gouges were deep and they covered a wide area of the door. As if the unknown prisoner had been shut in here for a very long time.

Michael was not exactly worried when Nell and Beth were not at The Pheasant, but he was slightly surprised. It was not like Nell to be late, and she and Beth had only been taking a look round the village.

He checked his phone for messages. There was one from the Director of Music at Oriel College, saying what a very positive, profitable meeting he thought they had had, and asking if Michael might be able to let him have some notes about the Romantic Poets and their influence on music fairly soon. For the last two days Michael had been so deep in Caudle's past and the story of Isobel Acton and Samuel Burlap, he had to think for a minute what the Director was talking about.

There was a second message, this time from his editor, saying they would like to bring forward the new Wilberforce book so as to have it in the shops in time for Christmas. With that in mind, could Michael send a fairly detailed synopsis so they could brief the illustrators? Michael began to feel somewhat beleaguered, and wondered if he could really manage to serve two masters – three if you counted Oriel College itself, which he should certainly do.

But there was nothing from Nell on the voicemail, so he sat down in The Pheasant's small oak-panelled snug, which overlooked the street, and drank a cup of tea, expecting to see her and Beth any minute. But by half past four there was still no sign of them, so Michael asked if they were in their room.

'No, and the key's still here,' said a youngish girl who was manning the bar-cum-reception. 'Is Mrs West's car outside?'

Michael had not thought of that. He checked and discovered the car was not there. This was puzzling but not very worrying. Nell might have gone anywhere and been delayed by traffic or by something mundane like a puncture. And the phone signal was so unreliable out here she might not have been able to phone. He tried her number but it went straight to voicemail. He went back inside and watched the clock crawl round to ten to five. By this time the puzzlement was giving way to something less comfortable. Might Nell have gone out to Stilter House? She had packed everything up this morning and put it in her car, but supposing she had forgotten something? He contemplated this possibility, and his mind turned up two separate, but equally sinister, facts. The first was Emily West saying she was uneasy for Nell, but especially for Beth. 'Because if Esmond is still there,' she had written, 'thwarted of Brad he may turn his attention to Brad's daughter.'

The second was Michael's own experience of seeing the unreal face looking through the grille in the tumbledown outbuildings, along with the certainty that someone had been standing close to him. He set down his tea cup and went back to the reception desk.

'I'm going out to Stilter House to see if Mrs West is there,' he said. 'Could you . . .' He stopped. It would be melodramatic in the extreme to say, 'If I'm not back in an hour send out a search party,' so he simply, said, 'Would you tell Mr Poulson where I've gone? I don't think I'll be long.' Poulson, knowing a little of what had been going on at that house, would surely be alerted if Michael or Nell were not back by around six.

Nell had no idea how much time had passed since the door was slammed. She had tried to break through it again, but had only succeeded in scraping what felt like half the skin off her hands. Was there any other means of escape? How about the ceiling, where it joined the walls? If there was a weakness anywhere it would be there. Could she knock through that? The ceiling was not high, but it was too high to reach from the ground so she dragged the chair across, but when she placed one foot on the seat, the rotten framework gave way and her foot went straight through. Nell swore, and turned her attention to the table. It would not matter if the thing collapsed under her, and it would not matter if she cut her hands to ribbons if it meant she got out and reached Beth.

The table was small and quite heavy, but Nell managed to drag it over to the wall, and pushed it against the timbers. So far so good. She was about to scramble onto it when she had the impression of slight movement near the door. She turned sharply, but there was nothing there, and she would have heard anyone unbolting the door. But there was something . . . Nell stood still, slow horror stealing over her.

Near the door something was moving. It was as if something was picking up the shadows and twisting them into an outline – as if long fleshless fingers were reaching down and gathering up the strings of darkness and decay to weave a human carapace.

There was a moment when the clotted shadows seemed to be fighting whatever was spinning them. Even the darkness doesn't like whatever this is, thought Nell, wildly. I'm not believing any of this – it's the light, it's some kind of disturbance of the dust because I've been stamping around . . .

But something was in here. Against the old door with its sinister nail marks something was struggling to take shape, using the darkness and the ancient cobwebs and the rotten spores clinging to the walls.

Nell snatched up a piece of the broken chair, which would at least provide a weapon, although this was absurd because when was a physical weapon ever any good against a ghost? Even if one believed in ghosts in the first place.

And then, like a bad connection finally sparking, or the pixels on a computer photograph clicking into place, the woman was there. The ravaged-faced creature of rain and darkness and ancient cobwebs. The woman who had stared through the windows of Stilter House, and who had stalked Nell and Beth through the dripping gardens, carrying with her a lump of twisted iron with spikes.

She was carrying it now. As Nell backed into the corner, ready to strike out with the piece of wood, the woman began slowly to walk towards her. Anne-Marie Acton, thought Nell, her emotions tumbling. Is that who this is? She swore never to leave until she had recalled Simeon. Can she really be still here, though? I really don't believe any of this.

The figure held up the piece of iron, and the vagrant memory that had nudged Nell's mind two nights earlier, finally fell into place. With sudden horrified understanding she knew what the brutal iron shape was.

TWENTY ONE

It was still light as Michael drove along the narrow lanes, but the sky was overcast and streaked with thin purple veins. It occurred to him that Caudle Moor had a remarkable talent for setting a scene.

He reached the house and with relief saw Nell's car. It looked fine – but it was possible it had refused to start and Nell and Beth had had to walk somewhere to get help. Or would they still be in the house? He went up to the front door first, and plied the knocker, willing Nell to appear. But she did not and Michael glared at the lock, which was a Yale, and therefore impossible to open from outside without the key.

He went around the side of the house. Here was the window that had been open last night – the window Nell and Beth had climbed through. It was shut now and all the other windows were shut. He tried the side kitchen door, which was locked. What about the French windows of the music room? He went around to the back of the house, and he had reached the moss steps when he heard the sound he had heard on his first visit. Soft, light piano music. Michael stood very still, the music jabbing little pinpricks of fear across his skin, then went forward. The French windows stood open and the faded curtains and thin gauzy stuff beneath them stirred slightly in the cool air. Michael took a deep breath, then went inside.

For a moment he thought he was seeing again the small shadowy figure from two nights ago – that it was the lost, long-ago Esmond who sat at the piano, rapt in the music. Then the figure looked up, and Beth said, 'Michael? Wow, you made me jump. I didn't know you were coming here. Is Mum with you?'

Speaking lightly so as not to alarm her, Michael said, 'I thought I might as well come out to the house. I haven't seen your mum yet. Is she around?'

Beth twisted round on the piano stool to look into the gardens with a faint air of puzzlement. 'Well, she was here,' she said. 'Only I whizzed into the garden and I thought she followed me, but then I saw she hadn't, so I came back in here to wait. I'm getting really good at this piece. Shall I play it for you? It's Chopin. It's called a Nocturne.'

'Let's find Mum first,' said Michael. 'Why did you whizz into the gardens?'

'Oh, because . . .' Beth stopped, guiltily. 'Um, well, actually, Esmond was here, and I went in the garden with him. I told you about Esmond, didn't I?'

'Yes, you emailed,' said Michael. 'Where did he go?'

'Home, I s'pose. I don't know where he lives, but I think it's quite near. I just went to the edge of the gardens with him. Down there,' said Beth, indicating vaguely through the windows. 'He doesn't like it if people don't say goodbye when they go away, so we played this duet as a kind of goodbye thing. Then we walked through the gardens, and he went and I came back here.'

'I see,' said Michael, concealing his unease. 'Listen, Beth, I'll find your mum, then we'll all go back to The Pheasant, yes?'

'OK. Shall I stay here while you get her?'

'Yes. Keep playing so I can hear you,' said Michael, thinking if he could hear Beth's unmistakable playing he would know she was all right.

He looked in all the ground-floor rooms, then, calling to Beth that he would check upstairs, went up to the bedrooms. He paused in the child's bedroom, looking around. On the old desk was a copy of *The Water Babies*. Esmond's book, thought

Michael. The book where Brad West left that letter. It had the carefully drawn jacket of its era, and inside were a number of the exquisite and faintly macabre illustrations the Victorians had thought suitable for children's stories. Michael hesitated, then thrust the book in his pocket and went up to check the attics, which were wrapped in their own brooding silence. Silence House, Ralph West had called this place. Silence from the Dutch word *stilte*. Because Esmond must be kept in silence.

The diligent piano playing was still going on when he got back downstairs, but Beth heard him and came out to the hall.

Michael said, 'Beth, can you show me where Esmond went? Just the general direction?'

'Of course I can.'

Beth led him confidently through the French windows and down the moss steps. And now, thought Michael, following her, she'll go to the outbuildings.

But Beth did not. She went through the shrubbery with the old trees dipping their branches to form a green shadowy tunnel – enough of them to just about warrant being called an orchard. In Esmond's day – probably in Brad's, as well – the apples would have scented the air, and in spring they would have frothed their blossom against the sky.

This looked like the edge of Stilter's land. There was a thick hedge and several sections of rather dilapidated brick wall, low enough to see fields beyond, and one or two houses in the distance.

'This is the way Esmond goes? Over the wall?' And then over the hills and far away, thought Michael. Or is it over hill, over dale, through bush through briar, through blood, through fire . . .? Why would I think about fire?

Because it burned in the end, that's why . . . Acton House burned to the ground and most of its secrets burned with it . . . But not all of the secrets, not all . . .

'Yes.' Beth looked across the fields, not quite puzzled, but with the tiniest of frowns, then back at Michael.

'Does he live in one of those houses over there?' Michael knew Esmond did not, but he was trying to find out how much Beth understood.

'I don't know.' She looked at him from the corners of her

eyes, and Michael thought: she knows there's something strange about Esmond, but she isn't letting her thoughts take a definite shape. Fair enough.

He said, 'Well, he's gone home now by the look of it. Let's find Mum.'

'I thought she was here.' For the first time there was a note of slight panic in Beth's voice.

Michael said, 'She's around somewhere. But let's look over there.' He took her hand and walked towards the old outbuildings.

Nell had backed away from the dreadful unreal creature as far as she could, but she could go no further. She was pressed up against the wall, holding up the splintered chair-leg, ready to hit out, but a whole new layer of fear and revulsion engulfed her when she visualized her hand and the wood sinking into that menacing spider-web of shadows, so bizarrely in the shape of a human form.

Her legs felt like cotton threads and she thought she might slide to the floor in a faint. But this made her so angry with herself that she yelled in fury at the approaching figure. It would do no good, and there would not be anyone to hear, but she yelled anyway.

Useless, of course. The figure was hovering over her and the stench of old, stale dirt, dank earth, and sapless human flesh gusted into her face. Nell felt a wave of sickness, then managed to lift the wood threateningly. But her fingers were so slippery with sweat it slithered from her grasp, and there was the glint of a smile from the creature in front of her. Before she could do anything else, the black iron shape was pushed into her face, and fingers – terrible hard bony fingers – were forcing themselves between her lips. There was the sensation of a cage closing around her jaw, then the sound and feel of a hinge snapping shut. A thick stave pressed her tongue down and there was the taste of iron and old blood. Dreadful. Unbearable. And the iron was constricting her mouth and her tongue so severely it was no longer possible to shout for help, even if there had been anyone to hear.

Somewhere beyond the spinning darkness, came the sound

of a door banging open. Light   rain smeared but wonderful, ordinary daylight – flooded into the room. Nell's assailant seemed to throw up her hands and cower back and Nell struggled to a standing position, clawing at the thing around her face. Through sweeping waves of relief, she was dimly aware of the outline shrivelling, as if the light was sucking it dry, causing it to dissolve in wizened strands.

Michael's voice said, 'Don't struggle, Nell – I'll do it.' There was the feel of his hands and the familiar scent of his skin against her face. The hinge snapped and the pressure of the iron stave withdrew. Nell gasped and half choked, but by taking several deep breaths managed not to be actually sick. Even so, it was several minutes before she could speak. 'Where is—?'

'There's no one here.'

'But—'

'It's all right,' he said. 'I don't know what it was, but I saw it as well. It's gone now.' He glanced over his shoulder and Nell saw a nearly formless pile of dirt and cobwebs on the ground. She shuddered, and said, 'Where's Beth? Is she all right?'

'She's outside. She's fine. She has no idea there's anything wrong. I said I'd check if you were in here, but I told her to wait under the trees because the buildings looked a bit unsafe. Stay here a minute.'

He crossed quickly to the door and Nell, whose legs still felt shaky and who could not have walked six steps to save her life, heard him say, 'Beth? Still there? Mum's here, and we're just negotiating some fallen brickwork.' There was a pause, then he said, 'Good girl. We won't be a minute. She's found some primroses,' he said, coming back. 'So she's picking some.'

'We need to play this down with her,' said Nell, who was starting to feel slightly better.

'We'll say the door banged shut and you yelled for help and I heard you.'

'I did yell,' said Nell. 'I didn't think anyone would hear, though. And then she – that woman – forced that thing over my face. And I knew once it was in place I wouldn't be able to yell at all.'

'What in God's name is it?' said Michael, looking at where the twisted piece of iron lay on the ground.

'It's what they call a brank,' said Nell. 'A scold's bridle. It was a medieval torture. The popular belief is that it was used for nagging wives. They'd fit it over someone's face and often parade them through the town, or leave them chained up in the stocks for two or three hours. There's a stave that forces down the tongue. You can't speak once that's in place.' The memory of those few minutes with the iron around her face and thrusting into her mouth washed over her, and she shivered again.

'You're safe now. It's all right.'

'I know. But Michael, I think someone was held prisoner here, and whoever it was, had that thing forced onto her – or his – face, so there wouldn't be any shouts for help.'

'Silence House,' said Michael, half to himself. Keeping his arm round her, he reached for the twisted metal. 'It's a vicious thing,' he said. 'That's the stave, isn't it? There's a spike halfway along.' He tested it cautiously with a fingertip and winced. 'My God, that's sharp.'

'I know. I felt it,' said Nell, in a half-whisper, and Michael held her hard against him.

'You might have been killed,' he said. 'Or maimed. I couldn't have borne it.'

'But I wasn't. I'm a survivor.' This time Nell managed a rather shaky smile. 'And I'm perfectly all right to walk now. Let's get out of this place. It's choking me. I don't mean just the dirt.'

'The despair,' said Michael, half to himself, thinking that later he would tell her how he, too, had been briefly trapped in here, and how, even in the outer room, he had experienced the thick suffocating loneliness and the helpless resignation. And the prisoner, said his mind. Don't forget that macabre glimpse of a face staring out through the bars – a face that had something wrong about it. I was seeing the brank, he thought. It had been clamped to her face.

To dispel this image, he said, 'We'll collect Beth and get back to sanity.'

'Are you leaving that – that thing there?' Nell looked at the brank which was still lying on the ground.

'I'm not taking it with me,' said Michael. 'I'll come back later and hammer it to smithereens, and bury the fragments. I've never seen such a thing before. Have you?'

'I've seen them in museums – when I was studying,' said Nell. 'But they were usually a bit better shaped than that. A bit more symmetrical. That looks as if someone cobbled it together in extreme haste.'

'Or,' said Michael, 'in extreme secrecy.' Then, seeing her expression, said, 'Let's head back to The Pheasant. Food, warmth, normality.'

'And a hot shower,' said Nell, summoning up a smile.

The hot shower was achieved immediately on reaching The Pheasant, but it was eight o'clock before Michael and Nell sat in the warm, reassuring dining room, Beth safely and contentedly in bed upstairs. Beth had no idea anything had been wrong. She had enjoyed going back to Stilter House where there had been no macabre figures tapping on the windows; she had met Esmond again and they had played the duet which she was going to practice when she got home, and they had taken some really cool photos of her at the piano, one of which would go alongside the one she had of her father. She ate an early supper, and went happily to bed to explore in more detail the hitherto-unknown world of the Malory Towers schoolgirls who played lacrosse and had midnight feasts.

Nell had showered, washed her hair, and scrubbed her teeth until there was probably no enamel left on them, but she still felt as if she would never be rid of the taste and the feel of the iron brank.

However, when she joined Michael in the small dining room, she thought a degree of normality was returning. The Pheasant's menu offered fresh salmon cooked *en croute*.

'Beautiful,' said Nell, eating hungrily. 'After this I'll feel ready to face the world again. Is there another glass of wine – thanks.'

The wine, which was a Chablis, was followed by two large brandies, which they drank with their coffee.

'What with wine and brandy and spooks,' said Michael,

leaning back in his chair, 'I suspect I'm slightly potted. But
I think I've reached a stage where I can cope with sorting out
that monstrous regiment of ghosts. How about you?'

'I'm slightly potted as well,' said Nell. 'But not so much I
can't stand shoulder to shoulder with you and confront the
spooks.'

'Whose existence you deny.'

'Yes, but I'm seeing things through a haze of Chablis, so
I'll go along with the premise for the moment.'

'Well, let's take the creature in the stone room for starters.'
Michael sat up a bit straighter. 'The one who seemed to attack
you? Can we assign an identity to her?'

'I think it was Anne-Marie Acton,' said Nell. 'Simeon's
sister. You haven't read all of Samuel Burlap's statements yet,
but there's a section where he describes seeing her when he
was a child, and she seemed to be – this sounds bizarre – but
she seemed to be trying to call Simeon back through the music.
She vowed she would never leave until she had reached him.'

'It's a preposterous belief, of course,' said Michael,
tentatively.

'Yes, but I think Anne-Marie was mad with grief and
consumed with bitterness and anger. And in that frame of
mind, one might latch onto anything that might provide a bit
of comfort,' said Nell, thoughtfully. 'Remember the reports of
a huge increase in spiritualism after the Great War? All those
poor women whose sons and husbands were killed flocked to
spiritualists and mediums in droves.'

'That's true. I've never heard of that music legend,' said
Michael, 'but it might have been some kind of local belief.
And there have been wilder notions throughout the centuries.
How does that explain Esmond's belief in the same thing,
though? Because that doctor who talked to him – William
Minching – seemed to think Esmond was trying to reach his
dead mother through music, as well. Could Esmond have seen
Anne-Marie or sensed her, and picked it up from her? I know
you don't believe any of this, but—'

'I might be just about prepared to make an exception when
it comes to Esmond,' said Nell. 'And from all the statements
– Burlap's and Ralph's and his servants – even though Acton

House had gone by Esmond's time, it sounds as if Anne Marie was still around.'

'Yes.' Michael thought for a moment, then said, 'You know, we still don't know what happened to Acton House.'

'Ralph wrote that it burned down.'

'So he did. I'd forgotten that. He said it was described in the Deeds as The Toft, and that "toft" meant ground where there was once a house, but it had decayed or burned.'

'Which begs the question—'

'Why and how did Acton House burn down?'

'Yes. But there's another question,' said Nell.

'What happened to Esmond?'

'Yes.'

'I looked for a death certificate on the web when I was at the police station,' said Michael. 'But I didn't find one. I might have missed it, or he might have died much later. Or the records might simply have been incomplete.'

Nell said, 'It's almost as if he was never in the world at all. That upsets me.' She reached for the small coffee pot left on their table and refilled her cup, then said, 'Violent death is a traditional motive for a haunting, isn't it?'

'Yes. Even people who don't believe in hauntings accept that one,' said Michael. 'You think Esmond might have died violently?'

'Don't you?'

'He seems to have vanished that night,' said Michael, recalling the police statements. 'The police archives describe searching for him at regular intervals for several years, but there was no record of him ever being found. He did exist though, Nell. Oh, in fact I picked up his copy of *The Water Babies* in that small bedroom.' He took the book from his pocket and gave it to her. 'I thought Beth might like it, if the aunts don't mind.'

'I'm sure they wouldn't. And I think Beth would like it very much.' Nell picked up the book, turning it over in her hands, and Michael watched her and thought: she's seeing it as a link to Brad, as well as to Esmond. Trying to strike a note of practicality, he said, 'It was very popular in its day, I think, although it probably wouldn't be very acceptable now. As far as I recall, it's got a lot of opinions and views that wouldn't be seen as politically correct nowadays.'

'It isn't a first edition,' said Nell, examining it carefully. 'So it won't be worth very much. And it isn't in particularly good condition – in fact it's slightly battered. I like that, though. I like thinking of Esmond reading and rereading it. Beth will, too.'

'The spine's split a bit,' said Michael.

'Yes. It looks as if someone tried to mend it – just there, can you see? In fact . . .'

'What is it?'

'Probably nothing. It's just that there's a wedge of something padding the spine.'

'Part of the binding?'

'I don't think so. The paper's a different texture.' With infinite delicacy, Nell eased the paper out of the book's spine, and unfolded it. There were three sheets, covered with careful writing, the paper badly creased and as brittle as spun glass, the ink faded.

'A child's writing,' said Michael, moving round the table to sit next to her so they could both see it.

'Yes.'

'Brad again?'

'No,' said Nell, staring down at the pages. 'No, it's well before Brad's time.' She looked up at him, her eyes dark with emotion. 'It's Esmond,' she said.

They took the pages up to Michael's room, and curled up on the narrow bed to read them.

'This is like old times,' said Michael, arranging an extra pillow against the headboard behind them. 'Remember Shropshire?'

'You're sounding like an extra from *Casablanca*,' said Nell, smiling.

'We'll always have Shropshire – no, it hasn't got quite the right ring, has it? Are you going to read this aloud or am I, or are we going to read it silently together?'

'Silently together, I think, don't you?'

'Because we'll each have a different perception of what he might have sounded like?'

'Something like that.'

The pages were headed: COMPOSITION BY ESMOND WEST, AGED 9, AT STILTER HOUSE, CAUDLE MOORE, DERBYSHIRE.

Beneath this were the words, MY FAMILY.

TWENTY TWO

MY FAMILY

Mr Bundy says people in schools have to write compositions about their families, so I am to do the same as my holiday task.

My family is my father who is called Ralph West. We live in a house with Mrs Hatfull the cook, and a parlourmaid. We have a lot of parlourmaids – not altogether, but one at a time, because most of them go away soon after they come, so we have to have a new one.

I don't have a mother because she died two years ago. Her name was Julia and my father says she was very beautiful and I must look at her photograph every day so I can always remember her. I do what he says, but even if I look at the photograph ten times a day, I don't really remember very much. The one thing I do remember is the day she died.

Michael and Nell looked at one another.

'The day she died,' said Nell, softly. 'Is this it? Are we going to find out what happened to Ralph's wife? Because if so—'

'You aren't sure whether you want to know.'

'Not if Ralph killed her, no. Because that would mean Brad – and Beth – have an ancestor who was a murderer.'

'I think you'll have to read it,' said Michael. 'Otherwise you'll constantly wonder. But Nell, darling, most people have a bad ancestor or two. If this was a story about a swashbuckling pirate in the 1700s, you'd probably even be enjoying it.'

'Swashbuckling pirates can be rather sexy,' said Nell.

'I'll buy a sword and a parrot tomorrow.'

'No need. You're sexy enough already.'

'Am I?' said Michael, astonished.

'It's my view that most of the female students in Oriel think so.'

'We'll go into that later,' said Michael, rather disconcerted. 'For the moment, concentrate on the wicked ancestor at Stilter House.'

> My father tells people my mother died after a short illness, but I know she was ill for a long time. She lay on a sofa in our house and had shawls and cushions and medicine, and everyone had to be quiet so as not to give her a headache.
>
> There was a silver tray in her room for all her pills, but the tray was kept behind a screen so no one could see it, because my mother said medicines were ugly. The screen was called tapestry, and it had lots of wool embroidery stuff, blue and green, in swirly patterns all over.
>
> I hated the screen. I had to visit mamma's room each evening after my supper and before grown-up dinner, which mamma and papa had in the dining room if mamma was well enough. Sometimes she had a tray. In mamma's room I had to sit on a chair and tell her about my day and my lessons.

Again Michael and Nell paused.

'The tapestry with the eyes,' said Nell. 'That's what Esmond drew for Minching.'

'Yes. He said the eyes told him he must never speak. So there was a tapestry,' said Michael.

'And there could have been someone hiding behind it the day Julia died.'

'Yes. And,' said Michael, thoughtfully, 'Esmond could apparently talk quite normally then. "I had to tell mamma about my day," he says.'

Mamma listened to what I told her, but she liked to talk
more about her pains, which were sometimes in her head
and sometimes in other places. Sometimes she had an
attack of the vapours. I don't know what vapours are,
but mamma often had them. I never knew what to say
when she talked about vapours and pains, so I used to
look at the tapestry and imagine I could see faces there,
and that there were people living inside the swirly blue
and green world. The person who made the tapestry had
not meant to put faces in, but I saw them anyway. There
was a man with a droopy moustache, and a lady with a
huge hat with birds on it, and a thin little man with
a long pointy nose like Jack Frost. Sometimes I found
new faces – new people. Mostly I liked them and I could
make up stories about how they had found their way to
the tapestry world, or how they had gone on an adventure
to get there because there was a legend about it being a
beautiful place to live.

One of the faces frightened me, though. It was where
there were two little slits – tears in the tapestry halfway
up – which were supposed to be mended, but never were.
They made slanting eyes, those slits, like you see in
drawings of the devil, and there was a curly bit of crimson
embroidery under them, which looked like a beard or the
top of a pitchfork. I thought it might really be the devil,
hiding inside the tapestry, peering out at the world. On
Sundays the vicar tells everyone about the devil being in
the world, and how he listens and watches in case he
hears somebody do something bad, which means he can
carry that person off to hell. You have to behave and be
good all the time so the devil can't catch you. If that's
true, the devil might have thought the tapestry world was
a very good place for him to hide and keep watch.

Mamma had a visitor the day she died. It seemed to
be a secret, because when I went to her room, as I was
opening the door there was a scuffly sound. Mamma did
not make scuffly sounds, so I knew someone must be
with her, but I went in anyway.

This is what I saw. I'm supposed never, never, to tell

about it, and I won't. But I want to write it down, even
though I shan't let Mr Bundy see what I've written. I
shall write another composition to show him, and I shall
hide this, and one day I might be brave enough to let
someone – someone grown-up – read it.

'Next page,' said Michael, turning over the fragile paper with
infinite care. Esmond had used both sides of each of the sheets.

'Something he saw in the room,' said Nell. 'Michael, was
it Ralph he saw? Ralph killing her? Was it Ralph who told
him he must never speak of it?'

'But Ralph took him to that doctor to see if the mutism
could be helped, remember?'

'Yes, but Ralph wrote about wanting to keep Esmond in
silence,' said Nell, reaching for the second page of Esmond's
composition.

The faces in the screen were not watching me when I
went into the room that day, not like they usually do.
They were watching mamma. And the screen was
wobbling as if somebody had just bumped into it. It
wouldn't be mamma, for mamma did not bump into
things, and she was lying on the sofa as she always did.
The screen was in a different place – nearer to the sofa
– as if being bumped had moved it a bit.

I sat down and asked how mamma was today, which
I always had to do, and mamma said she was a little tired
and perhaps I should go up to my room or into the garden
and come back later. I got up, but she leaned forward
and grasped my hand very tightly.

'Esmond,' said mamma, in a funny, harsh whisper.
'Esmond, find papa and tell him—'

Then she let go of my hand and her whole body jerked.
Her face twisted as if she had a really terrible pain, and
her back arched as if something had punched her from
behind. Her eyes went all stare-y and bulgy, and she fell
back against the cushions. Blood started to dribble out
of her mouth – it was dark blood, nearly black.

I said, 'Is it the pain, mamma?' but she just went on

staring at me, not speaking. I started to feel sick and my legs were so wobbly I didn't know if I could run to find papa.

The screen shivered, and mamma fell over to one side, and that was when I saw something was sticking out of her neck, just beneath where her hair was scooped up. A long narrow spear, like a huge splinter. Only this wasn't a bit of wood like you get from a tree or a rosebush; this was a thin steel needle and it glinted in the gaslight, coppery and crimson, exactly as you would imagine the devil's spear to glint. Blood came out all round it, soaking down into mamma's dress and into the silk cushions. It must be hurting her dreadfully. I leaned over and tried to pull it out, like you do with a splinter, but it was stuck in mamma's neck, and when I pulled harder more blood came out and went on my hands and the cuffs of my shirt.

That was when I saw that there really were eyes looking out through the devil's face in the screen – living, moving eyes that were watching me. It was the devil. He was watching me from inside the tapestry world.

And then – this is the bad bad part – the devil spoke. He had a horrid thick whispery voice, and he said, 'Esmond.' He knew my name. He knew who I was.

'Esmond,' said the whispery voice, 'you know who I am, don't you?'

'Yes,' I said. 'Yes, sir.' I had no idea what you called the devil, but sir was what you called grown-ups, so I thought that might be all right.

'Esmond, you must never speak of this – of what you have seen in this room. You must make a solemn promise. Never speak. If you do, something terrible will happen to you. You understand me, Esmond? Never speak or something terrible will happen.'

I said, 'Yes, sir, I promise.'

Then I ran out of the room, and papa was coming along the hall and I ran straight into him. I was shaking and sobbing, and he's a good, kind man, my papa for all he sometimes pretends to be so strict. He bent down and took my hands, and his hands were warm and comforting, but I still could not stop shaking. He said, 'Esmond? It's all right. I'm here. What is it? Is it mamma?'

Never speak . . . I nodded, and he kept hold of my hands and together we went into mamma's room.

Mamma was still lying where she had fallen, and she was still staring straight ahead. I stayed by the door while papa bent over her, hoping he would be able to pull the dreadful glinting splinter out of her neck and make her well again, but not daring to tell him it was there. The devil was no longer watching from the tapestry world, but he might still be able to see and hear. He would know if I spoke after I had made that promise not to.

I looked round the room, and I saw him dart past the big side window that looked over the gardens. He paused and stared straight at me, and put a finger to his lips. Never speak, Esmond . . . I nodded so he would know I meant to keep my promise.

Papa had seen the spear. He grasped it and pulled hard, and there was a terrible sucking sound, which made me feel sick again. As it came out, mamma seemed to become boneless and to collapse. There was more blood as well. Papa's shoulders shook as if he might be crying. I didn't know until then that grown-ups cry.

He stroked his hand over mamma's face and when he took it away mamma had closed her eyes as if she was only asleep. That was easier to look at than the staring eyes.

Papa said, very quietly, 'Julia, my poorest love.' Then he looked back at me, and he looked at my hands which had blood all over them, and he knelt down in front of me and put his hands on my shoulders and looked at me very seriously.

'Esmond,' he said. 'You must do exactly what I tell you and you will be perfectly safe. I will make sure that you are safe. You must never speak of this, not ever. Not if you live to be a hundred. Do you understand that?'

I managed to nod.

'Never speak,' said papa, in the same solemn serious voice. 'Never speak.

Nell was crying when Michael laid down the final page.

'Oh Michael,' she said, leaning into his shoulder, wanting the warmth and the comfort of him. 'That poor frightened little boy.'

'And all that imagination he had,' said Michael, pulling her against him. 'Seeing a world inside the tapestry, imagining people travelling there because it was a beautiful place.'

'It all fits,' said Nell. 'Ralph thought Esmond had killed Julia. Goodness knows what he thought Esmond's motive was – perhaps he thought Esmond was trying to help his mother's headaches in some way – but he was determined that Esmond wouldn't be punished for it. I suppose the authorities – doctor, police – would put it down to an unknown intruder.'

'And then he left his house in Derby and retired from his company, and brought Esmond to live in an out-of-the-way place to protect him.'

'Why did he pick Caudle, I wonder?' said Nell.

'Because he knew about it through his wife's family, I should think,' said Michael. 'The Susskinds, remember? I told you about the police reports. Isobel and Julia both had the same maiden name.'

'Yes, of course. So Ralph might have felt a connection to Caudle – as if it was a family place. He might even have thought the place brought him nearer to Julia.'

'It was more than just Caudle,' said Michael. 'He took considerable trouble to buy the actual land where Isobel Acton, *née* Susskind, had lived.'

'Yes, and it sounded as if he helped track down the owner of the land, as well. That could argue some family knowledge,' said Nell. 'She looked back at the pages. 'So Ralph told Esmond never to speak of his mother's death,' she said. 'And Esmond's frightened little mind interpreted that as never speaking at all. And coming minutes after the massive shock of seeing his mother die – and of hearing that other voice . . .'

'Who was that?' said Michael, his brows drawn down in a frown. 'For pity's sake, who was it hiding behind that grisly screen?'

'Julia West's murderer.'

'Yes, but who was it? And what actually killed Julia? Nell,

my dear love, don't cry, I know it's harrowing, but try to
remember it was a long time ago. Focus on the practicalities
if you can. The who and the how. Start with the how. That
spear thing – what could it have been?'

Nell had found a box of tissues and was mopping up her
tears, but she thought they might return if she dwelled too
much on Esmond West's fear and his heartbreaking obedience.
Never speak. But she forced herself to consider Michael's
words.

'It could have been something the murderer brought with
him.'

'That makes it premeditated,' said Michael. 'But it doesn't
sound like that, does it?'

'No. So it would have to be something already there.'

'What, though? What would have been in a lady's sitting-
room in those days? Knitting needle?'

'I shouldn't think it would be a knitting needle,' said Nell.
'I don't think someone in Julia West's stratum of society would
have knitted. She'd probably have embroidered or done crochet
work. Actually, there is tapestry crochet – I've seen it in
museums. That's a thought. It could have been a crochet hook
– one of the tapestry ones. They're a bit like a heavy-duty
darning needle.'

'That sounds a good bet,' said Michael. 'Let's say we've
got the method, then. That leaves us with the murderer's
identity. You're the delver into the past, far more than I am. I
suppose it's too much to expect you to turn up an undiscovered
journal again?'

'Much too much. Oh, wait, though.' Nell sat up abruptly.

'What?'

'That letter you found in the music stool at Stilter House.
The one Aunt Emily wrote to Charlotte. D'you remember what
it said?'

'Well, not all of it.'

'The gist was that Emily found Ralph's notes when she
borrowed the music score that had been Esmond's – originally
Isobel's.'

'And,' said Michael, slowly, 'when she sent everything back
to Charlotte, she said something about it being a good thing

for people to keep old family papers   she added something about historians owing a debt of gratitude to the likes of Samuel Pepys and the Pastons.'

'Then she said, "So I keep *all* old papers and letters, just in case".' Nell's eyes were shining. 'Michael, if anyone in the West family has any more old letters or notes about the past, it will be Emily.'

'You clever girl,' said Michael, and began to kiss her.

TWENTY THREE

E mily West was charmed to be invited to Oxford by Nell, and enchanted to meet Dr Flint who had collected her from the station and driven her to The Mitre, where Nell, the dear generous girl, had insisted on paying for a couple of nights' stay.

'Far too extravagant, my dear, but my word, what a beautiful place, and the staff all so helpful and courteous.'

'It's my pleasure,' said Nell, smiling at the small figure with its froth of grey hair and beaming snub-nosed face, and the scarlet jacket. Emily had explained she had worn the jacket so Dr Flint would be able to pick her out at the station. She had not, she said, wanted to risk getting overlooked in the crowds. Nell thought, but did not say, it was unlikely that Emily, with her air of finding such delight in everything, would ever be overlooked anywhere.

'And I know you offered to travel up to Aberdeen, Nell, but it's a very long journey, and you have your life here and your beautiful shop with all those lovely things.' Emily broke off to look with pleasure around the little sitting room of Quire Court, which Nell had furnished with several of her choicer pieces from stock. 'And I do enjoy travelling, you know, and meeting new people and seeing new places. Also, I've never been to Oxford before, isn't that a shameful admission?'

'I'll show you around properly tomorrow,' said Michael.

'Would you really, Dr Flint? Now that would be a great treat.'

'Only if you stop being so formal. Please call me Michael.'

'Well,' said Emily West, looking delighted, 'I do feel, you know, that if you've worked hard to achieve a doctorate you ought to be called by it as often as possible. But I'll manage Michael, on condition that I can be Emily.'

'It's a deal,' said Michael, smiling at her. 'Do you know, Emily, I wanted to meet you ever since I read your letters in Caudle.'

'Egg-nog Village,' said Beth, quietly, and Emily beamed at her.

'Now that's a very good name for it,' she said. 'We'll talk about that later, Beth. There have been some very interesting people who've lived there. And I'm glad to hear my letters made you want to meet me, Michael. Margery says they're nothing but rambles.'

'I like rambles,' said Michael. 'And yours are very vivid. Have you ever thought of trying your hand at fiction, Emily? A short story, perhaps? There's such energy in your writing.'

Emily became pink with pleasure. 'That's a great compliment from someone like you. As a matter of fact I met a very nice young man recently who has some kind of publishing interest – although I don't know quite what – and he said one can get stories published without all the fuss of sending them off to publishing companies and one only has to pay a very modest sum of money, and he offered to—'

'No!' said Nell and Michael in unison, and Emily looked surprised.

Michael said, 'Emily, when it comes to getting things published *they* pay *you*. Please remember that. But if you do decide to take a swing at a short story, let me read it first, and I'll advise you if I can.'

'He's good at helping people write things,' offered Beth. 'On account of writing about Wilberforce.'

'But Beth helps me to write about Wilberforce,' said Michael.

'Shall I meet Wilberforce? I'm very fond of cats.'

'Yes, certainly you can meet him. Would you like to have

afternoon tea in my rooms at Oriel? Wilberforce might not be very polite, though.'

'I would love that,' said Emily, at once. 'I don't care how impolite Wilberforce is.'

'Good. Beth, shall we make Aunt Emily a cup of tea before I drive her back to The Mitre?'

'Very nice,' said Emily approvingly to Nell, as the two of them went into the kitchen. 'Oh, very nice, my dear. Beautiful manners, and so good looking. English literature, did you say? The Romantic era in particular, I should think? Yes, I thought it must be, looking like that. I knew a young man – a long time ago – who studied poetry, in fact he even wrote some although it wasn't very good. He was very romantic, but he had great energy at certain times, if you follow my meaning, Nell dear.'

'Aunt Emily, you're a constant source of surprise,' said Nell, grinning.

'Am I? Nell, I'm so glad you and Beth came to no harm at Stilter House. I did worry about Esmond, you know. That's why I tried to contact you.'

'I'll tell you the whole story properly when we've got a couple of uninterrupted hours,' said Nell. 'But for now we're trying to find out what happened to Esmond, and that's why I phoned you. I thought you might have an odd letter or something that might provide a clue.'

'I've brought everything for you to look at, as I promised,' said Emily, happily. 'Charlotte had some work done on Stilter House some years ago, and she was all for throwing out all the old papers at the same time, but I said she would be destroying bits of history, and when she said she hadn't the room, I said, I had. So I took a couple of suitcases back to my house, stuffed with old letters and photographs and household books. They've been in a cupboard in the spare room ever since, and when you rang, all I had to do was tip them all into the carpet-bag. The man who cleans the drains helped me carry it to the taxi, and the taxi driver carried it to the train and a helpful person at the station leapt up and put it on the train by my seat. People are so kind.'

Nell thought that for Emily West there would always be

someone ready to be kind. It was to be hoped that not too
many people would kindly try to con her out of money.
Michael, who had come back in with the tray of tea, said, 'We
hoped you'd come out to dinner if you aren't too tired after
the journey.'

'I'd love to.'

'Do you like Italian food?' asked Nell.

'Last year I went to Florence and ate mountains of it,' said
Emily, happily.

'There's an Italian trattoria – family run – where they allow
children until nine,' said Michael. 'We could go there. After
nine the students tend to take over and it turns into a madhouse.
It won't be too bad tonight because it's end of term, but we'll
go fairly early if that's all right.'

'I once had a spaghetti-eating contest there,' confided Beth.
'I won.'

'It was a tomato-sauce nightmare,' said Michael 'They still
talk about it.'

'I'm having another contest when my friend Ellie comes to
stay from America,' said Beth, unrepentant.

After Emily had left and Beth had gone to her room to email
Ellie about Emily's visit and the possibility of a spaghetti
contest, Nell opened the carpet-bag with a sense of nervous
anticipation. It was half past four and she had two and a half
hours before Michael collected them for dinner at seven.

Would there be anything in these stored-away papers and
memories that would answer the remaining questions about
Stilter House and its ghosts? Would Julia West's murderer be
here? That sinister person who had hidden in Esmond's tapestry
world, and hissed that urgent command to him never to speak.

You never did speak, thought Nell, sadly. Esmond, I wish
I could reach out to you now. I wish I could put my arms
round you and reassure you, and make you shriek with glee
like Beth sometimes does. Her fingers brushed the neat bundles
of letters and old accounts in the bag, and for a moment she
felt – as she sometimes did with old furniture – the sensation
of other fingertips reaching out from the long-ago and touching
hers. She sat very still, but the moment passed. And anyway,

thought Nell, these particular ghosts are far away in Derbyshire, and I don't believe in ghosts.

Were there any ghosts in Emily's papers? It did not really matter if there were not; Emily would enjoy staying in Oxford and looking around Oriel College and maybe some of the others if there was time. They might take her on the river, too.

And, thought Nell, I can't delay opening up this carpet-bag any more. I'd better drag the past into the light, and see if there are any answers. There won't be, of course, but I'll have to satisfy myself that I've searched every avenue.

It took the best part of an hour to work through the miscellaneous jumble and sort wheat from chaff. There was a good deal of chaff, although most of it would be interesting to study at another date. There were household books and photographs; there were also receipts or accounts for goods purchased or services rendered, and handwritten recipes from a lavisher, cholesterol-unaware time when culinary directions began with such things as, 'Take a pint of thick cream and six eggs,' or, 'Lard the cutlets with fat pork.' There was also something called a Drunken Loaf, which apparently involved soaking hot bread with a bottle of red wine, then spreading it with 'as much cream as it will take.' Nell set this one aside for the medieval Christmas evening Quire Court was hoping to host.

And then, at the very bottom of the bag, she found a battered, but intact, cardboard folder, bearing the words, 'Caudle Moor Almshouses.'

Would this yield anything relevant? Hadn't there been something about Simeon Acton having a hand in building or endowing the almshouses? Nell reached for her notes. Yes, here it was.

Simeon Acton had built six almshouses in Caudle, for 'elderly people in the area who found themselves in difficult circumstances, or for people who had suffered hardship and were unable to work.' That fact had been taken from Samuel Burlap's notes, so it could reliably be regarded as primary source. And the tablet inset into the houses themselves had referred to 'the shelter, succour and sustenance of the old or the frail.' Nell thought this endowing arrangement was still in force in some English villages and towns, although in most cases, the Local Authority and assorted Social Services had taken over the responsibility, of course.

There was further evidence of a link between the Actons and the Wests in that Ralph West, keen to buy the land on which Acton House had stood, had seemed to know about a Nathaniel Acton who was Simeon's descendant, and had contacted him via the almshouses trust and its bank. The link was tenuous, but it was there.

Nell set her notes down, took a deep breath and opened the cardboard folder. The scent of old paper met her: the scent of old memories and forgotten loves and sadnesses and dreams and nightmares. The folder might contain the secret of Julia Acton's death or – what was far more likely – it would simply hold the unconsidered trifles of bureaucracy.

There was a modest wodge of papers in the folder, some typewritten, some handwritten, but on the top was a letter headed, *Caudle Moor Almshouses, Caudle Moor, Derbyshire. Matron and Chief Administrator: Miss C Pursefoot.*

It was dated 1940, and was addressed to Mr John West at Stilter House. Charlotte's father? Nell would ask Emily later, but the date seemed about right.

She smoothed Miss Pursefoot's letter out.

Dear Mr West

Since you are the last remaining Trustee of the Caudle Moor Almshouse Trust, I am sending you the surviving files pertaining to the Trust.

As you know, the Local Authority is to take over the administration of the almshouses next month, so we are in the process of packing away and generally removing all of the private files. It is a sad day for us to see the Trust dissolved, but times change, and we are hopeful that the new regime will be a good one and beneficial to our small community.

I think some of the past residents' papers may well be in the box; a number of them occupied their time writing about their lives in the village, and these could perhaps be of interest to those studying local history. If

Herr Hitler's Luftwaffe really do start dropping bombs on us, preserving fragments of Caudle Moor's heritage will probably be the last thing we will worry about. I do feel, though, that we should try to protect a few shreds of our history, so I am sending these random jottings to you for safe-keeping.

On behalf of my colleagues, may I express our sincere thanks for your help, support, and frequent financial generosity to the Almshouses Trust over the last few years. It is a matter for considerable regret that the Trust cannot continue, but in these days of rising financial costs and poor returns on investments, it is very understandable that people can no longer make the commitment that once they did.

Yours very truly,

C Pursefoot, Matron and Chief Administrator.

Written accounts of the past, thought Nell, trying to quell the surge of hope. Those dear souls who lived in the almshouses recorded their memories of Caudle Moor. People who lived there – people who could have known Ralph West – even Isobel Acton.

The first papers were merely exchanges of letters between the Almshouse Trust and the Local Authority and the Bank. There were smudgy carbon copies of letters sent, and sheafs of letters received. Nell ploughed on, going deeper into the past.

The 1930s – the Abdication, about which some of the residents had clearly felt strongly, one lady having written a very scathing account of it, and ending with the disgusted comment that Edward VIII 'could have married anyone.'

The 1920s – wonderful black-and-white photographs of people standing outside the almshouses, the younger women wearing tubular frocks with pleats and bobbed hair, the older ones possessing what Nell always thought of as the S-shaped silhouette of Edwardian ladies.

There was an inner envelope containing some handwritten lines of poetry – Nell glanced at these and saw they had been penned during the Great War. She placed this envelope carefully

on her desk, to study properly later, wondering whether the
unknown young man who had written them had come home.

Here were a few papers from the early 1900s, which might
be more fruitful. Letters which someone had deemed it worth
preserving – they seemed mostly to be an exchange of family
news, but remembering Emily's view on how Pepys and people
like the Pastons had handed down golden nuggets of domestic
history, Nell set these aside as well.

The next layer was a set of handwritten papers – rather
rounded writing, endearingly careful. At first Nell thought it
might be a child's writing, then she realized it was the writing
of an adult who was not very used to writing at all. Again, it
was probably nothing, but she would skim the first few
paragraphs.

The first paragraph said,

'I suppose I always knew my son was infatuated with Isobel
Acton.'

Nell blinked, read this sentence twice, glanced at the clock
and, seeing it was not yet six, took the papers over to the sofa,
and curled up against the cushions to read them.

> I suppose I always knew my son was infatuated with
> Isobel Acton. He wasn't alone, of course – plenty of men
> had felt the same. It was not so much that she was
> beautiful – although she was – it was that she had a
> quality that attracted men. In the privacy of these pages
> I'll admit that I would have welcomed a night with
> Madame Acton myself. But when I was whole and hale,
> there were quite a lot of ladies with whom I shared
> agreeable, if illicit, hours, so I'm not complaining.
>
> But my son's infatuation with Isobel was a different
> matter. I always felt it began when he was very young,
> for he was an impressionable boy. I did my best to guide
> him onto the right paths, but I was aware that my own
> reputation was at odds with any moral principles or rules
> I might want to instil in him. When you're known to
> have bedded most of the ladies in Caudle Moor and
> Caudle Magna – well, all right, Abbots Caudle and maybe
> Lower Caudle too – you aren't in any position to preach.

I left the preaching to the boy's mother, but I did my best. And until he was twelve years old I thought I had done a fair job.

That was when Isobel Acton was charged with the murder of her husband, Simeon, and my life was ruined.

We all knew Isobel was guilty, but the word was that the jury had been threatened or bribed to give a verdict of Not Guilty. None of those twelve men ever spoke of it, but there were some shamefaced expressions in the village for a long time after the trial.

Isobel went back to Acton House afterwards. 'Brazen as a church bell,' said the ladies of the village. They always liked to disapprove of her, although I'd have to say she gave them a good deal to disapprove of, and if the stories could be believed she'd had more men than you can shake a stick at. But then who am I to judge? Still, I'll always regret that she and I never had that night together.

For a time after the trial it seemed as if life might sink back into its normal pattern, which is to say it would return to being quiet and – let's be honest – a bit smug. The world hasn't really touched Caudle Moor, at least not so far. They say they'll be war with Germany in the next ten years, and it'll be the war to end all wars, and if that's so Caudle Moor might find itself shaken out of its placid complacency.

Nell sent another frantic look at the clock. Still only quarter past six. She would read as much of this as she could. It did not seem to be leading to any details about Esmond or Julia West's death, but if the writer progressed his story, it might do so later. She managed to resist the urge to flip forward to find his identity, and turned to the next page.

The ink was of a different colour now, so the writer must have made entries at irregular intervals. This might be useful or it might not.

But the next page began with words that made Nell's mind spring to attention.

'Today Mr Ralph West brought his boy, Esmond, to visit

us all, and the nightmare I had kept so deeply buried began
to claw its way back to the surface again.'

Esmond, thought Nell. *Esmond . . .*

TWENTY FOUR

Mr West used to visit the almshouses every two or three
months. Those of us living here knew he had taken on
some of old Simeon Acton's charity work. Philanthropy,
they call it, and we're supposed to be properly grateful,
although I never tugged a forelock to any man in my life,
and I'm not likely to do so now, never mind my affliction
or how well I've been looked after by the Acton Trust.
I have been looked after well, I'll admit that, but it's a
difficult thing for a proud man to accept this kind of
charity. When I was a boy we called it going on the
Parish, and it was as shameful then as it is now.
The Acton Trust and the almshouses aren't handed out
by the parish, but it's still charity as far as I'm concerned.
I hate it. *Hate* it. That's one of the reasons I make these
entries in my book. I reckon if I can pour out my anger
and bitterness onto paper, I shan't need to be angry or
bitter with the folk around me. I shan't need to rail against
the stupid rules that say almshouse folk have to be in
their houses by nine o'clock each night, for instance.
Nine o'clock! That's a harsh curfew for one used to
roaming around of an evening, without noticing the hour.
Still, my roaming days are behind me now. That's another
cause for anger and bitterness.

I wasn't bitter against Mr West, though. When he
visited I was polite. We all were. There'd be tea made
for him, properly set out in one of the parlours, for
we might have been poor, us almshouse folk, we might
have been brought low by ill-fortune or sickness, but we
knew the correct way to behave. We took it in turns to
offer him hospitality, and the matron always helped.

There'd be a fine old flurry of preparation, baking and suchlike, so you'd think it was royalty coming, instead of a man who bought and sold cups and saucers and bits of pottery from foreign parts.

Usually Mr West came on his own, but this afternoon he brought his boy with him. Esmond, his name is, and a nice-looking boy. He's what Dr Brodworthy calls a mute – not able to speak. But he's intelligent, you can see that from his eyes and the tilt of his head. I'd say there's not much that Master Esmond misses.

I took a bit of a fancy to him. The damaged attracting the damaged, people probably said if they noticed. But I never cared overmuch what people said, and I liked the way Esmond West didn't let his own affliction get in his way, just as I've tried not to let mine. I told him to sit by me and I talked to him about the village and the people. He listened, and nodded, and after a while he drew out a writing slate and chalk. He wrote, 'I like living here,' and I asked if he had lessons, and what he liked to do, trying to word the questions so it wouldn't make it too difficult for him to reply.

He wrote, 'I play my piano. I draw pictures.'

I said, 'I'd surely like to see those pictures,' and his little face lit up so much you'd have thought I'd promised him fifty pounds.

He wrote, 'If I come back I will bring them,' and I said that would be grand and I'd look forward to it.

Later, my wife said who did I think I was, inviting the son of Mr West to visit, and did I expect her to wait on him hand and foot. I said, peaceably, that I liked the child, and she could please herself about waiting, for I wasn't so maimed I couldn't make a pot of tea or pour a glass of milk for a child.

She said, 'He won't come, of course. Not to see the likes of us.'

I didn't think he would either, but we were both wrong, for one week later, Esmond, accompanied by a young man I had never seen, knocked at the door.

The young man introduced himself very politely as Mr

Bundy, Esmond's tutor. Esmond, he said, had asked if he could be brought to visit us again; he had promised to bring some of his drawings for me to see – this was right, was it? And was this a convenient time to call?

'Indeed it is right, and a very convenient time as well,' I said, pleased the boy had remembered and pleased that Mr Ralph West had consented.

'Then, if it suits, I'll come back for him in about an hour,' said Mr Bundy.

'That would suit very nicely. Come along in, Esmond.'

And if only I had known that with those words, the nightmare woke and flexed its bloodied talons.

He came several times, young Master Esmond. I liked seeing him. I liked telling him my memories of Caudle Moor and the work I had done here, and he seemed to find it all interesting. One day, I took him to see the forge. We walked well together, his small legs suiting my halting gait. I showed him everything and explained how it had all worked, and he nodded vigorously in the way he always did when he was interested. Then he wrote that he would make a drawing of it for me.

'That'd be very good,' I said. 'I'd put that on my mantelpiece – just over there, you see it? – for folk to see, and I'd tell them, "Master Esmond West drew that especially for me".'

I told my own son all about it when he came to visit.

'A clever young man, that Esmond,' I said. 'He could go very far if he works hard and keeps to his studies. They seem to have schooled him well before he came here.'

'Derby,' he said.

'Yes, that's right. I was forgetting you'd know. Sad for a boy to have lost his mother like that, isn't it?'

I remember thinking my son suddenly became very still, like a watchful animal that knows it's being hunted. When it's your own, you *know*.

Then he said, in a voice I'd never heard him use before, 'Does he talk about it? That's to say – does he write down anything about it?'

'No.'

'I don't think though,' he said, 'that you should let him come to see you again.'

'Why not? I like the boy. He likes coming here.'

'Nevertheless,' said Samuel, in a soft voice that sent an icy prickle across the back of my neck, 'I'd like you to stop.'

He was staring into the fire, and it might have been the firelight that reflected redly in his eyes . . . But I knew it was not. I knew I was seeing the madness I had seen in him all those years ago. When Isobel Acton was tried for the murder of her husband.

Samuel was twelve years old when Simeon Acton died, but he was not your usual twelve year old. Not how I ever thought a son of mine would be. I never understood him, not then and not now, although I hope I tried.

He used to come into the forge after school, or of a weekend – when his mother would let him, that is, for she was one who believed children should be given plenty to do, and she was always finding tasks and errands for Samuel. He'd have to help her if she was called up to Acton House to help with one of the house parties they had, or to Bondley Manor, old Sir Beecham's place for the shooting. Samuel always did what was asked of him and as far as I can remember he never had to be punished for anything. And that's a bit strange – you'll admit that, you who might one day read this. What child doesn't occasionally need a brisk smack on the bottom, or sending to bed without pudding after its supper?

But Samuel never did. I used to think back to my own childhood, and I'd hear tales of other children in the village who got into trouble and childhood scrapes – even that preaching old nuisance Edgar Gilfillan was caught stealing apples one autumn. So Samuel's goodness worried me. Children need to be naughty. They need to find out what the rules are and where the boundaries are. Young people need to rebel a bit. (Old ones too, but that's another story.) But Samuel never stepped over any boundaries or broke any rules.

He liked coming to the forge, though. He liked it when the forge was fired and the fierce heat would belch out in huge glowing waves. And he enjoyed watching the making or repairing of carriage wheels – the way I fired them, then cooled them, and hammered them into shape. And the forging of shoes for horses, of course. I let him try his hand at the simpler tasks and showed him how to work the bellows to control the forge's fires. He picked it all up wonderfully well. But I didn't want him to become a blacksmith.

Don't mistake that statement. The craft of the blacksmith is an ancient and honourable one. Blacksmiths are the only men who work with the four elemental substances: fire, earth, air and water. My father, who taught me my trade, told me the ancients believed those four things were put together to create the world. I used to remember that when I was working.

But it's a dying trade nowadays, and I believed Samuel, with his clever mind and his interest in houses, would do better in the building trade. I'd get him properly apprenticed, I thought. I had a little money laid by, and we'd manage it.

But in those days he was content to help me and I was content to let him do so.

Until, shortly after his twelfth birthday, the contentment ended.

Samuel had been almost bewitched by Isobel Acton. It's a strong word to use about a twelve-year-old boy, but that was what it was. And perhaps children are more open to bewitchment than adults. They're still fresh from God in their early years, still wrapped about in the celestial light and the dreams and stars. Still trailing clouds of glory, as the poem says. And if that sounds a strange, fanciful thing for a blacksmith to write, I'll add that since my affliction I've found time for reading and studying poetry and suchlike.

So I saw and accepted that Samuel was spellbound by the Acton woman – mostly by what he didn't say, rather than what he did. I saw that he listened to all the accounts of her trial, and I knew he sometimes hid himself and eavesdropped on conversations discussing it. I didn't like to see such a thing in my own son, and I tried to give his thoughts a different direction. But I believed he would grow out of it. We all become bewitched at various times in our lives – usually by a woman.

When the verdict of Not Guilty was given and Isobel returned to Acton House, I thought Samuel would return to normal. I didn't realize that the spell had turned inside out for him – that where once he had almost worshipped, he now hated. But he did. He hated Isobel for having feet of clay, he hated her for not being the beautiful sinless creature he had believed. He hated her because she was Jezebel of the Old Testament – a murderess and an adulteress. I almost wonder if, at that stage, he was entirely normal.

But I also believe he would have returned to normality if he had not fallen in with another who hated Isobel in the same way, and who, also, was no longer sane. Anne-Marie Acton.

Anne-Marie Acton came to Caudle Moor after Simeon died. She was a thin woman with a face that made you think she might have some hungry disease inside her, although that might have been the effects of grief. Rumour said she had a powerful affection for her brother.

Anne-Marie was convinced of Isobel's guilt, and when the verdict of Not Guilty was given, she vowed that if the law would not punish Isobel, she would do it herself. That's not repeating idle gossip. Miss Acton said this in full view of upwards of a dozen people, not once, but many times. Nehemiah Goodbody, who never missed a thing that happened in Caudle, said she went stravaging about the place like the wrath of God, but Nehemiah was always very strong about the wrath of God, especially since he had taken to repenting of his misspent youth, so nobody paid this much heed.

What was true, though, was that Anne-Marie took to prowling out to Acton House, and watching Isobel through its windows after dark. I know that to be true, for Eliza Stump, who had been housekeeper at Acton House for several years, told my wife. A lively, spirited girl, Miss Stump. Later, she married young George Poulson at The Pheasant, and it was generally thought it was Eliza who made The Pheasant so profitable. I suspect she led George a fine old dance at times, but he always looked well on it, and they had several sturdy children.

There was a change of ink and also of paper before the next entry. Nell checked the time again and thought she could probably just about finish reading the whole thing before scrambling into something suitable for dinner with Emily. If necessary she would phone Michael and ask him to put the reservation back for half an hour or so.

I finally come to that dreadful night in early autumn. I've spent some time making up my mind to write it all down, but it's festered inside me all these years, and perhaps setting it down will lance the boil.

I had been out that evening – it doesn't matter who I'd been with, but we had spent a very agreeable hour in her bedroom. I was walking back through the village around ten o'clock and everywhere was quiet, except for The Pheasant from which came sounds of laughter and modest revelry. Caudle doesn't indulge much in blatant revelry, but it does enjoy a modest glass or two of ale and a bit of a sing-song.

I wondered whether to look in on the taproom for half an hour, but I could hear they had started singing, *I'd choose to be a daisy if I could be a flower,* so I thought I wouldn't.

My way home took me past my forge, and I was just in sight of it when I saw, with alarm, that there were signs of activity inside. This was worrying, for I always locked up very carefully – apart from the valuable tools and equipment, the forge fire could stay hot for hours on end. My first thought was of burglars, but I thought it would be sensible to look through the windows to see what was happening before rampaging inside.

The windows of any forge get grimy with the smoke and the soot – my wife regularly takes hot water and turpentine to them, but they're as dirty as ever within a few days. So what I saw that night was smeared with a film of dirt. I suppose it distorted what I saw, because at first it seemed as if the window was a greasy, black-rimmed maw, through which I was seeing an Old Testament vision of hell. It was all there – the fiery furnace, *my* furnace – the clanging iron of the pitchforks, the moving to and fro of Satan's demons. And the squirming struggles of the damned . . .

The damned. She lay helpless across the anvil where I had hammered out countless horseshoes and numberless wheel spokes and dozens of various other things. Her arms had been stretched out and chains wound round her wrists then looped firmly into the thick staves behind her, where my tools were stacked in frames. Her ankles were tied tightly together by more chains. She did not shriek as the damned souls are said to, because a thick rag had been thrust into her mouth, but her eyes were bolting from her head, and the veins and muscles of her neck stood out like thick whipcords as she fought to spit out the gag.

Isobel Acton, chained and gagged, and at the mercy of the two people who hated her. Anne-Marie Acton. And my son, Samuel Burlap.

I was already tensing my muscles, ready to bound inside, but in the last moment I saw the madness glaring from Miss Acton's eyes, and I saw the same madness reflected in Samuel's. He was wearing the thick gauntlets I use for lifting heated pieces of iron from the fires, and in his hands he had a pair of tongs. Anne-Marie had a long hammer. Behind them the forge belched out its glowing heat, washing the old walls to crimson. When Anne-Marie moved, she trailed her shadow after her across the walls, dense black and grotesque. Samuel's shadow was smaller, more thickset, his hands huge and grotesque in the gauntlets. His eyes glinted crimson in the furnace's light.

I thought: they're just frightening Isobel. They won't do anything. I considered and rejected half a dozen courses of action in the space of as many heartbeats. My first instinct had been to run inside and put a stop to their macabre activities. But there was that madness, filling up the forge like a thick clotted fog. And they say the mad have the strength of three . . .

My second thought was to run for Sergeant Neale, but this was my son, and I defy any man to denounce his own child to the forces of law. Samuel might taunt Isobel and threaten her – and I would take him severely to task for that – but he would not cause her any actual harm. So I thought: I'll wait and I'll watch my chance. And if that sounds like the action of a coward, I can't help it, for coward I was when it came to facing two people with madness in their eyes and their souls.

Anne-Marie said something – I could not hear what – but Samuel nodded and reached for something that lay near the anvil, doing so cautiously as if fearing it might be hot. But it was not, and he smiled – a terrible smile – and held it up, nodding as if pleased. I couldn't see what it was from where I stood, but it was small, perhaps the span of a man's two clasped hands, and it was curved and hinged. With Anne-Marie's assistance, Samuel clamped it firmly over Isobel's face, and pulled the gag from her mouth. There was a moment when she let out a scream, but the scream was cut off at once. Her eyes widened in fresh terror, and as her two assailants stood back, I saw what they had done to her.

They had forced onto her mouth a brank. An iron muzzle with a curb that presses down the tongue. A vicious, brutal device of humiliation, it is, once used to silence nagging women or even women suspected of witchcraft. If Isobel Acton tried to speak, the spike would tear her tongue to shreds.

They pulled her off the anvil, and Anne-Marie opened

the door. Isobel's wrists were still bound with the chains and her ankles were free, but they looped some of the chain around her waist and pulled her across the floor, and out into the night. But still I hung back. I'm not proud of that, and you might say I was an arrant coward not to be able to face one skinny woman and a twelve-year-old boy. But I think anyone who had seen that glaring madness would have hesitated before approaching those two.

They did not go through the village square. Instead they led her around the side of the forge, across Pickering's Meadow and over the stile into Gorsty Lane. The image of a tethered beast being dragged to the slaughterhouse was impossible to avoid. I went after them, keeping to the shadows, watching for my chance to get Isobel away from them. I knew her for what she was and she sickened me, but what these two were doing to her was wrong by any reckoning.

As we went along Gorsty Lane, the trees dipped and sighed in the night wind. It was a chill, unreal sight to see those three figures. Anne-Marie and Samuel looked more or less ordinary, although Samuel still wore the huge smith's gauntlets and they gave him a deformed look. But far worse than that, was the woman they led. She looked like something from a nightmare. Her face, when she turned it from side to side, as if to escape the painful iron muzzle, looked like something from one of those children's storybooks. It looked like an animal – like a human whose face had been transformed into that of a half-beast. Once I thought she uttered a half-groan, and Anne-Marie thought so as well, for she turned sharply, and studied Isobel closely. But she appeared satisfied, and the grim little procession continued.

Acton House, when finally we reached it, was a dark shape against the night sky, and I remembered that all the servants had left after Isobel was arrested, and that since the trial she had lived there alone. A desolate place it looked, with the windows dark and the chimneys silent. A house needs light, warmth, people, or it dies. I had the curious feeling that Acton House had died – that all I was seeing was an empty shell.

I had expected them to go into the house, and I thought that would be my opportunity, but they took her around the side of the house and through the gardens. Those gardens were filled with rustlings and slitherings and the scuttlings of all the nocturnal creatures that inhabit any garden.

I didn't know Acton House, but my wife sometimes talked about a game larder where they'd pluck poultry or hang game for house parties, and I thought this was where they were taking Isobel. I was right; they went towards a small row of stone buildings, and opened the door of the furthest one. I edged nearer, but before I could step out from the concealment of the trees, Anne-Marie and Samuel came out by themselves, and walked across the grass. I heard Anne-Marie say, 'Food once a day. And she'll only have bread and water. It's all the bitch would get if she was thrown into Newgate.'

'Bread and water, yes.'

'We'll each have a key to the padlock. Nothing can go wrong.'

'How long will we leave her there?'

'Until I decide she's been properly punished.'

They were still talking as they went back to the house. Their voices died away on the night, but I had heard enough. I let them get out of sight and hearing, then I ran to the outbuildings, and dragged at the door of the far one. I saw at once it was indeed the game larder; there were marble-topped shelves and hooks driven into the walls and hanging from the low ceiling. It was larger than I expected, and set into the far wall was an inner door with a grille at the top, barred and covered with mesh. Isobel Acton, muzzled and helpless, was staring at me through that grille. Her eyes were wide and filled with terror, and even in the uncertain light I could see there was blood around the lower part of the brank, where she must have resisted it, and perhaps tried to speak against the spiked stave that held her tongue down.

I said, 'I'll get you out.' There were thick heavy bolts across the door, one near the top, one lower down. But as I reached up to the higher one, I saw the stout padlock holding the latch down.

They must have unchained her hands because her fingers were curled round the bars as if she was trying to tear them away, but each time she moved I heard the slither of a heavier chain, and although I could not see into the room I guessed they had left the chain around her leg, and secured it to the wall. Like an animal. If she had poisoned a dozen people she did not deserve this.

I must have torn half the skin from my hands trying to break that padlock, but in the end I had to admit defeat. The padlock was made of thick steel, and only a hammer and heavyweight pliers would snap it. And there was the chain inside to deal with as well.

'Listen,' I said, 'I can't break the padlock off. But I'll go back to my forge and get tools that will snap it open. It won't take me very long, and I promise I'll come straight back. Do you understand?'

She nodded, and I reached out my hand to her in a gesture that I think was meant to be one of reassurance. Her hand came up like a mirror repeating an image, and she nodded again. She trusted me.

I ran most of the way back to the forge, my mind racing ahead. I would need a strong hammer and the large pincers I used for fashioning cold iron. They had strong jaws that would snap through the steel padlock. I thought about this as I ran, because it kept at bay the knowledge of what my son – *my son* – had done and that memory of his eyes glinting with insanity.

Even through the windows I could see that the forge was still glowing, and when I turned the latch, the door was unlocked. That angered me at another level, for I had taught Samuel to be careful and never to leave the place unattended when it was hot. But once inside, the scents of hot iron and burning coals met me – they were familiar scents and they steadied me slightly. I crossed to the rack of tools against the wall, reaching for the deep leather apron, intending to put that on, the better for carrying the tools.

I was just reaching for the large hammer when I heard them come in. Samuel and Anne-Marie Acton. They stood in the doorway, and their furnace's glow washed over them, bringing back the earlier images of hell's caverns.

Anne-Marie said, 'You know what we've done, don't you? You saw us. You followed us.'

'You thought we didn't know you were there,' said Samuel, and there was a dreadful glee in his voice. 'But we knew.' He began to walk round the edges of the room, his face sly and calculating. I couldn't look at him. I turned to Anne-Marie.

'I don't care what you knew,' I said. 'You can't leave that woman there.'

'We can. We will.'

'No,' I said. 'I'm going back to free her.' I turned back to take down the hammer, and it was then that one of them shouted, '*No*.' The word sliced across the hot forge like a spear of lightning, and with it came the scent of burning metal.

Samuel ran towards me, and in the wild, hot light, he was a strange creature, a dwarf-demon scuttling across the fire-washed floor. He still wore the thick gauntlets and I saw that he carried a pair of long pincers, glowing with white-hot heat. In those confused moments I suddenly understood that while my attention was on Anne-Marie, Samuel had crept round to the open forge, and thrust the pincers into the heat. And the forge was still searingly hot . . .

'No!' he cried, again. 'You shan't free her! She's got to be punished.'

He ran straight at me, lunging with the pincers – lungeing low. Pain – screaming, burning agony – sliced through my leg and I stumbled back. There was a dreadful stench of burning on the air, but it was no longer burning iron, it was flesh, human flesh – my flesh that was burning and charring, and the pain was tearing me apart so viciously that I fell down into a sick unconsciousness and knew no more.

TWENTY FIVE

Nell laid this page of Jack Burlap's journal down, her mind filled with the nightmare images he had described. Samuel, she was thinking. That boy, that man who had wanted to build a beautiful house, and who saw images of fiery steeds, and flame-shod stallions in the forge when he was young. How dreadful. But how immeasurably sad.

Clipped behind this section of Jack's memoirs was another of the sheets of headed paper from the original almshouse trust.

CAUDLE MOOR ALMSHOUSES, CAUDLE MOOR, DERBYSHIRE
ADMISSION OF NEW RESIDENT

NAME: Jack Burlap
FORMER ADDRESS: The Forge, Caudle Moor
DATE OF BIRTH: Unknown. Resident, on being asked, said his age was no one's business but his own, and if being granted the residency of an almshouse meant he had to tell folk how old he was, he would go and live in a gypsy wagon and be damned to everyone.
[Matron's note: apologies here for reproducing the offensive language].
REASONS FOR GRANTING
RESIDENCY: Mr Burlap worked as village blacksmith for many years, making a good living for himself, his wife and his son. Following a tragic accident in the forge – sadly witnessed by his young son who had been helping him with some smithing work, Mr Burlap's leg was severely damaged. The injury was so severe that the lower part of the leg was later amputated, resulting in Mr Burlap no longer being able to pursue his trade. He therefore becomes entitled to assistance under the terms of the Acton Trust, viz. to wit, "for people who have suffered

hardship and are unable to work," and which was created
for "the shelter, succour and sustenance of the old or the
frail." No 4 Almshouse being presently unoccupied, this
cottage has been granted to Mr Burlap and his wife.
<u>*NEXT OF KIN:*</u>   Mrs Constance Burlap (wife). Master
Samuel Burlap (son), who cannot live at the almshouses
under the terms of the Trust, but who will reside with
the Gilfillan family for two years, after which, in
accordance with Mr and Mrs Burlap's wishes, will be
apprenticed to a firm of master builders in Ashbourne.

Anyone reading that Almshouse form will probably think
that was the end to my story – that I'd have no more to
tell, that I'd close these notes, and live out the rest of my
days in whatever peace I could find.

But there's a great deal more to write, and coming to
live in the almshouses wasn't the end at all. The real
nightmare was still to come.

They were very good to me in the infirmary where I
was taken after Samuel sliced the red-hot tongs into my
leg. They did what they could to ease the pain – I thought
afterwards, when I could think again, that they gave me
something laced with laudanum if not opium, for I
dreamed vivid dreams. Time ceased to exist – or to matter
– and I imagined myself travelling among the stars, and
exploring strange byways of the heavens.

(I make no apology for that flight of fancy, for if a
man cannot allow his imagination to slip the reins of
reality in such a circumstance, it's a sad thing.)

But there was a little piece of memory on the edge of
the pain and the dreams, depicting a woman's face
clamped inside a cage. A woman who had gripped the
bars of a small stone prison, and who could not cry out
for help. I tried to tell the doctors and nurses about her.
I struggled against the laudanum they gave me and against
the bone-wrenching pain, and I tried to say there was a
woman trapped.

'Acton House – you must send someone out there –
Acton House.'

But the hospital was some miles from Caudle Moor and I don't think they had even heard of Acton House. They thought I was seeing visions because of the laudanum, and that I was worried about someone being trapped in the forge. They said things like, 'Don't worry, you're perfectly safe. Your son came out of the forge with you, and he's at home being comforted by his mother.' The younger nurses said what a terrible thing for a young boy to witness, and told one another how Master Samuel had behaved very well indeed, running for help to the village police constable, shouting and sobbing that his father had dropped white-hot tongs on his leg. A son to be proud of, they said.

But for much of the time the pain swamped me. Somewhere at its height they told me they would have to remove the lower part of my leg. They used words like 'unhealed flesh', and 'tainted muscle.' They did not use the words putrefaction or gangrene, but ill as I was, I knew what had happened. When a portion of your own body stinks in your nostrils, you know it's rotting.

I'll just say the amputation took me to pain on a wholly new level. But I'll also say it was clean pain, if there can be such a thing. And they gave me a double, if not triple, dose of the laudanum and a gag to bite on. I didn't manage to float away from the dreadful infirmary room with its bone saws and knives and the leather straps at each corner of the table, but I managed to remember that the stars would still be there for me to travel to after it was over.

But although I came through those hours of agony, a different agony was waiting for me.

After the amputation they sent me home. 'Your wife will look after you,' said the doctors. 'A sensible woman, Mrs Burlap, and Dr Brodworthy will keep an eye on you.'

My wife had decreed that I should have our room to myself. I was still suffering considerable pain, and for us to have shared a bed – even a room – at that time would be intolerable for both of us. So Constance moved herself into Samuel's room and Samuel was sent to stay with the Gilfillans, Anne-Marie having left their house after the trial. Better for Samuel to be out of a house of sickness anyway, and we would pay the Gilfillans, of course. Everyone thought this a very sensible arrangement. The Gilfillans only charged a fraction of their normal lodging fee and were so puffed up with pride at being good Christians I should think they nearly exploded. Samuel went obediently enough, although I knew he disliked Edgar Gilfillan. But I thought, as much as I could think at all, that Samuel was glad not to have to face me and in truth I was glad not to face him.

Dr Brodworthy called the first day I was home, and I resolved to tell him what I had seen, and ask him to go along to Acton House, and see if Isobel was there. But Samuel foiled me. He came with the doctor, eager to help 'A very good son,' said Brodworthy as my wife and Samuel carried basins of hot water and towels up the stairs. He stood in the doorway while Brodworthy dressed the wound, and his eyes never left my face. When I started to ask about Acton House, Samuel crossed to the fire, which my wife had lit in the bedroom hearth, and picked up the coal tongs.

Brodworthy, seeing this, said approvingly, 'Mending the fire, boy? Very good indeed – your father needs to be kept warm.'

But I knew Samuel had no thought for the fire. He had deliberately picked up the tongs as a reminder. *Tell anyone what I did, and you'll suffer it again,* he might as well have said. And, helpless and weak as I was, I gave in. I merely said, 'What news is there of the village, Doctor? I've heard nothing all these weeks, and it'll take my mind off the pain to hear some gossip.' I glanced at Samuel, still standing by the grate, and risked asking about Isobel. 'What happened to Mrs Acton, for instance? Is she still at the house?'

Dr Brodworthy said, 'The word is that she left to travel. France and Italy, they say. No one's seen her for weeks. The house is shuttered and empty.'

I met Samuel's eyes again, and I knew – I *knew* without the smallest sliver of doubt that however much the house might be shuttered and empty, Isobel was not travelling anywhere. She was still locked away in that stone room.

I lay there that night, and tried to think what to do. I was not yet strong enough to even get out of my bed, never mind walk anywhere. The doctors had promised me a wooden peg leg when the wounds healed, but that was far in the future.

I kept seeing that imploring face staring through the grille, and those frightened trusting eyes. Isobel Acton had trusted me to go back to free her, and I had not done so.

It was after midnight when I was reaching the decision to call my wife and ask her to fetch Dr Brodworthy back. I wouldn't waste time telling my wife the story for she wouldn't believe me, but Brodworthy would. And I trusted him.

The old clock in St Mary's was striking one – I heard it clearly. Immediately after it I heard other sounds. Shouts and people running through the village street. Cries of, 'Fire! A fire at Acton House! Everyone to Gorsty Lane to help put it out!'

They all went out there, of course. All the village went, most to help form a chain, passing buckets of water, the rest to join in the excitement. My wife went, of course, telling me she would not stay long, but that her help might be needed.

Would the fire reach that grisly stone room? If it did, no one would regard a few ramshackle outbuildings as of particular concern. They would all be intent on saving the house and they would leave the outbuildings to burn. Were they burning now as I lay here? Was Isobel hammering to get out?

It was nearing dawn when my wife returned, full of how they had formed a chain and passed buckets of water along, but how the flames had such a hold of the house they had consumed almost all of it.

With her was Dr Brodworthy – kind, good old man –
who had brought several of the villagers home in his trap,
and was, he said, looking in to make sure the upset had
not disturbed me.

He listened to my heart and looked in my eyes and
did all the incomprehensible things doctors do. I was
trying to think how best to ask about the outbuildings,
when he said, 'Terrible thing tonight, Jack. We thought
the entire Acton place was empty, but when the men
managed to get through the rubble, they found a woman's
body.'

Then, seeing my expression, he said, soothingly, 'I
dare say she'd have suffocated from the smoke before
the fire actually reached her. Probably it was some vagrant
who was taking a night or two's shelter.'

After he had gone, I thought: the entire Acton place.
That must mean the outbuildings. Then it's over. That
poor woman is dead. I no longer need to dream about
her trapped there in the dark and the silence – that dreadful
silence created by the brank. It's at an end.

And yet somehow it was not at an end at all. Isobel
stalked my dreams every night. Sometimes she was a
scheming murderess, cold-hearted and merciless, offering
her husband the poisoned cup, but most of the time she
was a pitiful figure in the dark lonely silence of her
prison. Other nights she was a wild tormented thing,
choking on the stench of her own burning flesh, the brank
tearing her tongue to ribbons as she screamed through it
for help. I often woke believing I could hear her
screaming, but that was ridiculous, of course.

Three weeks later, Dr Brodworthy told me that by some
curious freak of fire or of wind, even though the whole
of Acton House had burned, the outbuildings, set apart
in the grounds, were unscathed.

'And we've identified that woman's body they found,'
he said. 'The police aren't making it generally known
yet, because they don't want to stir up local feeling all
over again. But I don't think there can be much doubt.

There was a gold locket around her neck with two pictures in it. The pictures were charred but the gold casing had protected them enough to tell who they were. Simeon and Anne-Marie Acton.' He straightened up from securing the fresh dressing around my leg.

'But that means—'

'It means the woman who burned to death that night was Anne-Marie Acton,' said Brodworthy.

I stared at him like the stupidest fool in Christendom, and all I could think was that Isobel must have been trapped inside that stone room and no one had known.

Nell laid the page down, her thoughts in a turmoil. So Samuel, that strange long-ago boy who had grown up to build Stilter House, had been the villain of the piece. And Anne-Marie, that tormented and yet tragic figure had burned to death.

But what about Isobel? What had happened to her?

There were three or four more pages left, but it was already a quarter to seven. She reached for the phone and dialled Michael's number. Hardly giving him time to answer, she said, 'Michael, I've found what I think is the end of the story, but I need another half an hour or so to reach the final details.'

She waited, willing him to understand, and was aware of a deep gratitude when he said, 'Of course. Would eight o'clock do? Or shall I just collect Emily and some food and bring it round? You can tell us what you've found while we eat.'

This suggestion was instantly appealing, but Nell hesitated. 'Emily was expecting to go out.'

'We can take her out tomorrow. She'll understand – she'll like being in at the finale, as well. We'll see you in an hour or so. Chinese or Indian? Or even Thai from that new place?'

Nell was still more than three-quarters inside the world of the nineteenth century and it took her a minute to realize what Michael meant. Then she said, 'Oh – Chinese if that's all right for Emily. I don't really mind.'

She replaced the receiver and, as she reached for the final pages, saw they were in a different-hand-writing.

I'm writing this because my father has forced me to. At my age it seems ridiculous that he can force me to do anything, but he says he wants everything set down, so there's a proper record of the truth. He says if I don't do that, he will tell the police what happened all those years ago – what I did to Isobel Acton.

I want to start by making it clear I did not murder Isobel Acton. That was Anne-Marie's fault. I can look back now and think that if Anne-Marie had never come to Caudle Moor, and if she had not talked to me after the trial, and if we had not discovered we shared a common hatred of Isobel – well, perhaps my life would have taken a different path.

Anne-Marie was not sane. I can see that now. I hated Isobel because she had spoiled my dream of a perfect sinless lady – I had wanted her to be like the ladies in the stories, threatened with death, rescued by knights and heroes – but she had turned out to be Jezebel in truth. Anne-Marie's hatred was different. She hated Isobel bitterly for killing Simeon, and that hatred and bitterness was so fierce it had eaten into her and devoured her sanity.

It was Anne-Marie who made the plan. How we'd imprison Isobel, stealing around the house and creeping into the music room as she played the piano.

'If we're quiet and careful she'll never hear us,' Anne-Marie said. 'Most evenings she leaves the French windows open while she's playing. We can go through the gardens and be inside that room before she realizes what's happening.'

And so that night, at exactly the hour Isobel always sat down at the piano, we stole through the gates of Acton House. This is meant to be a bald statement of fact, but I will say here that to creep through those shadowy gardens, knowing what we were about to do, sent spikes of pain and pleasure deep into my mind.

Isobel didn't hear us, so absorbed was she in her music. It was the music she had played the afternoon Simeon gasped out his life. I knew hardly anything about music

in those days and I don't know much more now, but I
knew that piece all right. I still hear it in my dreams,
even after all these years.

Anne-Marie half stunned Isobel using a large paperweight,
and then it was easy to tie a gag over her mouth and bundle
her in an old potato sack and carry her to my father's forge.
Halfway along Gorsty Lane she began to struggle, fighting
and clawing. (Feeling her body struggling against me to
get free is another of the secret memories.)

It was Anne-Marie, who worked out how we'd make
sure Isobel couldn't call for help from the stone room.
Perhaps that was prompted by the knowledge of my
father's trade. I don't know about that. I do know I
fashioned the muzzle in the forge, and at the time I was
proud of my skill.

'And I'll stay at Acton House,' said Anne-Marie. 'No
one will know, and I'll take food to her. Bread and water
– that's all she'd get if she were thrown into Newgate.'

We judged the length of the chain round Isobel's ankle
so that once in the stone room, she could reach the grille,
but that if the door was unbolted and opened she couldn't
reach its edge. So it was not in the least dangerous to
open the door a few inches and unfasten the brank for
long enough to allow her to eat and drink. Anne-Marie
said she would always feed Isobel at night, so that if she
shouted for help, no one would be around to hear. There
were no houses nearby anyway. Several times I wondered
how long Anne-Marie meant the imprisonment to go on,
but I never asked her and she never told me. I truly
believed she meant it to be a few days at the most.

I couldn't help with guarding Isobel or taking food to
her, because by then I was living with Edgar Gilfillan's
family. It meant my days were tightly ruled and it was
known where I was all the time. I had to walk to and
from school with Edgar himself. But occasionally, after
everyone was in bed, I'd creep out of the house. I had
my own room and they were all sound sleepers, and they
never heard me. I'd slip through the lanes and go in the
gates of Acton House, stealthy and furtive, afraid to be

seen, yet strung up with excitement. I'd creep through the gardens and stand outside the row of outbuildings, knowing Isobel was in there. On those nights I could hear Anne-Marie's music from the house – she'd play Isobel's piano for hours and there'd be the flicker of the candles she set near the open windows. 'Lighting the way back for Simeon,' she called it. In some ways she was very clever, but in others she was stupid – so stupid she actually believed she could call Simeon back. Several of us children had seen her doing that after Isobel was arrested; we stole out to the house, hoping to see ghosts, and we saw Anne-Marie in the music room.

I don't think anyone knew Anne-Marie was in the house. After the trial she spread a story about Isobel travelling in France, and she wanted everyone to think Acton House was closed up. 'But,' she said to me, 'if anyone hears music or sees candlelight – and if a little legend grows up that the house is haunted as a result, that's all to the good.'

'Because really, you're the ghost,' I said.

She liked that. Her eyes glowed with sudden life. She said, 'Yes, I am. I'll never leave while that bitch is there to be guarded.' The real madness came into her eyes then, the look that frightened me. 'And I'll never leave until I have Simeon back,' she said.

'Through the music?' I said it tentatively, because I was still unsure about that.

But she said eagerly, 'Yes, through the music. It's a very ancient belief, but it works.' Her eyes were suddenly strange as if her sight had blurred, as if she was seeing something I couldn't. Then, as if she had forgotten I was there – as if she was talking to someone else – she said, 'I won't rest until I've made it work. I promise I won't.'

It was Anne-Marie's music that caused the fire. There was one of those spiteful little winds that whip at tree branches and – if the windows of a house are open – snatch at curtains. The wind would have snatched at the long curtains in the music room that night, and blown them into the candle flames, and Acton House was an old house, its timbers dry and vulnerable. It went up like matchwood and by the time dawn was breaking most of the house was gone.

For a long time – several weeks – I thought the body found in the ruins of Acton House was Isobel's. It made me feel safe, because even if my father told what he had seen us do, there was nothing to prove his words. There was nothing to suggest to anyone that I had played any part in Isobel's death. People were slightly surprised to hear she had still been in the house, not travelling abroad as Anne-Marie had said, but no one thought her death was anything other than an accident. I never really thought my father would say anything, but to make sure I occasionally reminded him that what had been done to him once could be done again. I never let him forget that he was a helpless cripple. I didn't much like doing it, but I had to be sure he wouldn't talk.

It didn't occur to me that Anne-Marie wouldn't have escaped; that she wouldn't have had sufficient warning to get out. And I thought that with Isobel dead, Anne-Marie would have gone back to her own home.

By the time it became known that the body had been identified as Anne-Marie's, it was too late to help Isobel. She would be dead of starvation, of thirst, or both. I thought about it for a long time, and I had nightmares about it. I *saw* her, you see, trying to escape, beating her hands on the bars of her prison, unable to cry out because of the muzzle . . . I tried to push it all deep down in my mind, and cover it with a slab of darkness. But I knew I could not cover it up for ever. And I could not risk the body being found.

So on the next moonless night, I crept out of the Gilfillans' house once again, and went along the lanes. The gates of Acton House were fire-scarred, but they were still in place, although the police had padlocked them to keep people out. Not many people went along Gorsty Lane, but those who did scurried past the house, keeping their heads down and their eyes away from the

gates. The legend that had started with the murder of
Simeon had taken root.

I had brought a spade, a shovel, and a mallet hammer
with me, and also a small bullseye lantern. I slung the
lantern around my neck and threw the other things over
the gates. Then I climbed over and ran through the
gardens, treading carefully through the rubble from the
fire. The smoke-stench still clung everywhere.

The outbuildings were sunk in their own darkness, but
my hand found the latch of the game larder without
hesitation and I stepped inside. The smell of the fire was
in here as well, and thick cobwebs brushed my face. The
black memories swamped me, and for a moment I thought
I would not be able to do what I had come for. But I
could not waver now, and what I had to do would take
a couple of hours at the most, and then there would be
nothing to damn me.

I lit the lantern and set it on the floor. Dust-motes
swirled in the yellow light, and the layered cobwebs, like
old, grey lace, moved gently. I stared at the inner door
with its bolts and padlock, and I think even then I was
believing she might still be alive, that I might hear her
tapping on the other side of the door. But there was
nothing, and I finally managed to draw back the bolts,
and knock the padlock off with the hammer.

When I pushed the inner door there was resistance
and my heart lurched. But I pushed harder and something
scraped across the floor. Then the door was open and the
stench of decay – sickeningly sweet – gusted out at me.
It was like being hit in the face, and I gasped and recoiled,
one hand over my mouth. For a moment I thought I
would not be able to go on, but presently the air cleared
a little and I stepped inside.

The light fell across the stones, and I saw she had
been lying in a huddle against the door – that was what
had prevented it from opening smoothly. There were
scratches on the inside of the door, long nail gouges in
the wood where she must have tried to claw her way out.
Her face was still covered by the iron muzzle, but it was

upturned as if she had tried to catch any threads of light that might penetrate the darkness. Her eyes were fixed and staring in the last terrible stare of the dead, and one hand was stretched upwards, the nails torn, the fingertips bloodied.

In truth, I had expected to find nothing but a heap of dried-out bones – I could have coped with that – but there had not been enough time for the flesh to dry and shrivel on Isobel Acton's bones. The image of a piece of rotting fruit was impossible to avoid – her skin was discoloured and parts of the flesh had the appearance of wet bruises. Her hair was like black straw, speckled with grey dust and woven with spiders' webs. I looked down at her and I thought: so you've come to this, Jezebel.

Somehow I picked her up and somehow I detached my mind from the dreadful feel of that pulpy flesh. I carried her to the furthest part of the gardens – where the Acton land crosses into common meadowland, and where no one was likely to find her. I dug as deep as I could in the soft damp earth, and I tumbled the body in. Then I covered over what had once been my perfect sinless lady.

In the years that followed, I'd sometimes stand outside those gates – rusting and tarnished with the years – and think one day I'd re-create the beautiful house that had stood there. I liked thinking that. It helped me ignore that dark blood-tainted undertow – that memory of what lay inside those gates.

My father has said he will keep this statement locked away. He calls it a confession, which is a word that smacks of prison cells and judges with black caps, and a bell tolling the hour of eight.

What he does not understand is that if he hadn't meddled – if he hadn't tried to stop us – he would never have lost part of his leg. He would not have had to give up the forge and live in the almshouses. And I would not have been parcelled out to stay with Edgar Gilfillan's family in that cold house where everyone prayed all day, and the rooms were cold because all kinds of suffering purified the soul. If I hadn't been there, on the other side of Caudle Moor, I would have known about the fire that same night and I might have been able to get Isobel out of the stone room. Isobel . . .

I never really believed my father would denounce me. Arrogance, you'll say. Perhaps it might be better to call it hubris – a word I learned while I lived with Edgar Gilfillan's family. Hubris, meaning excessive pride, usually ending in downfall. But in the years immediately after my father lost his leg he was too sunk in his own misery to think much about me. He was too taken up with the loss of his work and the shame – as he saw it – of having to live in an almshouse. The once-cheerful blacksmith who had pursued a number of liaisons with local ladies (oh yes, I knew all about those) became a near-recluse.

Even so, as the years wheeled by I watched him carefully. I always knew I would deal with him if the need arose. There are things that can happen to a man with such a severe disablement . . . Things that can be made to look like an accident . . . He knew that, and I think he was always a little afraid of me. As the years slipped by he said nothing, and I believed myself safe.

And then a man called Ralph West, an importer of china and porcelain, commissioned me to build an extension to his works in Derby.

TWENTY SIX

The job for Mr West in Derby was a good one. A whole new wing to be added to his increasingly prosperous manufactory. He haggled a bit over the price, but most people do that and in the end we reached an amicable compromise.

I asked him if he would be so kind as to tell me why he had approached me; Caudle Moor is some considerable way from Derby after all.

'A colleague recommended you,' West said. 'Along with one or two other names. But when I saw where you lived – well, my wife has a slight connection with the place. Some of her family lived there many years ago. It seemed a happy augury.'

'Family?' I said. 'May I ask the name? Would I know them?'

'My wife was a Miss Susskind before we married,' he said. 'And a generation or so back, a Susskind married a man called Acton. My wife didn't know them, but she knew they lived in Caudle Moor.'

It was as if one of those skyrockets had exploded inside my head. Bright, hurting lights showered over my mind, lighting the dark shameful memories to dreadful brilliance. But I managed to think: he doesn't know. He doesn't know about Isobel or what she did, or anything that happened at Acton House. It's just far enough back for him not to know, and it sounds as if the family link is thin enough for him not to have heard the stories.

As if in reply, Ralph West said, 'I've recently been told there's a piece of land in Caudle Moor that the Acton family owned. It's sentimental nonsense, of course, but I have it mind to see about buying that piece of land some day. Of building a house on it, so my wife can live in the place where one of her ancestors lived. Her health is poor, you see, and I think it might do her good.'

I murmured something suitable, but I scarcely heard him. The images of Isobel had reared up out of the darkness to taunt me again, and as I prepared for the journey to Derby the knowledge that I was going to meet Ralph West's wife, this lady who was related to Isobel, set my mind and my body on fire.

And so now I come, finally and at last, to Julia West. Julia.

She was not Isobel, of course, but there was a strong family resemblance. The first time I saw her – she came to Mr West's office for some reason – the years looped back and I was twelve years old again, staring at the lady whose name blurred into Jezebel and whose voice was like velvet or moonlight or rose petals at midnight.

Julia West was a semi-invalid, seemingly. People said it was a shame for Mr West to have such a frail wife, and what a pity for their son that his mamma must needs spend most of her days lying on a sofa.

But for all her languid ways and her fragility, Julia West was as much a temptress as Isobel had been. And not all her days were spent on a sofa. She drove out to the works twice while I was there, inspecting the progress, nodding and smiling as if she were Royalty.

I knew at once that she was trying her lures on me. How interesting to see what I was doing, she would say . . . How wonderful the new extension would make her husband's factory and how clever of me to know how to build it . . . Oh, I knew she was spinning her silken spider's web, but I was no longer twelve years old, and this time I would respond, I would let myself be snared . . .

I waited until an hour of the afternoon when Ralph West was likely to be out and the child at his lessons. I went to my digs first and washed thoroughly and put on clean clothes. I combed my hair neatly and trimmed my fingernails. Every nerve in my body was strung out with anticipation, for I knew – I *knew* – that Julia West would welcome me with that intimate smile and that purring-voiced seduction. It would be smooth and sensuous and there would be a soft bed and silken sheets . . . If not this afternoon, then on some future afternoon. I had been married for fifteen years and my wife was – is – a good and worthy woman. But she was never a provider of the kind of bliss I knew I would experience with Isobel — Isobel? Why did I write that? I mean, of course, with Julia.

I went to the house – a fine house on the outskirts of Derby, but then women like Julia and Isobel always find wealthy men to marry, men who can keep them in pampered comfort.

I was announced by a maid – I had forgotten there would be servants – and taken to a long room at the back of the house. There were double French windows opening onto a flower garden, and a piano, and embroidered screens standing around. Useless things but you often see them in a lady's room. Isobel had had them all those years ago.

Julia lay on a velvet sofa. She wore a pale green gown, and in her hands was a piece of embroidery – what they call crochet, I believe. Soft, light cloth and thin fluffy wool, and long pointed needles for the crafting.

She did not get up. She looked at me with a tiny frown, and said, 'Mr – Mr Burlap? Forgive me, I don't think . . .'

Her words – her tone – struck against my mind like bruises and white hurting lights jabbed at my brain. I thought: she doesn't remember who I am. She's forgotten that she ever even met me.

But I gave her the benefit of the doubt. I sat opposite to her, but I leaned forward and took her hand in mine. Soft, silken little paws she had. But she pulled them free, and sat up a little straighter.

'Mr Burlap, I think you had better leave.'

I snatched her hand again, but perhaps I was clumsy, for she said, with real anger, 'Mr Burlap, this is intolerable. Please leave at once. If you had any thought of—'

I said, 'But didn't you have some thought of . . . Weren't you suggesting this all those times you came to watch my work?'

'How can you think that!' she said, and her voice was no longer the die-away tone of an invalid. Colour flooded her cheeks. 'How can you think I would be interested . . . in that way . . . in a . . . a *workman!* A country bumpkin – a yokel.'

She stared at me, her eyes furious. And the lights stopped being pinpricks and became huge ballooning globules, monsters that exploded in my mind, each one sending exquisite agony reverberating through my entire body. My heart pounded with a painful insistent rhythm . . . Just like the other one, said the rhythm. Just like that other slut, that Jezebel . . .

I snatched at the stupid handiwork she had been holding. I think I said, 'I'll show you,' and I grabbed the steel hook so that the threads unravelled. She made an ineffectual attempt to retrieve them, and somehow that fired my hatred even more. She was faced with violence – someone who might rape her for all she knew – but she had more thought for saving her frivolous crochet.

The door opened slightly and a small voice said, 'Mamma? How are you today?'

I moved almost without thinking, darting into the concealment of the screen behind Julia West's sofa. I almost knocked it over in my haste, but I managed to right it, and in doing so realized I could see through it into the room. There were two small tears in the screen – a prudent housewife would have mended them long since, but of course the likes of Julia West would not bother with such matters. The slits were at eye-level and through them I was able to see the boy sit on the edge of a chair, looking uncomfortable but clearly going through a ritual. How was mamma today? he asked. How were the pains? He had worked hard at his lessons, and practised his music.

I heard this, and I thought: it's going to be all right. He doesn't know I'm here. He'll go away in a few moments.

But then Julia leaned forward and grasped the boy's hand.

'Esmond,' she said urgently. 'Esmond, find papa. Tell him . . .'

I thought: she's going to tell them. She's going to tell them I'm here – what I did and what I said. That was when I realized I was still clutching the steel needle, and that the screen was within inches of the sofa – within inches of the back of her neck.

The feeling when the steel needle went through the

tapestry screen and dug into the base of Julia West's neck was the most extraordinary sensation I have ever known, or will ever know. I was twenty feet high, invincible, I held the power of the world in my hands, I held the strength to mete out death to the living . . . I watched her sag, and I felt – I actually *felt* – the life drain away from her.

The boy was puzzled. He backed away from the sofa, clearly unsure what to do. And then he saw me. I don't mean he saw me completely, but his eyes met mine as I stared out from behind the screen. His expression changed, I saw sheer terror in his eyes, and I knew I had to silence him – I *had* to . . .

God knows who or what he thought I was, but I said, quietly, 'Esmond.' And then, just to be sure, I said, 'You know who I am, don't you?'

He knew, all right. He had come to the site with his father once, and he knew me. He nodded. 'Yes, sir,' he said.

'Esmond, you must never speak of what you have seen in this room. You must make a solemn promise. Never speak.' I paused, then, because I had to be sure, I said, 'If you do, something terrible will happen to you. You understand me, Esmond? *Never speak or something terrible will happen.*'

He said, in a frightened whisper, 'Yes. Yes, I promise.' And ran out of the room.

I was out from behind that screen at once, and darting through the French windows. Esmond would have gone for help, and I had to be away from the house. If I ran around the side I could get to the carriageway and be hidden from view by the shrubs.

That was what I did. I went all the way around without anyone seeing me, but there was one bad moment, and that was when I went alongside the other window of Julia West's room.

Esmond saw me. Ralph West was in the room by then, and he was bending over his wife's prone body, but Esmond looked up and our eyes met. I hesitated, then

laid my finger over my lips. *Never speak of it* . . . He
nodded, and I ran the rest of the way, and keeping to the
cover of the trees, went down the carriageway and out
onto the road.

Safe. Once again I could feel myself safe.

Except I was not safe at all. Because at the end of that
year, with some stupid sentimental idea of being nearer
to his dead wife's family, Ralph West bought the Acton
land. And since he had been pleased with my work on
his factory, and since I was there in Caudle Moor, he
commissioned me to build a house.

Which meant Esmond would see me again. And would
recognize me as the man who murdered his mother.

I'm not proud of what I did to Esmond West. But I had
to be sure he would never tell anyone he had seen me
kill his mother, you see. His father sometimes talked
about how Esmond never spoke, but I later heard that
doctors were consulted about the affliction. Not just our
own Dr Brodworthy, but clever doctors from cities. What
they call specialists. It seemed to me it was only a matter
of time before Esmond would break that silence and tell
how he had seen me that afternoon in Julia's sitting room.
Even if he could not speak, he might write it down.

While we worked on Stilter House Esmond sometimes
came to the site with his father. I'd see the boy looking
at me and I'd know he was remembering.

And then my own father – stupid, stubborn old fool –
got to know Esmond. He actually invited him to the
almshouse and took him to the forge. He talked to Esmond
and encouraged the boy to write his thoughts and draw
his pictures. And I knew – I *knew* – it was only a matter
of time before Esmond would open up to this kind old Mr
Burlap who took him to interesting places in the village.
Esmond would write about his mother – about her death.
My father had let that business with Isobel go – I had not,
after all, actually killed Isobel, and I had been led along
by Anne-Marie. But the death of Julia was a different
matter entirely. My father would never let that go.

One night, when Ralph West and the servants were occupied, I got into the house through the garden door – I knew every twist and corner of that house, of course. I took Esmond from his own bed and I carried him out to the old game larder. He did not struggle; I think he was surprised more than anything. Perhaps he saw it as an adventure – there were several children's storybooks in his room, and I think he may have thought he was being taken into one of the books' exciting journeys.

I cannot write of how I killed him – I *cannot*. I can only say I took one of my mallets, and that a child's skull is vulnerable, and that it was quick, truly it was quick. He dropped at once and he wouldn't have known what hit him; he would have tumbled from full awareness into the deep darkness of unconsciousness and death. I have to remember that. I still remind myself of it in the night, when I feel my mind spiral down into that black chasm, and when the doubts come to taunt me and the dead stand at the end of my bed and hold out their imploring hands . . . Julia West – yes, she's there, the false double-faced creature. And Esmond, who posed such a terrible threat to me . . . And Isobel, my Jezebel with her painted porcelain skin and her voice like warm honey.

But I must keep to the facts, so I'll write that after I dealt with Esmond, ('dealt with' – oh God, I still feel that crunching blow in my own head at times) it was easy to call openly at Stilter House as if by arrangement, with estimates for Ralph West. To appear suitably horrified at the news of Esmond's disappearance, and to join in the search. Kind, anxious Mr Burlap, wanting to help. Taking over part of the gardens on his own account, concerned that the two servants did not stray into the old outbuildings and trip on unsafe bricks or masonry . . . 'I'll search that part – you stay safely on this side of the grounds.' I made very sure that I was the only one who went into those outbuildings that night, and all the nights ahead.

When the search had died down, I crept through the gardens at midnight and removed the body. It was a harrowing task, but what I had done before I could do again.

Isobel walked with me as I carried the small heap that had been Esmond West to the same spot in the grounds, and dug the small grave, and covered the body over with earth and leaves. She was wreathed in darkness and wrapped about in shadows, but I know she was there.

That night when I buried Esmond next to Isobel must have stripped something from me – some armour – for when I talked later to my father about the West family, I knew he saw through all the pretences and the deceits I had spun over the years. He was remembering what I had done to Isobel, and perhaps he was suspecting I had been part of Esmond's disappearance. There was a good deal of talk about that in the village – local people searched the lanes and the meadows for days on end.

It infuriates me that my father says I must write this account, but I've done as he asked, and it's all written down, and I shall sign and date it, as he asked, then take it along to the almshouses. My mother won't be there; in the middle of the afternoon she'll be busy-bodying in someone else's house and my father will be on his own. I know what he'll do. He'll lock this statement away in the Japanned box where he keeps his few papers, and he'll say that it makes an end to the matter.

But I'm the one who'll make the end to it, and the end is not what my father will be expecting . . .

And when I look ahead to the years left to me (I am no longer young, but I am not so very old), I do not think I can remain silent forever. I think there will come a day when I shall be compelled to accept the punishment due to me.

The final paper in the folder was a cutting from a newspaper. The date was 1901.

JURY'S VERDICT ON FATHER KILLER

A verdict of Guilty was today unanimously pronounced on Mr Samuel Burlap of Derbyshire, who stood charged with killing his disabled father, Mr Jack Burlap, in May of this year.

Mr Burlap had pleaded Guilty to the charge, declining to give evidence on his own behalf. The Court heard how Mr Burlap had visited his father on what the defence said was a normal family visit – a son calling on his elderly parents.

The dead man's wife had not been present, but neighbours reported hearing raised voices and sounds of a quarrel between Samuel Burlap and his father, followed by unmistakable sounds of violence, during which Mr Jack Burlap shouted for help. Sadly, by the time they got into the cottage, Mr Burlap lay on the floor with blood pouring from a head wound, and his son standing nearby holding a brass poker, covered in blood. One witness said Samuel Burlap appeared to be trying to break into a small cupboard which it was thought held Mr Jack Burlap's private papers, but this was never known for sure, and Samuel himself declined to answer questions.

Summing up, the judge said there could be no doubt about Samuel Burlap's guilt, and that the only possible sentence that could be passed was the death sentence.

Clipped to this were two further pieces of paper, both headed H M PRISON, NOTTINGHAM. The first said:

I, Henry Osgood, Surgeon of His Majesty's Prison of Nottingham, hereby certify that I have today examined the body of Samuel Burlap, on whom judgement of death was today executed in the said prison; and that on that examination I found that the said Samuel Burlap was dead.

Dated this fourth day of November, 1901.

Signed: Henry Osgood.

The second had the same heading and said,

We the undersigned hereby declare that Judgement of Death was this day executed on Samuel Burlap in His Majesty's Prison of Nottingham in our presence.

Dated this fourth day of November, 1901.

Several signatures followed.

TWENTY SEVEN

The various papers were strewn over the carpet, and the two low tables were littered with the remains of Chinese food. Beth had stayed up to eat her share of the food, and had finally gone, rather reluctantly, to bed.

Michael reread the execution notices, and laid them down thoughtfully. 'So that's what happened to Samuel in the end.'

'I can't help feeling just a little bit sorry for him,' said Emily. 'He had no real guidance, if you know what I mean. No parents to love him and understand him, or realize what was going on in his head.' She caught Nell's eye and smiled a bit sheepishly. 'I do know I'd find excuses for the devil, though. And I certainly can't forgive him for Esmond.'

'Nor can I. Jack did try to forgive him for Isobel, I think,' said Nell.

'But Jack was caught up with chasing the ladies, and then with his own tragedy,' said Michael. 'It was only later he became really suspicious.'

'Yes, but I don't think Jack ever really intended to tell anyone what his son had done,' said Nell. 'Even though Samuel seems to have subtly threatened him.'

'One thing I do find strange,' said Emily. 'That belief about the music calling to the dead. It's interesting, but I don't think I've ever heard of it.'

'Nor have I. Michael, are you having some more wine, or are you driving?'

'I'm not driving,' said Michael. 'Emily and I are sharing a

taxi back. So I'll have some more wine, please. In fact I'll even get the bottle of white Burgundy from the fridge.'

When he had refilled the glasses, Nell said, 'While we were in the house I heard Beth talking about the music – about it calling the dead back.'

'Was she talking to Esmond?' asked Emily eagerly.

'I'm not sure. Perhaps it was to something that might have been a leftover fragment of Esmond,' said Nell, firmly.

'You never will be convinced about ghosts, will you?' said Michael, smiling.

'I might allow you Esmond. I do think something of Esmond might have lingered in that house.'

Emily said, 'Was Esmond trying to pass the music down? Was that the "secret" he told Brad about?'

'It sounds like it,' said Michael. 'Nell will look sideways at this, but I think while Esmond lived in that house he picked something up about the music from Anne-Marie – Ralph seems to have seen Anne-Marie, remember.'

'What Ralph saw sounds like a kind of replay of Anne-Marie creeping up to imprison Isobel,' said Emily. 'I wonder if Esmond might have seen the same thing? He sounds like the sort of imaginative child who'd be receptive.'

Michael glanced at Nell. 'You saw Anne-Marie as well, didn't you? But I know that's another ghost you won't admit to.'

'I'll consider it,' said Nell. 'Emily, did Charlotte ever mention Anne-Marie? Or anyone who sounded like Anne-Marie?'

'No. Charlotte's ghosts were all quite happy, quite benevolent,' said Emily, and then, slightly startled, 'Do you know, I don't think I've ever taken part in such a bizarre conversation as this.'

'It's quite a bizarre situation,' said Nell.

'However it happened, Esmond somehow inherited the belief that music had a power,' said Michael. 'And he wanted to pass it to Brad. But Brad went abroad before he could tell him.'

'So Esmond tried again with Brad's daughter,' said Emily, nodding.

'Yes.'

'It does make a skewed kind of sense,' said Nell.

'There were a lot of lingering fragments of the past in that house,' said Michael, thoughtfully. 'Isobel and Anne-Marie's punishment. Anne-Marie's belief in the music's power—'

'And Esmond,' said Nell, softly. 'What are we going to do about that?'

'I've been thinking . . .' Emily broke off.

'Go on.'

'If we could . . . well, find where Samuel put Esmond . . .'

Michael said, 'Christian burial?'

'I wasn't going to go that far,' said Emily. 'Mightn't that involve police investigations and all sorts of complications?'

'I think there'd have to be an inquest,' said Michael. 'But I don't think it would be a very in-depth one, not for such old remains.'

'I don't think that would be a good idea for Beth,' said Emily. 'It would be far better if she could remember Esmond as a slightly unusual boy she met at Stilter House.'

'Yes, it would,' said Nell, at once. 'It would be confusing for her – macabre, even – if she discovered Esmond was murdered over a century ago.'

'Well then, I was thinking that if we could identify the spot in the grounds and mark it – that place where Beth used to say goodbye to Esmond – I should think that's where Burlap buried him, shouldn't you?'

'What kind of marking? You don't mean a headstone or something?'

'Oh, no. But I visited California last year and I saw some wonderful gardens while I was there. There's a very nice rose called "Nocturne" they have. I don't think it's available in this country, but it might be possible to arrange shipping.'

'Nocturne,' said Nell, staring at her. 'Chopin's Nocturne. Esmond's music.'

'Yes. It's a hybrid tea-rose – very attractive, quite sturdy. It might not survive at Stilter House, of course – well, it might not survive the journey from America. And it ought to have some careful pruning, which we probably won't be able to give it, not once the house is sold at any rate. But on the other hand—'

'On the other hand, it might flourish,' said Michael.

*   *   *

Michael and Nell walked slowly back through the gardens of Stilter House. The sun was beginning to set over the Derbyshire Peaks, and a spear of golden light fell across the newly dug earth and touched the small plant with its neatly printed label. *Nocturne.*

Emily and Beth had gone ahead of them, Beth enthusiastically talking about the rose bush, and Emily listening gravely.

Nell heard Emily say, 'And we'll come back here in the autumn because the house won't be sold that quickly, and we'll try to take some cuttings from that rose and strike them – I'll show you how to do that. Then you can grow a separate one of your own in Oxford. You can look at it when you play Esmond's music.'

'I'd like that a huge lot,' said Beth. Then, a bit uncertainly, she said, 'Esmond was real, wasn't he, Aunt Em? Because I was never ezzackerly sure.'

Nell saw Emily reach down to take Beth's hand. 'Yes, he was real,' she said. 'Here at Stilter House he was very real indeed. I don't think you'll see him again, but he'll stay real, because we'll still talk about him. And you'll play his music and perhaps you'll play it to me very soon.' She smiled. 'I'd like that a huge lot.'

'And if Esmond does go back to Stilter House, he'll see that rose bush and he'll know we put it there for him,' said Beth, pleased.

'Precisely.'

Nell had to blink hard because the stupid sentimental tears were suddenly clouding her sight. But it's all right, she thought. Beth's accepting it at face value. Jack Burlap was right when he said children were more open to enchantments than adults. That they were still partly in heaven's dreams, still trailing clouds of glory.

She paused to look back at the small shape of the Nocturne rose which would probably not survive, but which might perhaps flower for a season or so. And Beth would have a cutting and they would plant it behind their little shop in Oxford. Esmond, she thought. We won't forget you, Esmond, I promise we won't.

At her side, Michael suddenly said, 'Oh God, I do love you when you look like that.'

Nell turned to stare at him, startled, and found him looking at her.

She said, 'I thought you were waiting for the moonlight and roses to say that.'

'Well, we've got the roses, if not the moonlight. So I thought I'd seize the moment.'

Nell considered this. 'You did say we were booked into The Pheasant tonight, didn't you?'

'I did.' Michael took her hand.

'Will you say that again when we're in the bedroom? About loving me?'

'Oh yes,' he said.